THE
COLD
COLD
WAR

ROBB FELDER

ROBB FELDER

Published by Otter Falls Publishing
Cambridge, Minnesota 55008
Copyright ©2019 by Robb Felder

ISBN 978-0-578-57496-7

Printed in the United States of America

Fifty five years ago the mighty Russian Soyuz-1 space craft powered by the powerful N-1 rocket stood on the launch pad at the Baikanur Cosmodrome in the Soviet state of Kazakhstan. It was 1965. The Soviet's moon landing program was several years ahead of the US Apollo moon landing program. This was to be the first manned test flight of the Soviet's Soyuz spacecraft.

On board the Soyuz-1 spacecraft was a single cosmonaut, although the capsule was designed for four. The Soyuz-2 spacecraft would follow and they would test docking procedures for the moon mission. But the Soyuz-1 was plagued with problems and after only 18 orbits was ordered to return. However, upon re-entry, the parachutes failed to deploy properly, sending the space craft plunging to earth and exploding in a huge ball of fire, killing the cosmonaut, Vladimir Komarov.

Also killing the Soviet's possibility of landing a man on the moon, - - - - -.

After that incident, the Soviets cancelled the Soyuz moon landing program. Something was terribly wrong with the Soyuz-1 space craft..

Was it an inherent design flaw? - - - -

Or, was it sabotage? - - - - - -.

The Soviets claimed sabotage and executed one of the design team and fired the rest.

This is the story of how the US CIA brought down the Soviet moon mission and forever altered history.

Sixty years ago a young U.S. Army enlistee was in his second year of his three year enlistment and had just received reassignment orders to report for duty at Fort Greely, Alaska.

This is his story.

*To Barbara
who entered my world
and does beautiful things there*

.

*To Kira and McKenna
two angels, who
came into our lives on a moon beam
and light up our evening sky
like two bright twinkling stars*

*For all of our beautiful children,
and our grand and great
beautiful grandchildren.*

ROBB FELDER

PROLOGUE

Once upon a time, an old man sat on the bank of a river, the Ottertail River, his river, their river. As the river drifted past, ever flowing, like a river of time flowing on into eternity, his mind took him on a journey. Back in time, back up the river of time he journeyed. It was a bright, very warm, sunny day in the month of July. Just a hand full of cumulus clouds drifted overhead, like fluffs of whipping cream stacked high in a brilliant metallic blue bowl.

In the cat tails and willow trees along the shore, Redwing Blackbirds were busily flitting about, calling to each other and gathering food for their young in the nests. On the opposite shore a family of young mallards floated lazily by, on their way to join other ducks in a small bay just downstream.

A light breeze caused small wisps of ripples in the un-sheltered pools of the river. The bright sun sparkled off the ripples like shimmering diamonds floating on the water.

As the old man watched the ever moving pools of diamonds, he became mesmerized by the sparkle and movement.

Soon he began drifting away, - - - and as he drifted, he laid back in the tall, warm, soft grass; back, he drifted to another place and time of his life. He emerged on the 'other side' of yesterday with a clarity he couldn't even fathom.

CHAPTER 1

The train began to pick up speed as it left the station in Fargo. Soon it was speeding west, out across the vast prairies of North Dakota. This was his third time leaving home. He was a young soldier with one year into his three year enlistment. "This departure was a lot easier than the first two", he thought. He had grown up a lot since that first departure. Leaving home and his family and the farm for the first time had been a very scary experience.

His father had done it, so why couldn't he do it also? His father had served in World War One.

"Well, at least there isn't a war going on", his mother consoled herself and Bob. "This is nineteen fifty nine. This is "peace-time", she stated."

"You're going into the "Peace-time Army." Dad had said. "You'll get some training in your career field and at least you won't have to worry about being in combat."

Little did they know; there is always a war going on somewhere. Everyone thought that the First World War was going to be "the war to end all war". Well, for about twenty years anyway. Then right after the Second World War, everyone thought that, "Now the world will see peace, now that we have crushed Nazi-ism."

But the shortsighted leaders of the Allied Powers; Churchill, Roosevelt and De Gaul did not foresee that the other member of their alliance was not their friend. Joseph Stalin was a fiendish power-hungry monster who had been just waiting for Nazi-ism to be defeated so that he could unleash the next plague of terror upon humanity; ***Communism***.

Stalin moved quickly, after the war, to push his communistic agenda into the void of Eastern Europe and declared the newly formed state The USSR. In the process, he slaughtered thousands and thousands of his own countrymen and sent thousands more to the Gulag prison camps in Siberia. It was Churchill who declared that the USSR had formed an '***Iron Curtain***' around the newly formed federation. The allied powers of Western Europe stopped his advances to the west with the formation of NATO.

Meanwhile, The Big Red Dragon, China, was swallowing up Asia like a hungry monster. China next had its sights set on the Korean

Peninsula. However, the US already had military bases in the south of Korea. China began arming the northern half of the country as the US expanded its bases in the south. By 1948, with both North and South Korea 'armed to the teeth', the stage was set for confrontation. A line was drawn between the two factions. In 1949, the North Korean army invaded the South. The United States engaged them and so began the hard fought Korean War, which ended in a stalemate. A truce ended the conflict in 1954.

Throughout the rest of the 1950's and into the early 1960's; there were no major military conflicts. The world, it would seem; was enjoying a decade of peace. At least it would appear that way on the outside; however, under the surface, there was a continual war smoldering.

It was President Eisenhower who declared this period as *"The Cold War"*. Russia and the 'West' were engaged in an ongoing build-up of military power; most notably the stockpiling of nuclear weapons. This created a widespread fear of nuclear radiation, 'fallout'. Throughout the late nineteen fifty's, Americans built thousands and thousands of fallout shelters in fear of an imminent nuclear war with the USSR.

The soldiers in this war were the agents and the spies, engaged in a continual game of 'cat and mouse'. These soldiers were under the command of the four controlling agencies; the CIA, the KGB, Briton's MI6 and France's INTERPOL. The battlefield was anywhere in the world where there was top secret information to be stolen, bought, sold and swapped. These 'cloak and dagger' operations were carried out mostly at night in all of the dark corners of the world.

The irony of this scenario was, that right after the end of World War Two, and even before the end, the USA poured millions and millions of US dollars and equipment into the recovery and rebuilding of Russia, only to have Russia slam the door on the 'West' and lower the 'Iron Curtain' across Europe.

All this was in the ridiculous belief that in order for Communism to succeed, the entire world had to be consumed by it.

CHAPTER 2

The Northern Pacific's Vista Dome passenger train screamed on through the night. It was a three day, two night trip to Mc Cord Air Force Base outside of Tacoma Washington for the flight to Alaska. Bob had orders for a re-assignment from Fort Benning, Georgia, to the US Army's Arctic Test Center at Fort Greely, Alaska. He knew not what his exact job there would entail, but, he was schooled at the Army's Administration school at Fort Ord, California. He held a MOS (Military Occupational Specialty) of 7.11, which was classified as an Administrative Specialist. After one year of military service, he held the rank of PFC(Private First Class).

The flight took him from Mc Cord Airforce Base in Washington to Elmendorf Airforce Base just outside of Anchorage. After an overnight at Elmendorf, the next leg of his journey took him to Eielson AFB, just southeast of Fairbanks, Alaska. He arrived on Saturday, the fourth of July.

Fairbanks, located in central Alaska, in the Tanana River Valley, is Alaska's second largest city.

When PFC Bob Fellerer arrived in the summer of 1959, Alaska was celebrating its statehood. They were joining the union as the 49th state. He was transferred over to Fort Wainwright, an Army base, just a few miles from Eielson AFB. The city of Fairbanks was having a huge celebration honoring the states entry into the union. Because it was a weekend, he signed out and caught a ride into town for the big parade. Thousands of GI's from all over Alaska were in town for the celebration. The partying went on virtually all night, under the light of the 'midnight sun'..

This time of year in central and northern Alaska, they experience a phenomenon known as 'The Midnight Sun'. In the early summer months, the sun never sets. It does not go down below the horizon. Here at the top of the world, there are twenty four hours of daylight. At 06:00 hours the next morning, PFC Fellerer got on a bus and joined a busload of celebrators heading off into the wilderness.

Fort Greely is located about 100 miles southeast of Fairbanks. It lies at the confluence of the Delta River and the Tanana River and is located on the Richardson Highway at about five miles south of the junction of the Alaska Highway and the Richardson Highway and the town of Delta Junction. It is one of the US Army's largest military installations, area wise, and encompasses about six hundred and forty thousand acres. *Plenty of room for the Army to play with all their latest military toys.*

Fort Greely. home to the Army's Arctic Test Board, is one of the Army's most remote installations; except for, of course, Tule, Greenland. In terms of personnel, however, it is not so large. In nineteen fifty nine there were about five hundred soldiers stationed there. The main mission of the Army Arctic Test Board was, of course to test all forms of military equipment for performance in the extreme cold temperatures of the arctic. This included not only personal gear for the soldier; such as clothing, weapons, and outdoor gear, but also the heavy equipment, such as vehicles; trucks, tanks, heavy artillery and also the military's newest toy, the guided missile.

PFC Bob Fellerer arrived at Fort Greely late in the day of Sunday, the 5th of July, 1959. He was met by the Company Commander. Captain John Ellis and his First Sergeant, Master Sergeant Robert 'Bobby' Balleu, who spent about an hour or two explaining the mission of the Army's Arctic

Test Board and the nature of life at the Arctic Circle.

"Most of the testing we do here is classified with a security clearance of, 'Confidential', 'Secret', or 'Top Secret'." Captain Ellis explained. "You will not be required to handle any material of the 'Top Secret' classification. That level of handling requires an officer's rank. But, you will be handling material of 'secret' and 'confidential' classifications. You will be required to fill out an application to be granted those security clearances. Your application will be submitted to our command headquarters in Fort Belvoir, Virginia. They will grant the 'Confidential' clearance, however the 'Secret' clearance will come from the Pentagon."

With the high-level orientation completed, PFC Fellerer was introduced to the rest of the company staff; Company Admin Clerk, Specialist Fourth Class Roger Hammond and the Personnel Specialist, PFC Richard Davis. He was then given a tour of the barracks facility. The two main barracks buildings were three story concrete structures. One housed the longer term, permanently assigned soldiers. The other building housed temporary personnel involved in specific testing, and housed a mix of all branches of military as well as civilians overseeing their company's testing of their equipment. These barracks buildings were 'all-in-one' structures, containing; sleeping, eating, recreation and administrative facilities in each building. The buildings were painted with a pink color. No one knew why the Army had chosen the color pink, but, the soldiers all referred to them as the 'Pink palaces'. These buildings were located across the street from the base's nuclear power plant. All of the buildings on Fort Greely were heated by the super-heated water from the reactor in the nuclear power plant.

After his orientation and tour of the facilities, Bob got in line at the mess hall for a late dinner and after dinner was assigned to his sleeping area. He noticed that all the windows in the sleeping areas had heavy black shades on them. This was the month of July and the sun was still shining brightly at midnight. It was hard to fall asleep in the 'broad daylight' of the midnight sun. Not too surprisingly, Alaska is called 'the land of the midnight sun'.

"Wait until December and January," he was told, "Then the opposite effect comes into play."

In the morning he finished processing in. He was issued the special arctic clothing, which for 'garrison', or non-combat wear consisted of a heavy wool, army olive colored shirt and the 'Korean' combat boots. "These boots were battlefield proven in Korea", he was told. They were a rubber boot with a built-in very heavy felt lining, tested to minus forty below zero. Of course, there were wool socks to go along with the boots. Also, there were the 'long-johns' and arctic mittens, gloves and a middle-weight field jacket with a zip-in wool thermal lining. In addition, he was issued one of the arctic, heavy duty 'snorkel' parka that was also a remnant of the Korean War.

After he had all of his arctic gear stored away in his assigned sleeping cubical he was introduced to the soldier who was the current Test Site Courier and Mail Clerk. Specialist Fourth Class (SP4) Frank Krisinskey was from Philadelphia.

"I've had this position for about eight months," Frank said. "I don't have the MOS for it. I was trained to be a supply clerk. They assigned the courier and mail job to me after the previous courier requested a psych transfer halfway through his tour. He couldn't tolerate the winters up here; the bitter cold and the darkness twenty-four-seven. It's enough to drive most people nuts."

"Well the cold, I think I can handle," Bob replied. "I'm from Minnesota and we get temps. down to about forty below zero. As for the total darkness in the Winter, I guess I'll just have to see how that goes."

"Well," Frank said, "The winters up here begin in September and don't end until late May."

"I'll say this," he continued, "the Army has spared no expense when they designed this base. C'mon, I'll show you around the base. I'll give you a walking tour for now." He said as he led Bob outside. "Everything is located within about a five block radius of our barracks. Later, we'll take my truck and tour the complete base when we go to the airfield to pick up the mail. Even though it is a fairly small base, they've built in a lot of amenities to keep the guys from going crazy in all the dark days of the long winters up here. Here we have a gym. C'mon in, I'll show you around. Next to the basketball and volleyball courts is our work-out room and in this next section here is an indoor pool, of course." As they went back outside, Frank continued, "Across the street we have a movie theater, bowling alley, restaurant and snack bar. Next to that building is the Post Exchange shopping center. And over here, on this last block, across from our 'Pink Palace' we have an EM(enlisted-man) club with a lounge and a library and craft shop. In our barracks building basement, we have a TV lounge, ping-pong tables and pool tables. We have our own radio and TV station where they re-broadcast TV from the 'lower-forty-eight'."

After their walking tour, Frank signed out his jeep for the mail pick-up and deliveries and took Bob to the base headquarters building where he filled out the forms to be submitted for his security clearances. He was fingerprinted and photographed and the packet handed to the base commander, Colonel John Martin. Bob saluted him and handed him the packet.

"Welcome to Fort Greely and the US Army's Artic Test Board, PFC Fellerer. We'll forward this packet on to Fort Belvoir and the Pentagon. I'll let you know when it's all approved so you can begin your courier duties. I see in your personnel jacket, you have a flag in there that you have contacted your congressman; a Senator Humphrey, I believe. Usually, when a soldier writes his congressman, he has issues with the US Army. Want to explain that."

"Well, yes sir. When I was at Fort Benning, I was having issues with how I was being treated. They had me assigned duties outside my MOS and didn't allow me to continue my education, as promised by my enlistment agreement. They had me driving a five ton truck and tried to force me to file for a change in my MOS classification to a truck driver."

"I can appreciate your frustration with that, Private First Class Fellerer. Rumor has it that the Army is doing a big shake up and a buildup at Benning. There's another "hot-spot" brewing in this cold war. This next one appears to be in Southeast Asia. Well, we have our own war going on up here in Alaska.   I guess you could call this one the, "COLD, COLD WAR".

"Well, yes sir, I would agree. I will do my best to perform my duties as Courier, whatever that entails, to the best of my abilities. And, thank you sir."

"Here in the Alaska Command," Colonel Martin continued, "We have educational opportunities available to our soldiers. We have an agreement with The University of Alaska to offer off-campus extension classes free of charge here at Greely for anyone interested in advancing their education."

"That's fantastic, Sir," Bob responded, "I'll be checking that out and get signed up."

Bob saluted and returned outside where Frank was waiting. They drove out to the Main Post Office near the air strip to pick up the daily mail for the Artic Test Center. Frank introduced Bob to the Postmaster.

"Welcome," he said, "I look forward to working with you. Whenever you're ready to take your Postal Exam, we can give that right here at Base Post Office."

Frank and Bob returned to the Arctic Test Center barracks and unloaded the mail sacks. The bulk mail was transported in large canvas sacks.

"All the mail addressed to military personnel in Alaska," Frank explained, "Is flown in from the APO(Army Post Office) in Seattle, Washington."

The Mail Room was located in the main hall of the barracks building, next to the Mess Hall, so the guys could pick up their mail on their way back from dinner. Frank unlocked the door and they brought in the mail sacks. The mail room was about ten by twelve feet and contained a desk and sorting table and a mail rack with alphabetically labeled cubes. The room had a window with bars on it. Frank told Bob that he couldn't handle the mail yet, until he passed the exam. He pulled out the mail carriers rule book from one of the desk drawers and gave it to Bob to study.

"Well, let's go to lunch," Frank said, "Get used to eating lunch and dinner early, so you can get back to your mail room and hand out mail to everyone else after they have eaten. After lunch I will sort out the sacks of mail into the slots and you can spend the rest of the day studying the mail rule book."

After the dinner meal Frank opened the small cut-out door cut into the mailroom door. The cut-out dropped down and a window with bars with a slot in the base was swung across the opening. The soldiers would come up and give their name and their mail, if any was pulled from the alphabetized cubbies and handed out.

After lunch the next day, Frank said that they had a courier route to do. "Every other day," he explained, "You will have to travel off-base to the remote test sites to deliver mail and pick up courier packets containing test results and drop off any communication packets going to and from the test sites from whoever. Some will be from the manufacturers, some will be from Dept. of the Army. You will not know. Most of the information is "need-to-know" only and is Secret or Classified. Some of the test sites are close by and you can just drive there. Some are quite a distance and you will be flown to them. Some of the locations of those sites are either Secret or Classified and you will have to wait until you have your clearance."

"Today, we will drive down to the tank, artillery and missile testing range. It is located just about twenty miles from the main base, down in the Delta River valley. Keep in mind; there's not too much activity or testing done now in the summer months for obvious reasons. Most equipment is here for arctic testing. However, some is carried over into summer months for what is called 'terrain', or 'environmental' testing"

Frank checked his list of those soldiers getting their mail at the Delta River test site and put it into a special mail pouch. They arrived at the testing site headquarters a short time later.

Frank explained that most of the actual test sites were at various places far out on the Delta River Flats and only testing personnel were allowed access. They went in and Bob was introduced to the headquarters administrative staff. He was then introduced to the soldier; a Master Sergeant Ron Davis, who would be his contact. The person, from whom he would receive and transfer packets of secret documents.

"So, you're the 'newbie' we've heard about. Well, I hope you'll be as easy to work with as Frank was."

Then he gave Bob this kind of 'funny' grin that he thought was a little odd. Frank signed for and a sealed packet was logged out to him for transport to main base ATB, HQ. They then left and went directly to the main base ATB, HQ where Frank signed over the packet to the receiving officer; a Captain Muller.

After several days of studying the postal regulations, Bob said he was ready for the test. The next morning Frank drove Bob out to the Main Post Office so he could take the test. He waited there again for Bob, so he could take the Postal Exam to qualify him to be able to pick up and hand out the personal mail at various testing sites of the Artic Test Center. Bob passed the test and was given an ID card identifying him as the official Mail Carrier for the Army's Arctic Test Board.

Now he just had to wait for his security clearances to come up from the Pentagon and he would be also qualified for the position of the Courier for the Arctic Test Center.

About two weeks later, Bob was called to the office of the commander of the Army's Arctic Test Center, Colonel Ray Kimball.

"PFC Fellerer, Congratulations, I have just received your security clearances from the Pentagon for you to handle secret and confidential documents for the Test Center. This is a huge responsibility for you, PFC Fellerer. Remember, just the fact that you have a Secret clearance is to be kept secret. You are not allowed to divulge that fact to anyone, ever. That means; even after your enlistment is over and you are again a civilian, you still have to maintain secrecy about anything and everything that you were exposed to up here in Alaska."

"Understood, Sir," Bob responded as he saluted the Colonel and departed.

ROBB FELDER

CHAPTER 3

Late one Saturday night, right after Bob received his security clearances, after a night of celebrating the arrival of the new replacement soldiers, Private Fellerer and Specialist Frank Krisinskey stayed at the EM Club until everyone else had left.

After they had finished their last drink for the night, Frank said. "I asked you to stay a while, Bob. I've got something to talk about that is not for anybody else's ears. Now that all you newbies are getting settled in, I guess I can leave you in charge of the mail and courier services. My tour of duty and enlistment will be up next month. I'll be heading back to the 'lower 48'. I haven't decided yet if I'll reenlist, or not. I really want to go back to college. I had just barely started when I was drafted. I thought I'd have saved enough for tuition to get my degree; what with the 'foreign duty pay' that we get for our tour here in Alaska.

But, it turns out that wouldn't be enough, with the cost of tuition going up all the time. The cost is now, five dollars a credit."

"Frank, it sounds like I have the same plans as you do. But, listen, Frank, just before I left the lower 48, I heard that there is a new bill in congress to extend the Korean War Veterans Benefits to all the 'cold-war' veterans and that would include tuition benefits."

"Well, that may be true, but I'm afraid that by the time congress gets around to enacting such a bill, we may be too old to go back to school."

"What else can we do Frank? I suppose we could get a part time job while we're here to supplement our meager military pay, but, it sounds like even that wouldn't be enough."

"I have found the solution to our problem, Bob. I will share it with you, only if you are willing to swear to secrecy."

"Okay, I will swear to keep whatever secret you are about to tell me. So, Frank, what's this big secret plan of yours."

"The plan is actually, already in place. I have a little money-making scheme set up with some of the companies that send their equipment up here to be arctic tested. These companies are in very intense competition with each other for the huge military contracts to supply the military with the equipment that proves to be the best arctic qualified for the job. These companies will pay big money for information on the test results of their competitors equipment. For example, say GM has a new truck that they are testing for arctic performance and Chrysler has the same type of truck that they are working on. They would love to get their hands on the test results of the GM truck so they can design a superior truck that will outperform the GM truck and win the contract."

"So, it sounds like you're engaging in a bit of industrial espionage."

"Exactly. and it has paid me a lot of money over the last eighteen months; more than enough for me to finish my college degree. It could do the same for you, Bob."

"Yeah, but isn't it kind of risky. I mean, it is illegal, isn't it?"

"Probably, but it would be a civilian offense and not a military offense. This information is between civilian companies and doesn't involve the military until the military actually buys the equipment."

"I hope you're right about this. I sure as hell don't want to be involved in anything illegal with the military. They would lock you up and throw away the key. So explain to me what exactly would be involved in this endeavor."

"Everything is pretty well set up for you. It took me almost 6 months to get everything set up and working. You are just a small part of the flow of information from the Army Arctic Test Board to the civilian company requesting the information. As the Courier for the Test Center, you will be forwarding the documents from the test site to the requesting company back in the lower 48. The company that wants the test data on a rival company's piece of equipment will submit a request to you via the mail. You will forward the request to the test contact person at the site involved."

"You have been assigned a "Handler" who will coordinate all of the transactions. He will be the one who negotiates the price that the requesting company will pay. His name will remain a secret and he may, or may not ever have a reason to contact you. When the testing is complete, your contact at that test site will prepare two packets. One packet with test results, you will be forwarding to the USAATB headquarters. This one will probably be classified as secret or confidential and will be signed for."

"The other identical packet will not be labeled as secret or confidential and will not be signed for. This packet will then be forwarded to the requesting company by you. You will either be mailing this packet to your contact person at that company, or a person from that company will pick it up from you at some secret location which has been set up by your handler. When the packet has been delivered, a payment will be sent to your handler. He will disburse the money to all the people involved. You will need to set up a bank savings account for yourself to accept the payments from the handler."

"How will I know who my contact person is at all the different test sites?"

"I'll be working with you until we have visited all of the Army's arctic test sites. I'll let you know which ones will be providing "packets" for us, not all sites test the right type of equipment and some still have to be set up for the transfers. Of course, the new test season doesn't start until October or November."

"So, now I know why I got that peculiar look from Master Sergeant Davis when we were down on the Delta River Flats at the Artillery and Missile test site. Apparently he is my contact person."

"That's correct, however he should not have given you that look. That's a very bad public "tell". He is still new to that position. However, I'll have to reprimand him for that."

"So, I'll have to get to know all the other contacts at all of the remote test sites?"

"Yes, and you can't keep any list of these contacts. First of all it's against Army regs. to keep any written list of these people because they are also handing off regular legitimate 'secret' papers for courier back to Base Headquarters. So, what do you think, Bob? Do you want to make a lot of extra money while you're up here on your tour of duty?"

"Well, I'll have to give it a lot of thought. It sounds like it's a mighty risky business and probably border-line illegal."

"Well, you give it some thought, Bob. We can talk about it some more later. You don't have to decide right now. Like I've said the new testing season doesn't start for another month. Meantime, we'll be visiting all of the remote test sites anyway and I'll be introducing you to your contact people as we travel around."

They were about to break up their little discussion, when a waiter from the EM club came up and told them that they were closing, so, Frank and Bob headed back to the 'pink palace' for the night.

Monday morning, Bob checked out the new mail vehicle from the motor pool; a standard Chevrolet half-ton pickup truck, just painted the standard Army's 'olive drab'. He made his way out to the air strip and signed for the bags of personal mail for the USAATB. He took them back to what was now his mailroom at the ATB barracks building and sorted it all into the mail slots where it was now ready for the evening mail-call window.

The mail that was not picked up for two days, he would check against a list of soldiers that had been transferred and wrote the forwarding address on the mail piece. The next day he would return it to the Base Post Office to be forwarded back to the new address in the 'Lower 48'. Each Monday, he would get a new list from Personnel, of the transfers. A transferred soldier would stay on the list for ninety days.

After his administrative duties were completed, Bob checked his list of the soldiers who would be getting their mail at the Gerstle River test site. He locked up his mail room and got in his truck and drove over to the Supply Depot at the edge of the Base. This is where Frank was now working, until his EDS(Expiration Date of Service). He was still assigned to teach PFC Fellerer the remaining courier routes that Bob would assume when he was properly trained.

Bob and Frank drove out to the test site on the Gerstle River Flats, 30 miles southeast of Fort Greely on the Alaskan Highway. The Gerstle River flows out of glaciers in the Black Granite Mountain Range and flows into the Delta River.

"I've got to be honest with you, Bob, this is the one test site that scares the hell out of me. They test some scary shit out here"

"Why do you say that, Frank?"

"You'll see why when we get to the site headquarters and they give you the orientation presentation. This is where the Army does testing of their chemical weapons and quite honestly, some are right out of a horror movie. After you sit through the orientation session, I guarantee you'll have nightmares for the rest of your life."

A small sign identified the turn-off road into the Gerstle River Test Site. They drove down a winding dirt road, down into the river valley and followed the Gerstle River for about ten miles. Warning signs along the way warned of the potent and deadly chemical weapons being tested there. At about five miles in, they came upon the guard post and gate. The gate was manned by two soldiers with automatic weapons. Bob and Frank showed them their military ID's and Bob was asked to show them his vehicle trip log and explained why they were headed to the test site.

After they both signed in on the visitor log, his trip log was stamped with the name of the test site and time and date of entry. After one of the guards called in to the test headquarters for verification, they were warned that they could only stay a short while because some testing was scheduled about mid-day. They were given gas masks; in case of an emergency and asked if they knew how to use them, to which they said they were familiar with their use. The other guard opened the large steel gate and let them through. They continued down the dirt road to the site Headquarters, which was situated on a raised plateau above the river valley. As they pulled into the parking area, Bob commented on the number of civilian cars parked there.

"Most all of the test sites," Frank explained, "will have a number of civilians present when they are testing. These civilians are Reps. from the companies whose equipment or weapons are being tested. They are tech. people and are here to not only observe, but also to help and advise on the setup and use of the weapons."

Bob parked his pickup and he and Frank went into the headquarters building and reported in at the front desk. The test site headquarters was located in a series of connected trailers, for mobility. Here, they signed in and presented their ID's again and Bob had his trip log stamped with time and date.

Staff Sergeant Wilson greeted them and said, "Specialist Krisinzkey, you're back."

Frank introduced him to Bob, but wouldn't look him in the eye, but said, "This is PFC Fellerer, the new Courier for the USAATB. He will be taking over for me."

Sergeant Wilson told them that the Orientation session would begin in about ten minutes. He gave them name tags and directed them down the hall to the end of the main trailer, then left into the East module for the presentation.

When Bob and Frank got to the meeting room and got seated, Frank whispered to Bob, "Sergeant Wilson will be your contact person for courier packets going to and from Base Headquarters."

"What about the non-secret packets," Bob asked, in a whisper.

"I'll talk to you about that after our session," Frank replied.

Most everyone else was already seated. There were four civilian reps. and five soldiers, new to the test site. The main speaker, Colonel John Thompson came in and all the soldiers stood at 'attention'.

"At-ease, men," he said and everyone sat down as he introduced himself and proceeded to introduce everyone else.

"We have present, today, our civilian reps; John Thomas and Bob Erwin from the Bayer Company. We have Scott Brady and Ralph Swanson from DuPont. Welcome to the new soldiers assigned to our Test Site: Chief Warrant Officer Tom Mulder, Lieutenant Ralph Hanson, Staff Sergeant Joseph Thompson, Specialist Forth Class Martin Wilson and PFC Dwayne DeFoe. Also present today is our new Courier, PFC Robert

Fellerer and his Mentor, Specialist Forth Class Frank Krisinzkey. PFC Fellerer will be couriering our test results up to the Main Post Headquarters for disposition."

"Everyone here has a security clearance of at least "Secret", which will clear you for today's orientation; however, let me remind you that for witnessing these actual tests and being present, or viewing the testing, you are required to have a security clearance of "Top Secret". Are there any questions? If not, let's get started."

"Let me start by saying that Chemical and Biological Warfare are not a new thing. This form of warfare has been around for thousands of years, if not eons of human history. Think about it; it all probably began way back when Eve gave Adam a bite of that poison apple. Fast-forward to the Egyptian era. Poison-tipped spears were used extensively by armies of Egypt and Alexander the Great. The middle-ages saw poison-tipped arrows and pots of boiling oil poured down from castle walls upon the enemy.

"The renaissance saw the refining of natural poisons derived from plants such as; foxglove, digitalis and hemlock. Fast forward again to The First World War. Probably the first air-borne large-dispersion, poisons that come to mind would be Mustard Gas and Tear Gas, but there was also a nerve agent called VX, all delivered by artillery shells."

"Fast forward again, to the Second World War. We saw the wide-scale use of all of the previous modern-day chemical weapons, and added several more. Hitler used a chemical known as ZyklonB, a type of hydrogen cyanide and also used carbon dioxide and carbon monoxide in his gas chambers to kill millions of Jews. On the battlefield, the German army once again used Mustard gas, tear gas and the V-series nerve agent VX as well as the 'G' series nerve agent which contained Sarin(GB) and VX.
The US and the Allies used all of the chemicals that the Germans used and also Ricin, derived from the castor bean. Also used were; 'Flame' munitions(Incendiary bombs) and flame throwers. All of these chemical weapons have been previously tested and will generally not be tested in the future unless new versions are developed."

"Now, we'll discuss the new generation of chemical warfare, actually a new classification of weapons, called biological weapons. Also known as "germ warfare", is the use of biological toxins or infectious agents such as bacteria, viruses, and fungi with the intent to kill or incapacitate humans or plants as an act of war. Biological weapons are living organisms or replicating entities that reproduce or replicate within their host victims.

The definition of Biological Warfare is the use of living organisms or their toxic by-products to induce death or incapacity in humans and animals and damage to plants, crops, etc.

It is the use of micro-organisms capable of spreading and causing epidemics of disease for military purposes; the use of living organisms particularly microorganisms or their by-products to induce disease or death in a population.

Environmental warfare is also considered a type of biological warfare. This type of warfare is distinct from nuclear warfare and chemical warfare."

"Okay," Colonel Thompson said, "That concludes the verbal presentation. Are there any questions, before we move on to the film presentation of our operations here at the test site?"

John Thomas, the Rep. from the Bayer Company stood up and asked, "Do you think we have enough safeguards in place before we release any of our Bios. into the wild? All of our development thus far has been done in the completely controlled environment of our labs."

"A good question, Mr. Thomas. We of course want to be absolutely certain of the ability to contain and control these agents. That's why we have with us; Mr. Brady and Mr. Swanson from DuPont where they have developed the containment and arrest procedures to control and stop the spread of these Bios. Mr. Brady, would you like to respond to that issue?"

"These procedures and anti-agents that we have developed at DuPont, as with the Bayer Company, have been tested in a controlled lab environment and will be tested here in the wild, under arctic conditions with extreme cold temperatures, concurrently with the agents themselves."

"Well, thank you gentlemen, for that brief discussion. Now we will move on to the film presentation."

The film began with an overview of the Gerstle River testing area and a history of the test site. The GRTS was acquired by the U.S. Army in 1952. In 1954, the US Army's Dugway Proving Ground established operations at the GRTS for cold weather and surveillance testing of high explosive and chemical munitions and equipment.

The film then began showing an area of the test site where there were barns constructed which housed animals used in the testing process. All forms of livestock such as cows, pigs, goats, sheep and poultry were kept in the barns. Chemical weapons were being tested for effectiveness to kill and otherwise disable these test animals in the extreme cold temperature conditions. The film went on to document the effect of certain chemicals to cause mutations and birth defects in the offspring of the animals that had been exposed to the chemical agents.

The effectiveness of the cold temperature exposure was then measured against exposure at more moderate temperature exposure. The level of release of these agents was calculated to determine at what level of exposure, quantitatively was required for each body size of the test subjects to produce the desired results in the arctic cold. Those numbers were not shown or discussed in the film. Those figures were classified as Top Secret and kept only by the Pentagon. The test animals that had been exposed and either bred to test the condition of their offspring, or killed in the process, were then disposed of in a crematorium along with the mutated offspring, after autopsy analysis was completed and documented.

After the film showing, everyone filed out of the gathering room. Colonel Thompson and the civilian Techs from the Bayer Company and the DuPont Company, along with several of the soldiers left to travel out to one of the remote test sites for the afternoon testing of one of the biological agents. Bob and Frank signed out at the front desk and went out and got into Bob's pickup truck mail vehicle.

They turned in the gas masks and signed out again at the front gate and proceeded down the dirt road back out to the Alaskan Highway for the trip back to Fort Greely.

As they were leaving the main gate, they heard the sirens sounding the alarm that another chemical or biological test was about to commence.

"Boy, am I ever glad to get out of there," Frank exclaimed when they got on the road again, "That place, like I've said before, just gives me the creeps."

"Yeah, me too, "Bob replied, Now what was it you were going to tell me about those non-secret test packets?"

"Well, there may not be any from this test site. I think I kind'a blew it last winter. Just as I was picking up some of the packets from Sergeant Wilson, John Thomas from the Bayer Company came up and we got into a big argument."

"About what?"

"Well, I had read some background information on his company, the Bayer Company. This information stated that back during World War Two, the Bayer Company was the one who manufactured the deadly gas that was used in the Nazi death camps gas chambers. The Bayer Company manufactured and provided the Nazis with a deathly gas called ZyklonB, commonly known as Hydrogen Cyanide which was used to kill millions of the Jews all over Europe in the Nazi gas chambers, before and during the war."

"He argued and tried to deny it and I said that I would not be a party to any transactions with a company that had committed those atrocities and war crimes. I said that I would not be providing any testing information to his company. Then I stormed out and I haven't been back until today."

"How come you didn't get in trouble for not picking up the classified test packets and transferred them back to base headquarters?"

"I just told Sergeant Wilson he'd have to transfer them himself, he has the clearance for it and apparently, he has been, because nothing more has been said."

"How come you returned today?

"Well, I figured it was my duty to let you make up your own mind about the Bayer Company."

"Well, now I'm really torn between my duties as a courier for the Army and a company that has committed war crimes. Of course I'll have to do as ordered by the US Army, unless I can find a way around it"

"That's exactly what I have struggled with for the last eight months. I'm sorry, Bob, but it's now your struggle"

Bob and Frank drove back to the main base in silence, contemplating their dilemma. Bob dropped Frank off back at the Supply Depot and headed over to the Motor Pool to check his truck back in as required. He then made his way back to his Mail Room to prepare for the daily hand-out of the mail after dinner.

After dinner he got together with his two friends from the Company Orderly Room; Roger Hammond and Richard Davis. The three went downstairs to the rec room and played several rounds of pool. After the pool games, they walked across the parking lot to the EM club and had a couple of beers before calling it a night. The term 'night' was an ambiguous term this time of year. Although it was almost midnight, the sun was still well above the horizon.

CHAPTER 4

Tuesday, there were no special 'courier' runs, just the usual mail runs, taking the outgoing mail from the USAATB over to the base Post Office to be forwarded down to the 'lower-48' and picking up the new incoming mail for the ATB. All mail from Alaska was flown in and out of the APO (Army Post Office) in Seattle.

After dinner and after the evening Mail-Call, Bob locked up the mail room and headed upstairs to his bunk area in the third floor squad room. Several of the 'Admin.' soldiers were engaged in a discussion about a week-end canoe trip up to the Shaw Creek.

One of the benefits that the Army provided to Soldiers in this extremely remote area of Alaska was the availability of recreational equipment for their use in their free time on weekends. They had available: fishing gear, canoeing and camping equipment, and the use of military vehicles not involved in testing, to take the soldiers to the remote areas for the specific type of recreation.

The soldiers involved in the group discussion about the canoe trip were; Roger Hammond and Richard Davis from Company Headquarters, Frank Krisinzkey from Supply and now, Bob Fellerer from the Mail Room.

"I've signed up for two canoes for this weekend," Roger said, "that include the paddles and life jackets."

"I've signed up for the cooking equipment," Richard said, "Now all we'll need is the food. We can stop at the PX on the way out on Saturday."

"What about a tent?" Bob questioned, "Won't we need a tent?"

"Not on this trip," Frank answered, "We'll be staying in that old abandoned trapper's log cabin. It's right on Shaw Creek. This time I'll bring my 44 Magnum pistol along. That's bear country up there."

"I'll sign out my mail truck for the weekend. There's no mail up here on weekends," Bob added, "It has a topper with roof racks for the canoes."

"I'll drive my car up to the drop-off point at the Shaw Creek Bridge," Richard said, "that way I can pick up the groceries on the way out, you just have to get me a list."

"You have your car up here?" Bob questioned.

"Yup, drove it up the ALCAN highway. It got pretty beat up though, on the trip."

"Well, it looks like we have everything covered," Roger said, "I'll pick up several six packs of beer at the NCO Club, where I work part time. They don't sell any take-out beer at the EM club, only tap beer. They don't trust the younger soldiers with any quantity of liquor, too many under aged soldiers in the lower ranks."

"Don't forget," Frank reminded everyone, "Check out your fishing gear at the Rec Center. We don't need to worry about fishing licenses here in Alaska. GI's aren't required to have a fishing license, only a hunting license."

"You mean," Joked Richard, "We can't drop one of them Grizzly's that frequent that trapper's cabin?"

"Only if it's in season," Roger responded," and you have a license, or if you're a native Alaskan."

"How about if it's self-defense?" joked Richard again."

"Well, you'll just have to talk to your local game warden," Roger replied, taking him seriously.

With that, their little planning session adjourned. Everyone settled down for the evening; writing their daily or weekly letters home to family and loved-ones.

Wednesday, five A.M., Bob was awakened by Frank. "Come on, Bob, get up. Today we will be flying out to the test site at Fort Yukon, up on the Yukon River."

They got showered, dressed, ate an early breakfast at the Mess Hall and asked for bag lunches to go. Bob signed out his mail truck and drove over to the base Post Office and picked up the daily mail and brought it back to his mail room and sorted out the mail for the Fort Yukon site. Bob and Frank then drove out to the air field to catch their flight to Fort Yukon. They boarded the two engine turbo prop airplane called the Caribou and after a short 20 minute flight were at Fort Yukon, located about four hundred miles due north of Fort Greeley on the Yukon River, precisely at the Arctic Circle.

Fort Yukon, a town of about six hundred, mostly native Alaskan people was established in the eighteen hundreds as a fur trading post by The Hudson Bay Company.

There are no roads going into Fort Yukon. In the nineteen fifty's, the US Air Force established a base with an air field and radar site on the banks of the Yukon River. The Army established a test site there in the late nineteen fifty's, testing mainly equipment and vehicles used to travel over the countless miles of muskeg swamps and permafrost. This equipment and vehicles are flown in to Fort Yukon. Summer testing is extensively done on the partially melted muskeg and permafrost. Winter testing is also carried on, testing vehicle performance in temperatures as low as minus seventy eight below zero.

They were shuttled from the air field over to the Army Testing Headquarters, set up in a series of large trailers which housed both the administrative and housing facilities. A Sergeant Bill Wilson met them at the front desk.

"Welcome to Fort Yukon and the Arctic Circle, gentlemen, where the sun never sets in the summer and never happens in the winter. This is 'The Last Frontier'," he said, as Bob and Frank showed their IDs and signed in. Frank introduced Bob as the new courier.

"I've got very large packets for you today," Sergeant Wilson said, "They have been doing a lot of summer testing this year on a whole array of new vehicles for the arctic. C'mon, I'll show you around."

He led them outside and in back of the headquarters complex, to a large fenced-in area.

"Wow!" Bob exclaimed, "This place looks like the movie set for some new science-fiction movie."

"Boy, what Hollywood couldn't do with these vehicles," Frank added.

"Come on in," Sergeant Wilson said as he opened the gate, "I'll give you the run-down on each one."

"Wait," Bob said, "Aren't these classified Secret or Top Secret?"

"No, no," Sergeant Wilson explained, "These won't be classified until they're done testing them."

They walked over to one of the vehicles, a very large tracked vehicle. It was about twenty five feet long and had a set of two, very large rubberized tracks about four feet wide each. The vehicle had a large enclosed compartment on top.

"Boy, that's some swamp buggy," Bob said, "I'll bet it can carry quite a load."

"Well, actually I believe it's called the Arctic Weasel," Sergeant Wilson said, "It can carry an entire squad of fully equipped men in that enclosed cab and can travel at up to sixty miles an hour over almost any terrain, muskeg swamp, dry land, or snow. I understand that it'll be arctic tested this winter."

"So, what's this vehicle?" Bob asked as they walked over to another strange looking machine, "It looks like a weird pontoon boat, and what are those weird looking vanes or whatever they're called wrapped around the pontoons like a giant screw."

"I don't actually know what they call it. As I understand, those screw-like threads wrapped around the pontoons are what propels this thing. The entire pontoons spin like the prop on a boat. I've heard that they've had problems with the drive units being in the rear. They get clogged with snow and ice. They're working on changing the drive mechanisms to the front so they don't get clogged up. They're waiting for the new parts to be shipped up from the lower forty eight."

"Moving on, then, "Frank said as they moved over to another strange looking vehicle, "I think I know what this one is. I've seen pictures of these being used down in the everglades. It's a hover craft, right?"

"Right, Frank. perfect for our muskeg swamps up here. They've just completed summer testing on this. The results are in today's packet," Sgt. Wilson whispered, "There will be more testing done this winter."

"What are those strange looking vehicles?" Bob asked, "Parked over here against the fence. There are four of them and they are way smaller than the rest of the test vehicles."

"I think those are called 'snow cats'. I'm not totally sure what they are. They just came in and are scheduled for winter arctic testing. You can tell they are for operating on the snow. They have a pair of skies mounted on the front with a set of handlebars for steering. They have an engine driven rubberized belt about eighteen inches wide with cleats that runs along the bottom in the middle for propelling it along in the snow. The Bombardier Company of Canada makes them. They have already sold hundreds of them all over Canada. They claim they are the next big thing in the snow. They can carry one or two people plus gear. Bombardier claims that they can go like hell over the snow."

"They should be great for outrunning the enemy," Bob said, "And they look like they should be fun to drive. Maybe I could help you test them next winter."

"Maybe so," Sergeant Wilson said, "They aren't classified as 'Secret', because they are already in civilian use. I'll have to let you know when they're testing them."

"Well, gentlemen, that concludes my little tour of test vehicles. That isn't all of them by any means, but, it's all I can show you that are not classified as 'secret'. Most of those are out at our remote test sites in the muskeg swamps all over the Yukon River Valley. Plus, of course, we keep getting more of them all the time. This is shaping up to be our busiest winter yet for arctic testing."

"Well," Frank said, "It looks like it's about lunch time. Come on, Bob, I'll show you where their mess hall is located."

After lunch, they went up to the front desk and Bob signed for the classified test packet to deliver to Fort Greely Headquarters. Frank took the duplicate packet and said he would show Bob where and how to send it on to the requesting company. They walked back over to the air field through Fort Yukon, a town without streets or roads, just clusters of houses where the natives lived and subsisted on fish from the river and wild game.

"The Army brought in electric generators when they built the testing site and now supplied electricity to some of the homes." Frank stated.

They had to wait until about 2 P.M. for their flight back to Fort Greely. Bob dropped Frank off at the supply depot and made it back just in time to sort the mail and open up his mail room for the evening mail call.

Later that night, after midnight, Frank again woke Bob up. "Come on, he whispered, let's go down to your mail room and take care of that 'other packet'."

Bob slipped on a pair of pants and they crept downstairs in the twilight of the now fading midnight sun. Bob unlocked his mailroom and they entered and quietly closed and locked the door. Frank took an empty mail sack and laid it across the bottom of the door to obstruct any light from seeping out into the hall. Frank took the test packet out from under his shirt and placed it on the desk, then opened a desk drawer and took a large mailing envelope, placed the packet in it and took the necessary stamps from his wallet and stuck them on the envelope. He pulled a piece of paper from his pocket and copied the address from it, onto the envelope. The name on the addressee was The Chrysler Corporation, Detroit, Michigan. The Arctic Weasel vehicle was manufactured by the Military Division of GM.

"Here," he said, "When you go to the Post Office in the morning, drop this in the outgoing mail. And, that's how it's done, Bob. Simple isn't it? And for this you can make a lot of extra money. Your handler will be supplying you with the name and address for these mailings. What I do when I get them is tuck the list in the toe of my boot that I am not wearing. In other words, now in summer, I keep it in the toe of my winter boot. In winter, I keep it in the toe of my summer boot. So, what do you say, Bob, are you in?"

"I just don't know yet, Frank. I have to think about it some more. It seems too risky and somehow, just not right"

"Well damn it Bob, don't wait too long. The winter testing season starts in just a few months. Do you want to make a lot of money, or not. Make up your damn mind, I can't wait forever, or I'll have to find someone else to get these mailings out."

With that Frank opened the mail room door and stormed back upstairs leaving Bob to lock up and think about the whole plan.

ROBB FELDER

CHAPTER 5

Mosquitoes as big as dragon flies with stingers as big as hypodermic needles, were dive-bombing his face and neck and crawling all over his hands and arms.

"Boy, they weren't kidding in that orientation when they warned you about these pesky little devils," Bob said as he reached into his pack for more of the repellent and slathered more of the noxious smelling stuff on all exposed flesh, "When they bite, it feels like you're getting vaccinated with their venom. I mean, I thought we had mosquitoes back in Minnesota, but, those are like gnats compared to these monsters."

It was Saturday and the four friends, Roger, Bob, Richard and Frank were paddling up the Shaw Creek for a week-end trip into the wild. They had left Fort Greely about four in the morning. The Shaw Creek was about forty miles from the Base. They were all wearing their Army fatigues, hats and middle weight jackets, called field jackets.   Although it was late July, the temperature was only in the fifty's at this higher elevation.   They also wore knee-length rubber boots they had checked out along with the other fishing and camping gear.   After unloading the canoes and gear at the highway bridge from the two Army pickups they had signed out for the weekend, they had been paddling up Shaw Creek for about two hours.

"How much farther to the old trapper's cabin?" Bob complained.

"Only about another half mile," Roger replied, "I've made this trip last year summer. I know it's tough maneuvering around all the deadfall trees laying in the water everywhere, but, it'll be worth it when we get there. I guarantee it. We can get a big campfire going, that'll keep some of these killer mosquitoes at bay."

A little further on, they saw a large Brown Bear ambling along the shore of the creek with her two cubs.

"Brown Bears are very common in this area," Roger said, "In fact all over central Alaska. They're bigger than the Black Bear, but, not as big as the Grizzly, which are also sometimes seen in this area. We've seen some of the Browns at the cabin last year."

They paddled on in silence the rest of the way up Shaw Creek to the cabin. As they came around the last bend, they saw the cabin situated high up on the bank of the creek. They pulled the canoes up on shore and tied them up on a large deadfall log laying out into the creek. The cabin wasn't locked, so they began carrying in their gear, except for the food.

"Who owns this cabin?" Bob asked anyone who might know the answer."

"Nobody owns it," Roger responded, "This is all state owned land, and the cabin has been abandoned for years. The old trapper who built it probably either died or moved on, after the supply of fur-bearing animals became depleted and just left it. Guys from Fort Greely have been coming up here and using it for years."

"We can't store the food in the cabin," Roger stated, "We'll have bears trying to break in to get at it. It'll have go up in the cache."

"What's a 'cache?" Bob asked.

Roger pointed; off to the side of the cabin about ten yards was a tower of sorts, built with four large logs that were implanted into the ground supporting a small shed-like structure. The shed-like building was about six by four feet square, by about four feet high with a small door in front, mounted on the posts about eight or ten feet off the ground. The posts all had a band of tin about three feet tall wrapped around them about six feet off the ground to prevent any critters, including bears from climbing up to get at the food. An old aluminum ladder provided access up to the cache. The boys began storing all the food items up in the cache, including the ice chest with ice and the meat.

"These 'cache' structures," Roger explained, "are common all over Alaska, especially in bear country."

Inside the old log cabin there were four bunks and an old barrel stove that could be used for cooking on as well as heat. The cabin had only one window that overlooked the creek and had a large shutter that covered the window to keep out any bears. Outside, there was a lean-to with a stack of firewood under the roof.

The four men unpacked inside and went out and got out their fishing gear. They all started casting their lines in, all up and down the creek. The Trout and Grayling started hitting almost immediately; by noon, they had enough for a noon meal.

"Don't forget to bury the entrails," Roger reminded them, "If the bears catch a scent of our fish, they'll be all over this place, and won't leave us alone till we leave."

Bob began splitting some of the cut-up logs stacked next to the cabin and started a fire in the fire ring. When the fire was hot, he placed the steel grid over it. Frank, meantime, got out the frypan and greased it up, then dipped the trout and grayling in an egg batter, then corn meal and placed them in the frypan. In a few minutes the fish were ready. They ate them with chips and they all popped open a beer.

"Aah, this is the life," Richard commented, as they all sat on logs and feasted on their catch. After a couple more beers, they were feeling sleepy and spread out on the ground next to the logs and dozed off lying in the warm sun. After about an hour nap, they were awakened by the sound of snapping twigs. Across the creek they saw a large brown bear and her cubs.

"She probably caught scent of our fish fry," Frank said, as he dug in his pack and pulled out his forty five magnum, long barrel revolver. As the bear and cubs stopped right across the creek from them and she held her head up sniffing the air. Frank aimed his forty five in the air and fired off several shots. The sow bear and cubs bounded off into the woods.

"I hope that's the last we see of her," he said.

"Oh, I wouldn't bet on it," Roger said, "Now that she's caught scent of the fish, she'll be back. So from now on, we'll just have to be vigilant for her return. Hey, how about we do a little exploring upstream? Maybe we could hike all the way up to the source of this creek. I understand that it drains from a glacier about five miles further up in these mountains, up stream."

"Ok," Frank said, "As long as we can make it back by dark. I don't care to meet up with that 'mommy bear' in the dark."

"Well, we better get hiking," Bob said as he grabbed his backpack with some snacks and a couple beers in it. Everyone else did the same. Frank strapped on his holster and took his forty-five. The trail followed the creek through heavily wooded areas and across muskeg swamps as it gradually climbed. They followed the creek-side trail for several miles and stopped for a break.

"I noticed some boot tracks," Bob said, "among all the bear tracks in the soft spots on the trail. Looks like we're not the only ones hiking up to the glacier."

"Well, let's hope they're all friendly, both the humans and bears," Frank said.

They finished their beers and continued on up the trail. The terrain suddenly began to change as the trail ascended steeply and the creek now cascaded over large boulders and the trees thinned out in the rocky terrain. Soon they came to a waterfall about twenty or thirty feet high and they had to climb up over large boulders to reach the top. There, suddenly, they could see the icy face of the glacier where the creek came pouring out of the bottom of the ice. The face of the glacier was a jagged wall of sheer ice about forty feet high and wedged between the canyon walls about a hundred yards wide that contained it.

The air temperature suddenly became icy as well. There, just above the falls, on the bank of the creek, they spotted a camp set up with a tent and a campfire in front. As the four soldiers approached the camp, one of the guys who were sitting next to the fire stood up and greeted the four and said, "You must be the guys staying down at the log cabin."

"Why yes, we are," replied Frank, and introduced himself and the other three and said that they were from Fort Greely.

The other guy said, "I don't give a damn about your names and I already figured you were from Greely. Now, why don't you just turn around and head back down to that log cabin, which is our cabin, by the way."

Roger started to argue that point with him, stating, "That cabin is an abandoned cabin on public land."

Just then, the other guy stood up and pointed a gun at them and said "Not anymore, it isn't. we're claiming it, and we want you out of there."

"That cabin was built by my grandfather back in nineteen forty eight when he was prospecting here, along Shaw Creek. You damn GI's from Greely seem to think you own the whole friggin state. We want you the hell out of there. Now, why don't you just get back down there and clear the hell out. We'll give you till morning to pack up your shit and be out."

Richard thought about drawing his own gun, but, decided he didn't want to start a gun fight and get someone killed. The other three were looking at him, kind of expecting him to. But instead he said,"Well, it is getting late, guy's, we may as well head back down."

With that they climbed back down the steep trail at the falls, and made their way along the trail all the way back to the cabin. About half way back, it began to rain; lightly at first, but by the time they got back, it was raining pretty good and getting late. They were glad to get inside, out of the rain. Roger lit a lantern because outside, the midnight sun was waning as the thunder clouds darkened everything.

"Before we settle in for the evening," Roger said, "We'd better go out and flip our canoes over up on the creek bank so they won't fill with water."

When that was done, Frank said, "I guess, we'll have to cook and eat inside tonight."

So, as Bob brought enough firewood inside for cooking and keeping warm through the cold rainy night, Roger climbed up into the meat cache and brought down hamburger and cheese for dinner. Richard brought in some beers from the cooler outside and after Bob started the fire, everyone shed their outer garments and hung them up to dry, while Roger got out a frying pan and made up the hamburger into patties and got them cooking. Soon everyone's clothing was dry and they proceeded to feast on cheeseburgers, chips and beer. Outside rain was coming down heavily and a thick fog settled into the Shaw Creek valley. Inside, the foursome began a game of poker and began to discuss the incident up at the glacier.

"I don't think," Roger said, "we should knuckle-under to that guy. Dammit we were here first and I'm pretty damn sure this cabin is still public property."

"I agree," Bob said, "I think we should stand our ground and not leave tomorrow until we are good and ready to head back to the base."

"Yeah," Richard said, "But what about the fact that they have a gun and are probably willing to use it."

"So," Frank said, "So do we have a gun."

"Yeah, I do have a gun, but I have no intention of shooting someone over this damn cabin. There are plenty of other places in this huge state of Alaska where can fish all we want."

"Ok, how about this?" Roger said, "In the morning, we load our stuff into the canoes and just fish all along this section of the creek. I know for a fact all waters are public waters in Alaska. We can then take our fish back to the base and have them cooked up in the mess hall. I've seen that done before."

After a couple more rounds of poker, the four soldiers decided to hit the sack. They were pretty bushed after their hike up to the glacier. Bob stoked up the fire, adding several large logs.

"There, that should last us till morning. It's going to be a long cold night."

They all fell right to sleep with several beers in their bellies. But, the wood didn't last all night. By about midnight, the fire died down. Bob got up. He added more wood and found the poker and stirred up the red hot coals, then crawled back into his bunk. However, in his half-asleep state, he forgot to remove the poker from the stove.

At about two, A.M., they were all awakened by a loud crackling and crunching sound.

"Who's there?" Frank yelled, thinking someone was trying to break in the door, "I'll bet it's those damn prospectors from up at the glacier."

But, Frank was wrong, a few seconds later, the window shutter came crashing in, along with the whole window. There in the window opening appeared a huge grizzly bear, clamoring to crawl in through the opening.

"What the hell?" Roger yelled.

Frank got out of bed and scrambled around trying to find his gun. Bob suddenly spotted the poker still stuck into the red hot coals of the stove and jumped out of bed and grabbed the red hot poker and began jabbing at the huge grizzly bear head coming in through the window. The grizzly opened his huge mouth to snarl at him. Bob jabbed the red hot poker into the grizzly's mouth and down his throat. The smell of burning flesh filled the cabin as the bear backed down from the window, howling in pain. But, a few seconds later he again stood on his hind legs and was trying to get up into the window. By this time Frank found his forty-five pistol. Bob stepped aside as Frank aimed and fired two of his forty-five magnum rounds into the head of the grizzly. The huge bear took one step back and dropped to the ground, dead.

Bob, Frank. Richard and Roger all quickly slipped on a pair of their fatigues and ran outside to look at the huge grizzly bear lying on the ground, dead. "What the hell are we going to do with a huge dead bear carcass?" Frank questioned, rhetorically.

"Well," Bob said, "We can't do much tonight. Let's get back to bed and try to get some sleep."

They went back inside, Frank lite the lantern again and they put the broken window back into its frame, along with the window shutter, as best they could, while they each had another beer to celebrate their bear kill. Soon, they were sleepy again and crawled back into their bunks, after Bob again stoked up the fire. They slept soundly until about six o'clock.

The rain had ended and the sun was already well above the horizon. Roger, the self-appointed cook went to work and cooked up some grub for breakfast, after climbing again, up into the meat cache to retrieve some bacon and eggs they had stashed there.

"What should we do about that huge grizzly that we killed last night?" Bob asked as breakfast was being prepared.

"We'll just have to leave it for now," Roger said, "When we get back into Delta Junction, we'll call the Alaska Fish and Game Dept. and explain what happened."

They, devoured the breakfast, packed up all their gear and hurried over to the canoe landing, only to discover that the canoes were not there.

"What the hell is going on around here, Roger shouted angrily. "Where the hell are our canoes?"

"We had them pulled up and overturned right here, yesterday, Bob stated.

"Those damn prospectors," Richard said, "I'll bet it was those two asshole prospectors that we had that run-in with, up at the glacier yesterday. They said they wanted us out of here today. Now how the hell can we get out of here if they stole our damn canoes? I'll bet they are just getting a kick out of harassing us."

"Well, I guess we don't have a choice but to hoof it back to the bridge and see if we can catch up with them there," Frank said, "I think I know of a shortcut back. It's about a two hour paddle back to the bridge by canoe, but, the creek zig sags back and forth so much. We can make it back in about an hour using the short-cut trail. "

Richard first took the camp ax and cut four walking sticks for the hike back to the bridge. They set out down the trail, which was good going on the higher ground, but the going became difficult where the trail cut through the muskeg swamps. The rain from last night had flooded the swamps and they had wade through water and mud that at times came over the tops of their boots. The mosquitoes were horrific, after the rain and they didn't have time to stop to apply repellent. So they slogged on through the muskeg as the little devils chawed on them ceaselessly. After about an hour, they saw the bridge through the trees.

"I don't see those two prospectors anywhere near the bridge," Bob said, "

"I do see an old beat-up pickup parked off to the side of the road. That must be theirs," Frank said, "Which means, we beat them here. Now we just have to get the drop on them when they get here."

They crept through the brush, up to their own two pickups parked on the shoulder of the highway close to the bridge and threw their gear and walking sticks into the back and quickly crawled into the two trucks; relieved to be in out of the ravages of the mosquitoes. Then, they waited.

They didn't have to wait long. In about twenty minutes, they spotted the canoes rounding a bend of the creek. The four soldiers quickly and quietly got out of their pickups, grabbed their walking sticks and went over and crouched behind the two thieves' truck and waited for them. The two thieves landed the canoes at the bridge and began carrying one of them over to their truck to load it. Our four soldiers split up, two went around the back of the truck and the other two went around the front.

Frank drew his forty four magnum and yelled, "Okay, just set our canoe down nice and easy and get your hands up in the air."

The two canoe thieves complied and set the canoe down. However, the one that had pulled his gun on them the day before, went for his gun again. Bob quickly raised his walking stick and swung it hard and fast and came down on the guy's forearm. His gun went flying as he howled in pain.

"You son-of-a-bitch, I think you broke my damn arm," He yelled, grabbing his broken arm with his good hand.

"Okay, one at a time, climb into the back of one of our pickups. The one with the broken arm went first and painfully climbed up into the back of the truck. Bob helped him and climbed up after him. He forced the guy to lie down and took some of the rope they had used to lash down the canoes and hog-tied the guys' hands and feet to each other.

"Okay, now you," Frank said to the other one that he held at gunpoint, "Nice and easy, climb up and join your partner in the bed of the truck. Then we're going to take a nice little ride back down to Delta Junction, to the county sheriff's department."

Bob took some more of the rope and hog-tied the second one down on the floor of the truck. They all four loaded their one canoe that the two thieves had dropped next to their truck into their other pickup and got the other canoe and doubled them up in the back of that truck. Richard picked up the thief's gun that had gone flying. The four soldiers all got in and they turned their trucks around and headed back down the highway to Delta Junction.

"Well, I'll be damned," Sheriff Gene Turner said when he saw the two thieves. These are the two we've been looking for. Did you know that these two are wanted fugitives? This here is Bart Mc Gee and his partner Will Black. There's a bounty posted for these two. There's a reward of five thousand dollars each for their capture. Lock them up, deputy."

"Oh, really," Bob said. "We thought they were just a pair of crazy prospectors. As he began to explain how he and his three friends stumbled across their camp up at the Shaw Creek Glacier.

"They pulled a gun on us," Bob went on to explain, "They tried to tell us that old trapper's cabin was theirs."

"Just what are the two wanted for," Frank asked the sheriff,

"Oh, they have a long 'rap sheet' of crimes listed against them; among them is murder," the sheriff began to explain, "These two have a hideout up on the Jarvis creek, north of Fairbanks. They apparently robbed a bank in Fairbanks and shot and killed one of the tellers then murdered their other partner over a poker game at their hideout. We tracked them to their hideout, but they got out before we arrived. That's when we found the body of the other gang member. They apparently wanted that cabin up on Shaw creek for their new hideout."

"Wow," Roger said, "Who knew they were that dangerous."

Bob explained to Sheriff Turner about the run in with the grizzly bear up at the trappers cabin and how they had to shoot it after it started climbing through the window. The Sheriff said he would notify the DNR, and they would take care of the carcass.

"Well, I'll get some paperwork and take a statement for you guys to sign," The sheriff said. You'll probably want to get back to your base. It's getting late and you have to clean up your gear and get it turned in."

"Right," Bob said, "Just let us know when you want us back in to sign the paperwork and file for that reward."

So, the four, Bob, Frank, Richard and Roger headed back to Fort Greely. When they got back to the Rec Center to turn in their fishing gear and the two canoes, they rented a storage locker and stashed the camping gear from the two fugitives. A lot of the guys on base had their own personal gear stored in their own lockers. They thought they could use it again next time they went out. As they were transferring the gear from the canoes to the locker, Bob discovered a small leather pouch in the bottom of one of the canoes. The pouch seemed quite heavy for such a small container. He put it in his own pocket and didn't say anything just yet. He didn't really know what might be in the pouch. It was too small to possibly contain any of the loot from the fugitives bank heist.

They proceeded to finish cleaning up the canoes and then took the pickups back over to the Motor Pool and washed them and checked them back in.

CHAPTER 6

On his way to the Mess Hall, later that Sunday evening, Bob stopped at his mailroom and dropped the strange pouch into his desk drawer, then locked up and joined his friends for supper. After supper, Richard went down to the company armory to lock up his forty four magnum pistol, then he and Roger went upstairs to their cubicle bunk area to clean up their gear and shower before hitting the sack. Frank and Bob went down to the basement rec room for a game of pool. After a couple of games, the rec room became deserted as everyone else headed upstairs to bed down for the night.

Frank then asked Bob, "What was in that strange little pouch that I saw you take out of the canoe earlier, up at the bridge on Shaw Creek?"

"I don't know yet, I haven't had a chance to open it. I locked it in the mailroom. I'll let all you guys know tomorrow."

"I think I know what it might be. I've heard rumors about Shaw Creek, up in Fairbanks, at Fort Wainwright, when I make supply runs up there and back. Let me know when you get a chance to look into the pouch. I've got a very early supply run to make, up to Fairbanks tomorrow, but I should be back about four o'clock. Call me."

They both headed up to bed, but didn't mention anything yet to Richard and Roger. All four of them were pretty whipped-out after their ordeal on Shaw Creek.

Monday morning dawned early, at about 0200 hours, now, in late July. Bob however, and most of the Army Arctic Test Board got up at six. He quickly showered, dressed and ran downstairs to the Mess Hall for breakfast. After breakfast, he headed over to the Motor Pool, walking past the Nuclear Power Plant, just across the street from the barracks building. Down another block was the Motor Pool. His pickup truck was parked in the outside lot this time of year, but in winter would be parked inside the huge vehicle work shop and vehicle parking building when the temperature started dropping below forty below zero, which was from about November to April. He signed out his pickup and headed back over to the barracks building to pick up the outgoing mail from the mail drop box mounted on the wall just outside his mailroom. He then headed out to Main Post Office to pick up the company's mail.

After sorting the mail and filling the alphabetical mail slots, Bob worked at his Monday morning task of completing the updating of transfers forwarding addresses and adding new arrivals to his roster.

All this while, Bob had been thinking about his friend Frank and his proposal to sell test information to competing companies. It was just not sitting right with him. He was almost sure it would be illegal and could get him sent to jail. Just as he was prepared to do his Monday morning courier pick up down on the Delta River flats test site, his phone rang. He picked it up. It was Master Sergeant Ron Davis from the Missile Test Range. He called to tell him that there would be no courier packet today. Bob was very relieved. That would give him time to work on a plan for his dilemma.

After about another hour of struggling with the problem, he began to formulate a solution. He opened a drawer of his desk and pulled out the phone book for Fort Wainwright. He looked through it and found a number for the Inspector General Office. He dialed the number and asked to speak to one of the investigators.

Lieutenant Ray George picked up his phone. "Special Investigator, Lieutenant George, sir." He stated, "How may I help you, Sir."

"This is PFC Bob Fellerer, Sir. I'm calling from Fort Greely's Arctic Test Center. I am the new Courier and Mail Clerk for the ATB. I would like to talk to you about a possible breech of security that I have discovered, regarding some of the testing data that I believe is being compromised."

"Well, Private Fellerer, any breech of security of any classified material, we will take very seriously. Why don't I come down to Greely immediately and let's talk about this situation. I have an opening tomorrow afternoon. I'll set up a meeting at the Arctic Test Headquarters there in Greely. I'll call you back with a time for us to meet there."

"Very good, Sir, I should be done with my morning run to the Base Post Office for the daily company mail by about nine o'clock."

They both hung up and Bob gave a huge sigh of relief at having taken the first step in resolving the issue with Specialist Frank Krisinzkey and the transferring of secret test results to competing manufacturing companies.

"But what will happen to Frank?" he wondered, "He could be in some serious trouble and he was becoming a friend," Bob thought, "But

I have to take care of myself, first, for the sake of my family. I'll just have to wait and see how this all plays out."

He sat and worried about it until lunch time, then he went to the Mess Hall for his early lunch. He came back and opened up his mail room for the noon 'mail call'. After he had completed his mail call, Bob closed up the mail window and went over to his desk. He unlocked the drawer with the mysterious pouch. He opened the pouch and was so shocked, that he nearly jumped out of his chair. The inside of the pouch literally glowed with the sparkle of gold, lots of gold. There were gold nuggets the size of marbles and lots of gold granules the size of gravel. Bob had no idea what the value of the pouch of gold would be. He went over to his postage scale and took the gold out of the pouch and weighed the gold. It weighed thirty six ounces. Secondly, he had no idea what the value would be for that weight of gold. It would have to be weighed in at an assayer's office, then, split four ways with his three buddies. He checked in the Delta Junction phone book, but there wasn't an assayer there. The pouch of gold would have to be taken to Fairbanks, there was an assayer's office listed in the Fairbanks phone book. Bob locked the pouch of gold back into his desk drawer. It was about 1300 hrs. in the afternoon and he was scheduled to work for a few hours over at the ATB Headquarters Personnel Department, doing some typing of lists of the new arrivals by rank and MOS, to be sent out to the various test sites that needed replacements for those soldiers whose tours were completed and had returned to the lower 48.

He returned at 1700 hrs. for an early supper and opened up his mailroom window for the evening mail-call. But first he got a phone call from I,G, Inspector, Lt. Ray George.

"I'll be at your ATB headquarters tomorrow afternoon at thirteen hundred hours, PFC Fellerer, can you make it?"

"Okay, yes sir, I'll be there."

After all the mail was handed out and everyone headed upstairs for the evening, Roger, Frank and Richard came up to the window and Bob told them to wait just a minute. He closed the mail window and unlocked the door and carefully checked up and down the hall to make sure no one else was around. Bob's three friends all filed into the mail room.

"First of all, I just got a call from Sheriff Turner in Delta Junction. He wants us to sign the statment paperwork on those two criminals that we captured and turned in, what's their names again?"

"Bart McGee and Will Black," Frank added.

"Yeah, those two, we also have to sign the forms to get our reward for their capture."

"So, what's in this mysterious pouch?" Roger asked.

"Before I divulge that to you, I want you three to swear to secrecy about what's in the leather sack. Further, I want an agreement by all of us that we split what's in the pouch four ways. Everybody agree?"

"Okay, agreed," Both Richard and Roger said.

"I'll agree to it as well," Frank said, "Cause I think I already know what's in the bag."

"I'm in as well, of course," Bob said.

He got out his key and unlocked his desk drawer and took out the leather pouch and emptied the gold contents out onto his desk.

"Holy crap," Richard yelled!

"What, the fuck. Are you kidding me?" Roger stated.

"Hot damn," Frank said, "I knew it!"

"Now, how the hell did you know what was going to be in the bag?" Roger asked Frank.

"Well, I just assumed that's what it would be, based on what I heard from the guys up in Fort Wainwright when I make my supply runs. The rumor has it that there's gold up in Shaw Creek, under that glacier, and as it melts, the gold is exposed."

"So, what you're saying is that those two crooks that we captured and turned in, were panning for gold up at the glacier," Richard questioned?

"That's exactly correct," Bob said, "And, we've got to get back up there and get more before somebody else gets to it,"

"How much do we have here already?" Roger questioned, "And what's it worth?"

"I've weighed it on my postage scale and we have about thirty six ounces. I think the value of gold right now is about one hundred and fifty dollars an ounce. So doing the math, we have about five thousand, four hundred dollars, worth of gold here."

"Holy shit, no kidding," Richard said, "You're right. Bob, we've got to get back up to that glacier and get more."

"Well," Roger said, "I guess the only question now is; how do we sell it and get our money?"

"I've already done some checking on that," Bob said, "First, we have to have the weight verified by an assayer. There isn't an assayer's office in Delta Junction, but I found one listed in the phone book in Fairbanks."

"Oh hell, I know right where that is," Frank said, "It's right on Northern Lights Blvd. I go right by it on my way into Fairbanks to pick up supplies. It's called the 49th State Gold Buyers. Their sign says that they buy raw gold, 'right from the pan'.   Hell, I could take our gold in next Monday, on my next supply run."

"That sounds like a good idea. If we can trust you," Richard said.

"Well, damn right you can trust me. You've trusted me to deliver your damn mail for the last eight months, till Bob took over. Besides, we all now know approximately what the gold weighs, and what the current value is, and I'll get receipts when I cash it in at the assayer's office."

"Okay, okay, let's not argue about it," Bob said, "Here's what, let's do. First we'll need to get a lock box to safely transport the gold. I'll pick one up at the PX, tomorrow. Then next Monday, Frank, you can pick up the lock box before you leave for your Monday supply run. Meantime, let's plan another trip up to Shaw Creek and see if we can pan some more gold."

"We can check out some panning equipment from the Rec Center," Roger said, "Hell, a lot of guys go out gold panning every weekend. I'll call and reserve some panning equipment and some camping equipment for us for this weekend."

With that, Bob took the gold nuggets and granules, put them back in the sack and locked them back up in his desk drawer. He locked up the mail room and they went out to Roger's car and headed out to Delta Junction and signed all the statements and forms and returned back to Base and headed over to the EM club to have a beer to celebrate their newfound fortune and discuss further plans for gold panning beneath the Shaw Creek Glacier.

CHAPTER 7

Tuesday morning, right after breakfast, Bob checked his pickup out of the Motor Pool and picked the ATB's mail from the Main Base Post Office. He brought it back to his Mail Room and sorted it into the slots for mail call. All this while, he was mulling over in his mind, his dilemma with Frank and his industrial espionage practice. Frank was sure to be prosecuted for his illegal operation. Other than that, Frank was his good friend.

"What would the other guys in our little group think, if they found out that I turned him in," he thought, Maybe I should have just refused to pick up the test docs., and let Frank work out his own way of transferring them to the other manufacturers."

Eleven o'clock came and went and Bob didn't go to his early lunch, or lunch at all. His stomach was tied in a knot fretting about the meeting with the I. G. Investigator. At 1200 hrs.

he opened up his mail window and handed out mail to the guys coming out of the Mess Hall. At 1230 hrs, he closed up and headed out to his truck and made his way over to the ATB headquarters building. The receptionist directed him to one of the meeting rooms.

He entered the room and introduced himself, "I am PFC Robert Fellerer, Sir."

Lt. Ray George introduced himself and said, "I believe you've met Colonel Kimball, your Arctic Test Board Commander. He will be sitting in on this meeting so that he will be apprised of situations regarding the men in his command."

"PFC Fellerer, Lt. George has only briefly explained why you have contacted him regarding your suspicions of a possible breach of security regarding some of the testing results that you believe are being illegally passed to the competitors of the manufacturers of the equipment we test. You may proceed with your investigation, Lt. George."

Lt. George placed a tape recorder on the table and started it. The two Officers also began taking hand written notes.

"Okay PFC Fellerer, you said on the phone that you believe that test results were being passed by Specialist Frank Krisinzkey, and that he would then send them on to the competitor manufacturer of the equipment being reported on. Would you explain just how this takes place."

"Yes, Sir," Bob began, "As Frank was taking me around to the various test sites, he introduced me to the contact person who would be signing over the classified packets of test results for me to provide transport back to the ATB base headquarters. As I was signing for the packet, the contact person would then produce a packet of copied test results, not stamped classified or secret and hand them to Frank. When we returned back to base, I would take the classified packet and turn it in to the ATB test coordinator at Headquarters. Frank would then take the copied packet and mail it to the competing company. Sometime later, Frank would say that he had received a check in the mail from that company."

"Has he said where he gets the information on where, and to whom to send this copy of the test results?"

"No, Sir, only that he is working with a handler who provides this information."

"How many of our test sites have been compromised by this pirating of test information?"

"Well, Sir, Frank has, so far, introduced me to the Delta River Missile and Artillery Range, the Girstle River Site and the Fort Yukon Site."

"Has he accepted those copies of the test results from all three of those test sites and forwarded them?"

"Yes, Sir, he has."

"What's the next test site that you two will be visiting?"

"Prudhoe Bay. Sir. I believe Frank has said that we will be flying out on Thursday and returning on Friday."

"Well," Lt George said, "It appears that Specialist Frank Krisinzkey has quite an operation of industrial espionage going for himself. And, he wants you to continue the operation after he leaves, is that correct?"

"Yes, Sir, that is correct."

"Have you said yet that you would consider taking over the operation?"

"Well, Sir, I have all but said that I would not consider it, even though he keeps pressuring me to take over after he leaves. He keeps saying that I could make a lot of money, but if I turned him down, he would just have the contact person at the test sites do the mailing instead. He said that they don't really want to do that because that puts them at too much risk of being discovered. He said that he needs someone in the 'mail system' to do the mailings. That's less risky than the test sites doing it."

"Well, PFC Fellerer, I think we now have enough information on what's going on. We will analyze what you've told us here today and come up with a plan on how to proceed with this issue. Meantime, do not discuss any of this with Specialist Krisinzkey, or anyone else; understood, PFC Fellerer."

"Yes Sir, understood, Sir."

"Thank you," Colonel Kimball said, "For coming forth with this information. I know this has been difficult for you, deciding what to do. But, believe me, you've done the right thing. One of us will get back to you with instructions on how you should proceed. That will be all for now."

Bob stood up and saluted the officers and left the room and the headquarters building. He was still wondering, as he drove back to the Motor Pool to turn his truck in.

ROBB FELDER

CHAPTER 8

Wednesday, just after Bob returned to his mail room with the morning mail, he got a phone call from Lieutenant Ray George.

"Good morning, PFC Fellerer," He said, "We, here at the I. G. office at Fort Wainwright held a meeting this morning to discuss the issue that you brought to our attention yesterday. It has been decided that you will proceed as follows:

No.1. You are to take Specialist Krisinskey up on his offer to take over his business of passing on test results to the competing companies.

No.2. You will continue to accept the second copy of the unclassified test results from the test sites. You will, however, mail those packets to me, here at Fort Wainwright instead of the mailing address that Frank has supplied to you.

No.3. You will forward all of the mailing names and address of those companies that Frank gives to you, as well as any future ones, to me. Here is my address: Lieutenant Ray George

c/o Inspector General Office
1924 Alcan Street N.W.
Fort   Wainwright,   Alaska
APO 49240

No.4. You will attempt to acquire, from Specialist Krisinzkey, the names of all of the people that he has worked with; the persons at the various companies, as well as the name and address of his handler. You will forward these names to me ASAP, along with the names of all of your contacts at all of the test sites..

No.5. You will open up a savings account at the Wells Fargo Bank in San Francisco, where you will deposit any and all of the money that you collect for this operation and forward the account number as well as your monthly bank statements to me, here at the I.G. office.

That's the complete set of directives for you to follow. Are there any questions?"

"No Sir, not right now. Could I get a copy of these directives to have on hand for referencing?"

"Absolutely, PFC Fellerer, I will be sending you a copy of these, today. Keep in mind, these are classified material and as such, they are to be kept under lock and key at all times and not discussed or shown to anyone. These directives are FYO(For Your Eyes Only), not your First

Sergeant nor Company Commander. Not anyone; understood?”

“Yes Sir, I understand completely.”

“Very good, PFC Fellerer. If you have any further questions, call me right away. Also let me know immediately of any changes to the system of receiving these documents, or, any threats made to you by Frank or anyone else regarding your involvement in the process.

I also need to inform you that you may, from time to time, hear from my counterpart, someone from the I.G. division at Fort Belvoir Virginia, because Fort Greely is under their command. You may even hear from someone at the Pentagon or even the CIA. Keep in mind, PFC Fellerer, this issue of espionage is a very serious issue and has far-reaching implications.”

With that, Lt. George hung up and left Bob wondering just what the hell he had gotten himself into.

* * * * *

Thursday morning early, Bob packed a duffle bag containing his winter socks, boots and his winter parka and gloves, also his sleeping bag. He had been told that the temperature was considerably colder and the accommodations were sparse in Prudhoe Bay, which was located on the Arctic Ocean. He completed his morning mail pickup from the Base Post Office, brought it back and sorted it into the mail rack. He then went down the hall to the company Orderly Room where his friend SP4Roger Hammond worked. He turned his Mail Room keys over to SP4 Roger. Roger was his back-up mail handler. He was a certified Mail Clerk and would open the mail window and hold the noon and evening mail calls while Bob was up at Prudhoe Bay. Bob then drove out to the airfield where he was met by his friend Frank, who would accompany him on the flight up to Prudhoe Bay, on the Arctic Ocean.

Prudhoe Bay is about four hundred and sixty miles due north of Fort Greely. The plane ride took about two and a half hours to complete. During their approach to the landing strip, they could see the vast Arctic Ocean covered mostly in ice, stretching off to the horizon. There was just a narrow strip of open water near the coast and in the bay. As they got off the plane, Bob commented, "Boy, Frank, they were not kidding when they said it would be colder up here. That wind coming off the Arctic Ocean has a definite bite to it."

They were met by a friendly soldier who introduced himself as Master Sergeant Gene Mc Cafery. Frank then introduced him to Bob.

"Welcome to Prudhoe Bay, the U. S. Army's northern most outpost on the planet. Well, let's get you in out of that cold arctic wind."

They walked over to the edge of the airstrip where there were about a dozen varying sized Quonset huts. He took them to a small hut that had eight bunks, stacked two high. The hut had a kerosene heater in the center and a storage cabinet on the end wall, and that was all.

"Slip into your arctic gear, and I'll show you around." MSG. M Cafrey said.

As they put on their arctic gear, Bob commented, "Boy, they were not kidding when they said sparse."

"Yeah, I know, but this is just the guest quarters. Us permanent residents have much more comfortable accommodations. These Quonset Huts are set up off of the Tundra on pilings drilled down into the permafrost,. that way they have minimal environmental impact. Keep in mind, we're about two hundred miles north of the Arctic Circle and about five hundred miles from the North Pole. Up here, our summer is just about over, now at the end of July. In a couple of weeks we will start seeing snow and by the end of September the bay will be frozen over. We have about ten months of winter and two months of summer, June and July. The midnight sun has already begun to significantly recede. We will be in total darkness by the middle of October and stay that way until the middle of March."

When they were geared up, MSG. McCaffery led them outside and along one of the narrow streets of Quonset huts. Just like Fort Yukon, there were no motor vehicles in this road less wilderness. Everyone walked in summer and when the snow came, there were Dog Sleds everywhere. He took them over to the Headquarters building, which was a larger Quonset hut. He introduced Bob to the soldiers who worked there.

"We're at about half-staff right now. We'll be at full strength again by October when the winter test season begins. We do a fair amount of testing on equipment that is designed for the Tundra in summer months, which is much different than the winter Tundra. We've been running tests on the Arctic Weasel, which you probably saw at Fort Yukon. We test it on the Tundra, and not on the Yukon River flats. I'll introduce you to some of the other pieces in a few minutes. First, I'd like to show you a project that is under way out on the Tundra right now."

He took them over to a very large display table that contained a layout of the Prudhoe Bay region. Scattered all across the terrain were miniature scale models of oil well derricks.

"We have been testing oil drilling equipment here in the arctic. In the process, we have discovered a vast oil deposit lying beneath the entire Prudhoe Bay area. It could be the largest oil deposit ever discovered in North America."

"How are they going to get the oil down to the lower forty eight?" Bob asked, "The Arctic Ocean is frozen over most of the year."

"They're working on designing a special oil pipeline to transport the oil south across Alaska to the port of Valdez. Right now the U.S. Army is accepting bids from various oil companies to do the drilling and build the pipeline."

"Well, let's get some lunch. You guys must be starved. You had a very early start today."

Sgt. McCaffery took them over to a large Quonset Hut that was the Mess Hall. After lunch, they continued their tour. Bob and Frank followed him outside to an open area where they saw this immense vehicle sitting on huge wheels.

"What is this thing called?" Frank asked, "It looks like some sort of train with an engine and four freight cars."

"This is what is called the Arctic Train," Sgt. McCaffery replied, "Some like to call it the Tundra Buggy. Up front is the engine unit which powers and controls the train. A very large diesel engine generator supplies electric power to each of the wheels, just like a railroad engine, and has an electric motor that powers each wheel independently. That's how the monster is steered. Each wheel is eight feet high and three feet wide to float over the delicate tundra terrain. With those wide tires, they cause minimal damage to the Tundra. The, 'train' cars are not quite as large as a regular railroad car, but, can carry quite a large load. This is how all of the building material for the Quonset Huts and the landing strip were hauled up here. And now it is hauling all the oil well equipment as well as all of our supplies and most of our food. It was arctic tested several years ago, and the Army has ordered two more just like it for when they start building on the oil pipeline."

"Wow," Bob said, "That is some kind of a monster machine. Although, it appears to have more civilian use, than military."

"Well, if you want a strictly military vehicle, then this next one should fill the bill."

Sgt. McCaffery took them into another one of the Quonset buildings. Here they gazed in awe at one of the latest all-purpose Arctic vehicles, designed to transport both men and hardware across the Arctic ice-pack. It was another enclosed tracked vehicle designed to climb the ice ridges and shards of Arctic ice. It was larger than the Arctic Weasel they had seen down at Fort Yukon. It was not as fast, but capable of much heavier loads.

"We just got this one in," he said, "We'll be testing it this winter out on the ice flows of the Arctic Ocean. This one is designed to transport a platoon of soldiers, and equipment, or artillery rocket launchers out across the North Pole, if necessary. The Pentagon's thinking is that if we were to have to engage The USSR, in an all-out war, it would be out on the ice of the North Pole. They'll be bringing in about five or six more of these, each one a little different that the others. They are manufactured by the Chrysler Corporation. Well, men, that concludes our little tour. I trust you can find your way back to your guest quarters. Dinner tonight is at 1900 hours. And I'll see you right after breakfast at 0600 hours, to pick up your test packet, or should I say 'test packets'. Your flight back to Greely is scheduled at 0700 hours."

Bob and Frank found their way back to the guest quarters. Bob discovered that the quarters were equipped with a stereo system. He found several eight-track tapes and put in a Buddy Holley album and he and Frank stretched out on their bunks and zoned out until nineteen hundred. After evening chow, Bob found a Kingston Trio eight-track album, which he but in and they crashed to the music for the night.

At 0500 hours, the sun, which now dipped below the horizon during the midnight hours, was already well up in a clear blue sky. The two Fort Greely soldiers got dressed and packed up again. They made their way to the Mess Hall for a breakfast of pancakes, sausages and scrambled, powered eggs. Fresh foods were a rarity in this remote arctic station.

After breakfast, they headed for the Headquarters Quonset hut. Sgt. McCaffery greeted them again. "Well, here are the two test packets for you to transport back to the ATB in Greely."

Bob signed for the classified packet and Sgt. McCaffery started to hand the other copied packet to Frank, but Bob grabbed it first saying, "I'll take both of them."

As they made their way back down the narrow streets of Prudhoe Bay, Frank said, "so, it looks like you've changed your mind about handling the extra copy of the test packets."

"That's correct, Frank, I've worked past the 'risk factor' involved, and decided that I may as well be handling both packets from now on."

"Well, Bob, that's great, because I'm really busy now. They've got me making extra runs up to Fairbanks for supplies. Everyone is stocking up for the long dark winter ahead."

They stopped by the guest quarters to pick up their duffle bags and Frank handed him the slip of paper with the mailing address for the duplicated packet.

"Thanks for deciding to do this, Bob, now I won't have to set up a whole new strategy for getting these duplicated packets sent out. You'll be making tons of money, I guarantee it."

They caught their 0700 hrs flight back to Greely. Back at Greely, Bob signed over the 'classified' packet at the ATB headquarters. He dropped Frank off back at the supply warehouse and stopped back at his mail room and placed the duplicated packet in a mailing envelope and wrote the address on it; not the one Frank had given him, but, instead, the name and address of Lt. Ray George in Fort Wainwright. He wrote a duplicate slip of paper with the 'Franks' name and address on it and placed it inside the mailing envelope. The original, he stuck in his pocket. Later, he would keep it and all the other address slips in the tip of his 'off-season' boot. With that prepared, he headed out to the Main Post Office to pick up the morning mail for the ATB and to mail the duplicated packet.

As he drove back to his mail room, he started thinking, "Well, here goes, the wheels have been set in motion. There's no turning back now."

ROBB FELDER

CHAPTER 9

Late July across the Arctic, the midnight sun was now only a memory of that very short time when the sun never set. Everything, now, was done with an urgency about it in preparation of what was about to come. It was the week end and the foursome was ready for another adventure up the Shaw Creek to check out the possibility of successful gold panning at the base of that glacier.

Frank had taken that first pouch of their gold up to Fairbanks, to the Assayer and cashed it in. He had split the cash four ways, thirteen hundred and fifty dollars each, and handed it out to the four of them. Bob had opened up a savings account at the Midnight Sun Savings Bank in Delta Junction. The other three had probably done something similar with their take from the gold.

Bob signed out a vehicle again, for the trip. This time, a three quarter ton military truck, the military version of a pickup, equipped with four-wheel drive and the box had a thermal high-top covering and seating in the back. They had decided to not take the canoes this time, so there was plenty of room for their gear and two of them to ride in the back.

The gear that they packed with this time consisted of course; of gold panning gear along with fishing gear, again, and camping gear. They decided not to stay at the old trappers cabin, it was too far of a hike from there up to the glacier, but, instead to camp up near the mouth of the glacier. With their gear loaded and Roger and Richard seated in the back, they hit the road up to Shaw Creek. They didn't stop at the bridge this time. They had discovered on that fateful last hike back from the cabin, that there was actually an old road, back up through the brush to the cabin. The old road although fairly firm to drive on, was covered with brush. Bob shifted into four wheel drive and they crunched over the short brush all the way up to within about a half mile of the cabin. There, Bob had to stop. The road ended there at the edge of a large muskeg swamp.

"Well, this is it men, the rest of the way in is through the muskeg, same as we came out last time."

They all donned their backpacks with all their gear, slathered on the mosquito repellent, and followed the narrow trail through the muskeg. It wasn't quite as muddy as the last time, right after the rain, but, they were glad for the boots. They paused for a break at the cabin, then, continued on up the trail and climbed up the cliff next to the waterfall to the glacier.

"Let's set up camp over there," Frank said, "On that little rise. It's up off the creek, in case it rains and floods the creek, and it's also about a hundred yards back from the glacier, so we won't be freezing to badly."

They set up the five man tent and stored their gear inside. They also built a fire ring and gathered firewood for later. For lunch, they just had sandwiches and chips, and topped that with a beer, of course.

"Okay. men," Roger said, after lunch, "Let's go to work and see if we can strike it rich."

The four prospectors got out the gold panning gear and went to work, scooping up a small amount of the sand and water from the bottom of the creek, carefully sloshing the water over the sand to wash out the lighter sand and gravel. What's left in the bottom of the pan after all the sand and gravel is washed out is the heavier gold granules. They each had brought a small leather pouch to store their gold granules.

"Yeah," shouted Roger, "I've got some."

He was a little more experienced than the other three, having done this several times during his tenure in Alaska. Soon all four had some of the gold granules to add to their leather pouches. They worked that section of the creek for a while longer, then, moved up stream a little further. They had fairly good luck, and soon they each had about a quarter cup of the gold granules. After several hours, they took a break, went to the cooler and got a beer and sat on the creek bank to rest.

"Boy, oh boy," Complained Richard, "This is more work than I thought."

"Oh, quit complaining," Frank said, "We've probably made a couple thousand dollars each in gold already today."

After the beers, they all went back to work. They worked the creek all the way up to near the mouth of the glacier then broke for supper. Bob started the fire. Roger got out the campfire grill and a package of brats and began cooking them. When they were done, they all cracked open another beer and had the brats with chips and the beers. They sat on the creek bank again and ate their supper.

"Well," Frank said, "We've got several hours of daylight left. We may as well keep working our way right up to the glacier. There may actually be some larger nuggets of gold right under the mouth of the glacier."

"How about I take my pick ax and chip away some of the ice at the mouth of where the creek comes out of the glacier," Bob said.

The other three agreed; they would, meantime work their way, panning, up the creek to the glacier mouth. Bob grabbed his pick and they all went back to work. He began chipping away at the ice around the mouth of the glacier where the creek flowed out from underneath.

This glacier, like most, was made up of, not one huge chunk of ice, but, thousands of boulder-like chunks. As the glacier ever so slowly slid down the canyon, pushed by the immense weight of the ice forming further up the mountain side, it crumbled and broke up as it slid over the rocky surface of the canyon. As it did so, the sheer weight of the ice broke apart the rock of the canyon walls and over thousands of years, ground the rock into gravel and sand. Some of the rock that was crushed into gravel and sand contained veins of gold that were molten into the rock. Thusly the gravel and sand at the bottom of the glacier contained granules of the gold, and sometimes larger nuggets of the gold could be found.

"Hey, look," Bob shouted, "I've found one of the nuggets."

"Where," Roger questioned, as the other three dropped their panning and ran up the creek to the glacier where Bob had been chipping away at the ice.

"It was actually imbedded in one of the ice boulders that was right on the ground. It must have become imbedded as the ice slid down the mountain."

Excitedly, the other three ran over to the campsite and grabbed their picks and joined Bob as they all feverishly picked away at the ice, hoping to find more nuggets. But, alas, they didn't find many more of the large nuggets. So after about an hour of futile effort, they all returned to panning, but they panned right at the mouth of the creek. They did, however, pan out some very large granules of the gold. The gold seemed to be rather prolific right in that one area.

"The glacier," Frank said, "must have sheared off a rather large vein of gold further up the mountain and carried it down here. Then, when the glacier melted away, the gold was exposed in the mouth of the creek."

They worked at the panning until it was too dark to see the gold in their pans.

"Guess we should knock off for the night," Richard stated, "It looks like we've had pretty good luck here at the face of the glacier."

They picked up their pans, the gold pouches and their picks and returned to camp. Bob lit the lantern and they all held up their pouches of gold and assessed the results of the day's work.

"Holy crap," Roger exclaimed, "We've had a really productive day. I can't believe we've panned all this gold today. We must have about two pounds of gold each."

"If there's two pounds of gold each at one hundred fifty dollars an ounce, we've got about five grand in gold, each," Bob stated, "But we've got to get it secured it for the night. There's no telling what night creatures roam this area at night. I'm talking about 'claim jumpers'."

"I think we should keep the campfire burning all night and take turns standing guard," Frank said.

Bob stoked up the fire again and they all went into their tent and placed the gold pouches into the small safe that they brought with.

"How about we do this," Bob said, "We dig a hole and bury the safe until morning, when we're ready to head back."

"That sounds like a great idea, Bob," Roger said as he got a small shovel out of his pack. Soon he had a hole dug about a foot deep, just outside of the fire ring. Roger got the safe and placed it into the hole and covered it up. Bob placed one of the firewood logs on top of it.

"I'll take first watch," Frank said, as he sat down on the log, "I've got my gun with."

The other three all went into the tent and crawled into their sleeping bags and fell asleep in minutes after a long day of panning for the gold. At midnight Frank went into the tent and woke Bob up.

"See or hear anything?" Bob asked.

"Nah," Frank replied and gave him the gun and holster and crawled into his sleeping bag. Bob went out and stoked up the fire and settled down on the log. It was a very quiet night, albeit very chilly as the glacier gave off its icy air. About 0100 hours, a fog started forming in the canyon. Bob got up and went into the tent and got his field jacket on.

By 0200 hours, just before sunrise, the fog had formed a very thick blanket that engulfed the entire glacier canyon and their campsite. Bob couldn't see more than two feet in front of him. A few minutes after two, Bob heard a faint muffled sound from the back side of the tent. He went around back to check. As he shined his flashlight around, what little he could see in the thick pea soup fog was just Frank who had gotten up and out the back door of the tent to take a piss. Bob returned to his log and again stoked the fire to try and gain a little heat from it in the icy fog. In about twenty minutes, he felt warmer, however, the warmth caused him to become a little groggy.

He was almost dozing when he heard a voice saying, "You, on the log, get up."

Bob jumped to his feet, yelling, "What the fuck."

He could barely make out two guys standing right in front of him with guns drawn on him.

"Who the hell are you?" He asked.

"I'm Joe, and this here is Tom, and we're friends of Bart McGee and Will Black," The taller one said, "And we're here to get back dat gold dat they prospected out'a dis here creek b'fore you got dem throwed in jail."

"Well, first of all, we don't have any of Bart and Will's gold. Talk to the Sheriff down in Delta Junction. Secondly, those two are murdering criminals and will be locked up for good. And thirdly, we're in the U.S. Army and if you want to fuck with us, you'll have the U.S. Army on your asses."

Suddenly Bob was struck from behind by an apparent third intruder. He went down on his knees, but, apparently not knocked out. Meantime, Frank, who was out in back, just finished taking a piss and heard the argument. He quickly picked up a broken tree limb about the size of a baseball bat and snuck quietly around the side of the tent. He could barely see the three guys standing there in the thick fog. But the campfire gave off just enough light. He wound up and came up the side of the head of one of them with the tree limb. The guy went down, but fell against one of the other guys. His gun went flying, but, the third one still had his gun out. Frank saw it and dropped his club and ducked around to the back side of the tent and took off running. Two of the guys started running after him, shooting and cursing as they ran.

"Come back here, you son-of-a-bitch," they yelled.

Meanwhile, the third guy that had been clubbed by Frank came to and got up, but, he was a bit wobbly and staggered over to the other side of the campfire from Bob, near the edge of the creek. He raised his gun and aimed toward Bob and fired, but his aim was bad in the dim, smoky light and the shot went wild. Meantime, Bob drew his gun from his holster and fired at the guy at the edge of the creek. Bob thought that his aim was bad too in the murky mix of fog and campfire smoke. But apparently he hit the guy because he fell backwards into the creek.

The other two heard the shot and abandoned their pursuit of Frank and came running back around the side of the tent. Bob heard them coming back and ducked around the other side and watched to see what would happen. The two of them just stood there for a few seconds as Bob tried to decide if he should shoot them as well.

Just as he was about to yell at them to drop their guns, the man in the creek started yelling.

"Help, help, I've been shot and I can't swim."

One of the other two said, "C'mon, Joe, we've got to save Jimmy."

They started running toward the creek, but, didn't get there in time as Bob heard Jimmy yelling again just as he was being swept over the falls. Joe and the other guy started running over to the trail with their flashlights on. Bob could hear them scrambling down the boulders to get to the bottom of the falls; yelling as they went.

"Jimmy, - - - Jimmy, you alright ol' buddy. we're c'omn on down, try to hang onto something."

At that same time, Roger and Richard had finally woken up and scrambled out of the tent.

"What the hell is going out here?" Roger said, "Christ, we heard gunfire and yelling. What the hell!!"

Bob said, all panicky, "No time to explain, come on, we've got to get our shit and get the hell out of here before they get back. They're trying to kill us."

"What, - - - who?" Richard asked as all four of them scrambled back into the tent and started grabbing their gear. They grabbed all they could and stuffed it into their backpacks and followed

Frank out the back door of the tent and into the woods.

"What about the gold?" Roger said.

"We'll have to come back for it," Bob said, "We don't have time to dig it up now."

"Follow me," Frank whispered, "I found this trail when I went running out here before. It's like a deer or maybe a bear trail."

Frank led them down the trail in the thick fog that still enveloped the glacier and surrounding woods. They all had their flashlights out and aimed straight down at the ground. Somewhat slowly they made their way down, where the trail dropped steeply over the ridge that held the falls. The trail appeared to run parallel with the falls and the creek, but about fifty yards away from the creek. They could hear the two intruders, at the falls yelling, even over the roar of the falls; for their third man who went over the falls.

CHAPTER 10

With Frank in the lead, they very carefully and quietly made their way down the descending trail until they could no longer hear the two guys at the falls, yelling for their drowning partner. The trail kept parallel with the creek for about another half mile then joined up with the main trail along the creek and after another couple of miles led them to the old cabin. Here, they finally felt safe enough to talk to each other. They dropped their packs and sat down on some logs, exhausted from the long fast hike down from the glacier.

"Holy shit, Bob, what the hell is going on?" Roger demanded to know, "Who are those guys?"

"They are, apparently some friends of that Bart and Will that we captured and turned in to the Sheriff last weekend," Bob replied."

"But, what the hell did they want with us, and how did all that shooting start?"

"Well, here's the story," Bob began, "At about 0200 hours, I was half dozing, sitting on that log, when all of a sudden, out of the fog, there they were. Two of them came up to me with guns pointed and ordered me to stand up. They started demanding the gold that those other two had panned up there at the glacier. I, of course lied and claimed I didn't know anything about their friend's gold. They didn't believe me apparently, because the third one came up behind me and 'cold-cocked' me and knocked me to my knees. Meantime, Frank, who had been out back taking a leak, heard us arguing and came around the tent with a tree limb and clubbed one of the other guys, knocking him to the ground. But, as soon as he realized that they were armed, he turned around and ran back around the tent and off into the woods. The other two began chasing Frank and shooting at him. Meantime, the one that Frank had clubbed, slowly came to and staggered around and ended up over by the creek on the other side of the fire. He raised his gun and fired at me but missed because he was still groggy and because of the smoke and the fog. I pulled my gun out and shot him, and he fell backwards into the creek. The other two heard the shooting and came running back and were standing there, when we heard the one that I had shot, down in the creek yelling for help. The two started for the creek, but, it was too late. Their partner went over the falls."

"That's when you two woke up and came rushing out of the tent."

"Hot damn," Richard said, "That's some story. Sorry to have missed all the action and shooting."

"Well, you're lucky to have missed it all. We had only one gun on our side, you know, against their three. But thanks to Frank clubbing one of them, that evened the odds a little."

"Do you think we could barricade ourselves in the cabin and hold them off?" Richard asked.

"Hell no, Richard," Frank said, "It'd still be two or three guns to one. And the cabin isn't that hard to break into. Remember that Grizzly last weekend."

"We're almost to our truck, we may as well make a run for it," Roger said, "We can't know when they'll be coming down the trail. It all depends on if they find their third member alive, or, if he drowned and his body will come floating right past this cabin. Either way, they could be coming through here at any time."

After a few more minutes break, they picked up their backpacks and headed out across the muskeg swamp to their truck.

When they arrived, Richard said, "What do we do now? Do we wait here till they pass by down the creek trail to their truck? I can see their truck from here, parked at the bridge."

"No," Bob replied, "We get the hell out of here. I sure as hell don't want to risk another confrontation with their guns. Let's just hightail it back to Delta Junction and hole up there for a while. Hopefully they will clear out in a couple hours, then we can come back and hike back up to the glacier and retrieve our gold and the rest of our gear."

"I agree with Bob," Frank said, "Beside, I don't know about the rest of you, but, I'm starved."

"You're right, Frank," Roger said, "now that you mention it, so am I. In our panic to escape, we haven't had time to even think about breakfast."

With that, they threw their gear into the back of the truck, Roger and Richard climbed in back, Bob and Frank in front again, and took off for town.

Delta Junction was not a large town, but not a small town either by Alaska standards. It is so named because it is situated at the Junction of two of the major rivers; the Delta River and the Tanana River. It is also at the junction of two of the main highways in all of Alaska. The famous Alcan Highway, was the one land link with the lower forty eight states. The 'Alcan' begins in British Columbia, Canada and ends in Delta Junction.

The Richardson Highway, which begins in Alaska's southern coastal town of Valdez, comes north and joined up with the Alcan and then goes on up, all the way to Fairbanks.

The town, like perhaps thousands of other small towns in America, consisted of; a gas station, a grocery store, a hardware store, a motel, a saloon, a restaurant, and a church which was jointly owned and shared by multiple denominations.

Bob pulled his truck and crew up in front of the 'Midnight Sun, Motel, Bar and Restaurant'. The hungry and weary crew went in and sat at the bar. They all ordered the special; the famous thick-cut bacon, three eggs and hash-browns, and of course steaming hot cups of coffee, even though it was already well past noon. They all ate like starving grizzly's. When they got their tabs, they were appalled at the forty five dollar tab each.

"What the hell," Bob complained.

"This is pretty typical for Alaska," Roger said, "Keep in mind, all the food has to be trucked in from the lower forty eight, three thousand miles via the Alcan Highway, or shipped up the Inland Passage to the port of Valdez and trucked up the Richardson Highway. Alaska can't raise much food of their own, due to the mountainous terrain and the short growing season.

"Well, shit," Bob said, "We could have gone back to Greely for lunch for free. The Army does all their own shipping, and the taxpayers pay for it all."

"Well, these Alaska prices won't be a problem once we cash in all that gold," Frank whispered, "Let's get back up to that glacier and get our gold."

They all had a second cup of coffee and paid their bills and headed back up the road to Shaw Creek. It was about 0400 hours when they got to the Shaw Creek Bridge. To their dismay, when they got there, the other truck belonging to the three hooligans was still parked at the bridge.

"Damnit," Bob said, "I wonder what is holding them up." He was becoming irritable with the guilt and worry about the guy that he shot and may have killed."

"We can't go back up to the glacier until they clear out. We can't just wait around someplace, either, for them to show up, and, dammit, it's getting too late. We'll have to head back to Greely. I've got to check this truck back in and get it cleaned up by eighteen hundred hours. It's just getting too damn late. We'll have to come back next weekend and retrieve the gold. Sorry, guys."

Bob turned the truck around and headed back to Fort Greely. They turned in what gear they had salvaged from their escape from the glacier and signed for another week on the equipment left behind.

Bob signed the truck back in and they all helped wash it. They headed back to their 'Pink Palace' for the night.   At supper time, they discussed their strategy for the next weekend.

"We won't need to check out any new gear," Bob said, "Everything we need if we have to stay overnight is already up there. I'll just sign out the truck and we'll head out."

"The one caveat," Frank said, "Is that we will have to go up on Friday and stay overnight, get our gold early Saturday and get up to Fairbanks to that assayer's office to cash it all in, because the assayer is not open on Sunday."

"Okay," Bob said I'll see if I can sign out the truck on Friday after work. So we can get up to our campsite before dark."

ROBB FELDER

CHAPTER 11

The first week of August was a pretty uneventful week. Bob continued to pick up the unclassified test packets along with the classified ones, and mail the unclassified ones to Lt. George at Fort Wainwright.

The summer testing season was winding down, so the number of test packets decreased as the test sites began gearing up for the upcoming winter season.

On Friday morning after Bob had completed his morning mail run, Bob, Roger, Richard and Frank were called into the Company Commander, Captain Ellis's Office. They all four went in together and saluted.

"Gentlemen, he began, "It has come to my attention that the four of you have become involved in an incident up on Shaw Creek. You have been ordered by the Base Commander,

Colonel John Martin to report to his office at thirteen hundred hours today. So; dress sharp, Class A's, and present yourselves promptly on time."

"Yes, Sir, understood sir," They all responded as they saluted.

"You are dismissed," Captain Ellis said.

The four soldiers left his office and gathered in the hall outside.

"What the hell do you suppose that is all about?" Bob asked.

"I suppose something to do with us capturing those two murderers up on Shaw Creek," Roger said.

"I hope we're not in trouble for interfering in a civilian criminal matter," Frank said, "I hope this doesn't have something to do with our run-in with those other three recluse friends of the two murderers that we encountered this past weekend."

"I guess we'll find out at thirteen hundred hours," Bob said.

They all went back to work for the morning. At eleven hundred, Bob ate lunch and opened op his mailroom window for mail call. The other three came in at twelve hundred and had their lunch. After lunch, Bob closed up his mail room and they all went upstairs and got changed into their class 'A' uniforms, which consisted of the army green dress uniform with dress shirt and tie.

It was a pleasant, sunny, early fall day with the leaves just starting to turn as the foursome walked the three blocks over to the Fort Greely Base Headquarters.

They checked in with the receptionist, who said, "Oh, good, you're plenty early," and led them to a large waiting reception area outside the Base Commanders office.

As they were waiting, their Company Commander, along with their First Sergeant came in and entered the Base Commander's office. They had to stand at attention when they entered. A few minutes later, Colonel Martin, the ATB commander came in. They came to attention again as he entered the Base Commander's office. After another few minutes they saw Sheriff Turner from Delta Junction come in and enter the commander's office.

"Isn't this just so like the Army?" Frank commented, "In any given situation, the soldiers who are the most affected by a given directive are always the last to know about it."

"Are they convening a Court Martial Board?" Bob asked, rhetorically.

After about five minutes, the door to the commander's office opened and all the 'Brass' stepped out, which included Lt General Brady, the commander of the U.S. Army, Alaska Command from Fort Wainwright. Bob, Frank, Roger and Richard all jumped to attention.

"At Ease, men," General Brady began, as the four relaxed their stance, "Gentlemen, The four of you have exhibited exemplary bravery and profound courage in the incident at Shaw Creek, Alaska on the weekend of July twenty third and twenty fourth, nineteen hundred and sixty, in the apprehending of two very dangerous criminals. The United States Army wishes to recognize your courageous actions and is hereby awarding you each with this commendation ribbon. The General then went down the lineup of the four friends and handed out the ribbons and shook each of their hands and said, "Congratulations, soldier," and saluted each of them. Company Commander Captain Ellis followed and handed out sheets of parchment printed verbiage of the incident and the award. He shook each soldier's hand and congratulated them and saluted.

Next, Sheriff Turner spoke, saying his department was awarding each of them the citizens award for bravery and courage in bringing the two fugitives to justice. He then proceeded to hand out the awards.

Meanwhile, photographers from the Arctic Test Board's newspaper, The Arctician , The Delta Midnight Sun, the Fort Wainwright North Star and The Fairbanks Aroura Borealis; all were snapping pictures of the brave foursome and all of the Brass handing out the rewards. After all of the awards were handed out and pictures taken, Colonel John Martin announced that there would be a reception in their honor at the EM Club that evening. He then gave the command, "Dismissed". Everyone then filed out of the base headquarters.

As the four were walking back to their barracks, Bob said, "We are totally screwed, guys. Remember, we were going to go back up to Shaw Creek and retrieve our gold tonight. Now we have to be at that stupid reception. We won't be able to get it tomorrow and still make it to Fairbanks before the Assayer's office closes. I guess we'll have to get our gold tomorrow and stash it until next week."

CHAPTER 12

More bad news hit them on Saturday morning. Just as they were about sign out for the weekend in the Orderly Room, to head out for Shaw Creek, the First Sergeant, MSG. Balleu caught up with them.

"Come into my office, guys, I've got something you might want to pay attention to before you head out."

They all filed into the First Sergeant's office. He picked up a sheet of paper off of his desk.

"This just came in from Fort Wainwright. I was just about to post it on the bulletin board."

He handed them the sheet which stated that; "The Alaska command at Fort Wainwright has hereby declared that due to recent dangerous incidents; the area of Shaw Creek, from the highway bridge to the glacier, is now "Off-Limits" to all military personnel until further notice."

"But Sergeant," Bob said, "We still have some of our gear up there."(He didn't mention anything about their gold).

"I can't advise you on that, all I can say is that the directive says Off Limits, and Off Limits is Off Limits. You'll have to deal with it as you see fit. Maybe you can get someone from Delta Junction, a civilian; to go up and get your gear."

"Okay, Sergeant Balleu, we'll see what we can work out."

They left his office and went over to the EM Club and each poured a cup of coffee to discuss they're dilemma.

"The Army giveth, and the Army taketh away," Bob said, "First, they give you an award for doing the right thing, then they take away the access to our campsite and our gold."

"Now, we really are screwed," Roger said, "How the hell are we going to get our gold out now?"

"Now, now, don't go getting all bent out of shape," Frank said, "I have a plan. I have talked to some of the guys that I deal with when I go up to Fort Wainwright for supplies. They tell me that there's another way to get into that glacier without going up Shaw Creek."

"What? How?" Bob asked.

"North of Shaw Creek, on the highway; is a place called The Harding Lake Roadhouse. Just north of the roadhouse is the bridge over the Salcha River. This river drains from the northeast; from the same low mountain range that harbors the Shaw Glacier. It also drains from a glacier on the northwest end of this mountain range. About thirty miles up the Salcha River, there is an old prospector's camp with an old log cabin just like the one on Shaw Creek. Branching off from there is a hiking trail that heads east and skirts the mountain for about twenty miles and comes out at the Shaw Creek glacier."

"That sounds like the solution to our problem," Bob said, "If we were to come in from that trail, although we would be still in the, "Off Limits" zone of Shaw Creek at the glacier itself, we could get in and out of our camp undetected."

"And, we could dig up our gold and get it out of the camp," Roger added.

"The only problem with this plan," Richard said, "Is that we obviously won't be able to do it this weekend. There's just not enough time to get up the Salcha River and hike in twenty miles and out again."

"Yeah," Bob said, "We won't be able to do it on any regular two day weekend either, it'll take almost two days just to get to our camp at the glacier. We'll have to wait until the Labor Day weekend. We'll have to gear up for a very cold trip. The leaves are already turning and the temperature is dropping to almost freezing at night."

"Not only that," Frank reminded them, "The days are getting shorter very rapidly now. Long gone is the midnight sun. We have only about ten hours of daylight to work with now. Hell, in about three months we'll be in almost total darkness, twenty four hours."

"Here's what I better do," Roger said, I'll reserve a flat bottom boat and motor from the Rec. center for Labor Day weekend. That'll be way quicker than canoeing up the Salcha River. Hell, we can probably get up to that prospector's camp in about two or three hours."

"Well, it sounds like we have a solution to our dilemma," Bob said, "Everybody agree?"

"Sounds like a good plan to me," Frank agreed.

"Well, I think we can make it in and out again without any trouble," Roger said.

"I'm in," Richard said, "But, we've got to make it on Labor Day weekend. That will be our last chance to get in there and out again before the winter weather starts. The snows will start early at that higher elevation."

With that consensus, they all drank another cup of coffee and headed over to the gym for their weekly workouts for a couple of hours. After a workout on the machines and a couple games of hoops at the gym, they went back to the barracks for lunch. At fourteen hundred hours they headed over to the theater for an afternoon matinee. After evening chow, the foursome changed into their civilian clothes and they got into Richards car and headed out down the Alcan Highway about ten miles, to a place called The Malamute Saloon. It was your basic saloon and dance hall. It was part restaurant, part bar and dance hall. They had a band on Saturday night and a strip show.

As they got seated in the bar area and ordered a round of drinks, Richard said, "I wonder if my girl Sylvia is dancing tonight."

"You do realize, Richard," Frank said to him, "If you have to pay for sex, she's not really 'your' girl. She belongs to everyone, Hell, I've even had her a few times."

"No, no, God dammit, she's mine!" he shouted as he slammed his hand down on the table, "She's mine and I love her, she even said she was all mine."

"Richard, Richard," Roger said, "You've been in Alaska way too long. Hell, I'll bet even Bob, here, will have a crack at her before his tour is over."

"No thanks, Roger, I'm practically a married man, and intend to remain celibate for my tour."

"Yah, yah," Frank said, "That's what we all said too, when we first got here."

"Just you wait," Richard said, "Before this long, long winter is over, even you'll be wanting to claim one of these fine pussies for your very own. Hell, you know you can't suppress the urges forever. You try to hold it in for eighteen months; your balls will explode"

And so went their weekend and the next three weekends. On the work front, the courier pickups from the test sites had stopped altogether. The summer test season was over, and winter testing wouldn't start until October.

CHAPTER 13

Finally, the long awaited Labor Day weekend arrived. Saturday morning, September fifth, 0500 hours; breakfast finished and their winter gear packed for the long weekend and the long hike up to their gold camp at the glacier. They all signed out in the Orderly Room for the weekend. Bob signed out the three quarter ton truck from the Motor Pool again. They met Richard and Frank, who had bought the groceries last night. They signed for and picked up the flat bottom boat, along with a thirty horse Evenrude motor and five gallon gas tank and an extra gas can from the Rec. Center, and were on their way after a stop to fill the gas tanks. After a two hour ride to the Harding Lake Road House, they put the boat and supplies in at the Salcha River Bridge.

Roger got the motor fired up and they were off, up the river. The Salcha river wound its way through muskeg swamps for about the first half hour, then they moved into an area of short stunted pine forest, typical of the tundra-like terrain near the Arctic Circle. Other, smaller streams flowed into the Salcha; draining the vast muskeg swamps. As they journeyed further up the river, it began to narrow and flow faster, flowing over rapids as the river climbed into the foothills of the small mountain range up ahead. Roger maneuvered the boat around large boulders and over the rapids. After about a three hour trip, they could finally spot the cabin, situated on a raised bank, in a clearing above the river. They discovered that they were not the only ones at the cabin. Another boat was already tied up at the dock.

Roger maneuvered the boat up to the small dock, next to the other boat and Bob jumped out and tied it up. They all got out and stretched their legs, then climbed up to the cabin to check it out and see who their fellow river travelers were. This cabin was quite a bit larger than the Shaw Creek cabin. It had a fireplace and a kitchen area with a table and cupboards, a large sofa and a pair of chairs. Along two of the back walls were rows of stacked bunks. As they entered, they were greeted by three other occupants who introduced themselves as; John, Edward and Ralph. Frank introduced himself, Bob, Richard and Roger.

John said, "We're from Fort Wainwright. We're here to hunt caribou. The herds are starting to migrate south for the winter, from the Tundra in the far north. They winter in these foothills where they get protection in the wooded terrain from the harsh Tundra winds. How about you guys, are you hunters too?"

"No," Frank replied, "We're fishermen, actually. We're headed over to the Shaw Creek where we still have some of our gear that we want to get out before winter."

"Don't tell me you're the guys that captured those two murderers up on Shaw Creek. We read about you guys in the Fort Wainwright and Fairbanks papers. You got some kind of award for it, I understand. How'd that happen?"

"Well," Bob began to explain, "Actually, they tried to run us out of that cabin on Shaw Creek. They stole our canoes, so we ambushed them at the highway bridge when they attempted to load our canoes into their truck. So, now dammit, as a result of that, the Army has placed the Shaw Creek area "Off Limits", probably for the winter. So we're going in the back way to get our gear out."

Bob didn't mention that they were actually going into their glacier gold camp to get their gear and their gold out.

"Well, that's a clever way to do it. We wish you guy's good luck with that. By the way, don't stay too long, we heard that they're predicting a snow storm up in the high country."

"Well, we gotta get going. It's a long hike up there and we want to make it up there yet today before dark, and then back by tomorrow tonight. Maybe we'll see you again here on Sunday. Good luck with your hunt."

With that, the four gold prospectors went out to the dock and took their packs out of the boat and took the motor off. They pulled the boat up on shore and overturned it behind some bushes and stashed the motor and gas cans under it.

They donned their backpacks and found the trailhead behind the cabin and began their hike up into the foothills, traveling east toward Shaw Creek about twenty miles away. The trail wound around through the foothills for about the first five miles, traveling through a heavily forested area. But, it soon began to climb up into the foot of the mountain itself. As they climbed, they noticed the trees were beginning to thin out and soon they were above the tree line. As they climbed, the temperature had been dropping, it felt like it was well below freezing. They stopped in a sheltered spot to take a break. They had been hiking for over two hours.

"I think we've come about ten miles so far. We must be about half way there," Roger said.

As they looked up to the mountain top they noticed thick dark clouds were swirling around the top.

"I guess those guys weren't kidding about the snow," Bob said, "Those look like snow clouds surrounding the mountain top, We'd better get going if we're going to beat the storm back to the cabin on Salcha River."

They got up and continued hiking along the rocky trail, which followed along the edge of a steep cliff. After a mile or so, the trail began to decline, back down into the tree line and wound its way around to the south side of the mountain. It was easier going there. The trail was smoother and sloped downhill. After about another hour's hike under ever darkening skies, they began to hear the sound of the waterfalls on Shaw Creek. Soon they came to the edge of the canyon that held the glacier. They climbed down into the canyon and skirted its face until they came to the creek. They crossed Shaw Creek and entered their old campsite. Everything was just as they had left it in that hasty retreat three weeks ago. They shed their backpacks and sat down on the logs that they had assembled around the old fire pit and had their lunch, and discussed their options as light snow began to fall.

"Here's our options, guys," Roger said, "We can stay here for the night and hope the snow wouldn't be too deep by morning for the trip back. Or, we can quickly pack up our camp and make a run for it and try to beat the storm back to the cabin on the Salcha River. Let's have a show of hands. Who says we stay the night and wait out the storm?"

Richard raised his hand and said, "I think we should stay. It's already getting late, and our camp here is already set up. It's already two o'clock, and it's a good four, or more hours back to the Salcha River cabin."

"Okay," Roger said, "who says we make a run for it?"

Frank, Bob and Roger raised their hands and Frank said, "What if the snow is so deep by morning that we can't pack all our gear out of here. We'd be screwed."

"Okay." Bob said, "Let's get cracking and get out of here as quickly as possible."

They all went into the tent and got their sleeping bags rolled up and attached to their backpacks. Bob got out a shovel and dug up the strong box that held the gold and put it into his backpack, while the other three took down the tent, rolled it up and attached it to Roger's backpack. The packed up all the gold panning equipment; the picks and shovels and the pans. Richard and Frank divided up the food that they had left from that ill-fated trip of three weeks ago and packed it into their packs.

As they crossed over Shaw Creek again and picked up the trail back, snow was falling quite heavily already. It was starting to become difficult climbing up the rocky trail out of the glacier canyon. The snow was already deep enough to make the ascending trail slippery and slow going. They struggled on up the trail for about an hour. Some places where the trees hung over the trail were a bit easier, but they could tell they weren't making very good time. After another hour, they weren't even out of the tree line yet. It took them yet another hour to get that far. Then as they came up out of the tree line they discovered that the wind had picked up and was swirling the snow around creating a 'white-out'. They could barely see the trail anymore as they struggled along the barren trail until they came to where the trail skirted the sheer cliff. They then realized they weren't going to make it. The wind was howling so badly it threatened to blow them over the edge of the cliff, they couldn't even be heard shouting to each other.

They carefully turned around and stumbled back down the trail into the protection of the trees.

"We'll have to make camp here for the night until the blizzard blows over," Frank said.

They found a protected spot under the trees that was level enough to set up the tent. It was rapidly growing dark. They all huddled into the tent as the temperature was plummeting. There was no way they could have found firewood, let alone get a fire started in the howling wind and snow already about a foot deep. Bob glanced at his watch and found that it was already almost eight o'clock. They had been on the trail almost six hours.

For dinner, they each had a cold hotdog wrapped in a slice of bread, and some potato chips and a beer.

As darkness descended and the blizzard howled across the mountain side, they crawled into their down filled sleeping bags. They just removed their boots, but, left all their other clothes on for extra warmth and quickly fell asleep from the sheer exhaustion of battling the howling blizzard and carrying their heavy backpacks up the slippery, snow packed mountain trail.

CHAPTER 14

Bob was the first one awake in the morning. He had to turn on his flashlight to see his watch. He thought it must be middle of the night, and still dark outside. But, his watch told him it was already eight o'clock in the morning.

"What the hell?" He thought, "Why was it still dark?"

He shined his flashlight around the tent and discovered that part of it had collapsed. Then it dawned on him. The weight of the snow had collapsed part of the tent and blocked out the daylight. He woke up the other three and told them that it was already eight o'clock and they had better get going. They all crawled out of their sleeping bags and put on their boots, then rolled up their sleeping bags and secured them to their backpacks again. For breakfast, they again had cold hotdogs wrapped in a slice of bread and a beer.

As they crawled out of the tent, they had to squint their eyes. The morning sun was blazing brightly and reflecting off of the new snow in their mountain campsite. The blizzard had abated during the night after dumping about three feet of snow on them. They brushed the snow off of their tent and rolled it up and attached it back onto Rogers backpack. They struggled out from under the trees, back onto the trail and after a pause for a morning piss, they discovered that on some parts of the trail the wind had swept away some of the snow. But they were now rested from yesterday's struggle and re-energized by a good night's sleep. They pushed on up the trail again through some of the drifts that were waist deep.

To their delight, they discovered after they broke out of the tree line that the howling wind of the blizzard had swept away most of the snow from the trail. Soon, they were at the section of the trail that went along the rim of the sheer cliff. The trail was quite icy here and the going was much slower. Just as they were near the end of the cliff trail, they saw the three guys from the cabin; John, Edward and Ralph approaching them. As they came closer, they pointed their rifles at Bob, Roger, Richard and Frank.

"Okay," John said, "We want that gold that you've got."

"What gold?" Bob asked.

"Don't fuck with us," John said, "we're not stupid. We know you went back over to Shaw Creek to get your gold out. You see, we're not stupid soldiers from Fort Wainwright. We're friends of Bart McGee and Will Black, the one's you guys got thrown in jail. When we went to visit them, they told us about the gold up at that glacier. Our other friends Joe and Tom couldn't make it out this weekend. They're staying at the hospital with our other friend Jimmy that you shot over there at Shaw Creek. Now, give us that damn gold or we'll blow you right off this cliff."

Bob wasn't about to argue with him anymore so he took off his backpack and took out the lockbox. John stepped over, closer to Bob to receive the box from him, but as Bob was about to hand him the box, he appeared to stumble a bit and fall towards John. In the process, Bob grabbed John's rifle with one hand and swung the box with the other hand and hit John in the side of his head. John let go of the rifle as he was stunned and started to slip on the icy trail and went sliding over the edge of the cliff. They could hear his screams as he went flying over the edge and down the fifty foot precipice to his death. Bob turned the rifle on the other two assailants and they turned around and ran off down the trail, back toward the cabin.

Bob put the lock box back in his backpack and took the rifle with him. The foursome again made their way down the trail and back into the tree line. Frank, however, took his gun out and kept it ready in case they should meet up with the two gang members on their way back to the cabin. As the trail descended, they noticed that the snow diminished as they came down the mountain into the lower elevation. After about two hours, they were nearing the cabin. By the time they got to the cabin, there wasn't any snow at all.

They quietly approached the cabin with extreme caution. They carefully peered into the back window, but, the cabin appeared to be empty.

"Could the two surviving gang members have cleared completely?" Bob whispered.

As they crept around to the front of the cabin, they noticed that the other boat was gone from the dock. With less caution then, they entered the cabin and found that it was true. The two gangsters had indeed cleared out.

"Well," Bob said, "it looks like we have the place to ourselves. We may as well get comfortable."

"Yeah," agreed Frank, "It's probably too late to make it back down the river tonight. Besides, we don't want to take a chance of running into those two gang members again. Although without their leader, John, they appeared to be completely disoriented."

"Well, it's getting quite late," Roger said, "we'd better fix some supper and get to bed. At least we've got a decent kitchen here. We'll have to get up very early tomorrow morning in order to make it back down river and into Fairbanks to get to the assayers office before it closes."

As Bob got a fire going in the fireplace, Roger made up some hamburgers and some dehydrated potatoes and vegetables. They washed it down with the last of their beers. They all crashed into bed early after first making sure that the door was locked and window shutters were hooked securely.

Later that evening, Bob got up, grabbed his flashlight and went out to use the outhouse. It was a crystal clear night with a near full moon. On his way back, he heard the sound of an outboard motor coming up the river. He quickly got back into the cabin and locked the door again. He debated with himself, if he should wake up the others but, decided against it and wait and see what happened. He watched, in the moon light as the boat pulled up to the dock. Four men got out and proceeded up toward the cabin. Bob was just about to wake the other guys, but then he watched as the four from the boat went around back of the cabin and headed up the trail. That's when he knew that his hunch was correct. He went back to bed and immediately fell back to sleep.

Sometime after midnight, Frank got up and likewise had to make a trip to the outhouse. He grabbed his gun and took his flashlight and went out, but just as he was finished, he heard a noise and the sound of someone talking, coming from up the trail. It sounded like a couple of people were struggling with something, coming down the trail. Frank quickly turned off his flashlight and picked up his gun and opened up the outhouse door just a crack. As the troop came down the trail and passed right in front of the outhouse. In the bright moonlight, Frank could see they were struggling with something that appeared to be wrapped in a blanket and bound by rope wound round and round the blanketed something inside.

Then suddenly it dawned on him. "These were the guys they had encountered yesterday, up on the trail at the crest of the cliff. They were bringing out the body of their comrade John, who had gone over the edge of the cliff."

He recognized the voices of Edward and Ralph, but who were the other two?

Just then one of the other two spoke, "I'm so glad we're back to the cabin, my back is killing me. I always thought John was the skinniest one, but, he sure seems heavy now."

"That's who the other two guys are," Frank said to himself, "those are the two that accosted us over at the glacier on Shaw Creek last month. They are all part of the same gang."

Frank followed them and watched as the four pallbearers made their way on down the bank of the river and laid their buddy in the bottom of the boat and climbed in after him. They started the motor, backed the boat away from the dock and rather silently slipped away, down river. Frank went back into the cabin, locked up and crawled back into the sack and fell sound asleep.

After breakfast, very early the next morning, they turned their boat back over and put it back into the river, attached the motor and added more gas to the main tank. All four of our prospectors climbed aboard with their gear and set off, back down the Salcha River.

As they cruised back down the river to their truck at the highway bridge, they saw no sign of the two attackers and their two comrades from the previous day's confrontation up on that cliff trail. Bob and Frank discussed their midnight visitors from last night as they traveled down the river toward the bridge. The trip back down river took quite a bit less time, going with the flow of the river. They encountered no one at the bridge, so they loaded the boat, motor, gas tanks and all their gear into the truck, tied the boat down and headed north to Fairbanks. They turned off The Richardson Highway onto Northern Lights Blvd.

About a mile down, on the right they found the assayers office. The sign on the building said "49th State Gold Buyers." Bob parked in front and they got out. He went into the back of the truck and dug into his back pack and pulled out the lock box.

The four prospectors were greeted at the door by an armed guard at a small desk. He had Bob open the lock box and show him the contents. The guard opened each pouch and peered inside, and directed them to the front desk. They showed their I.D's. and had to sign in, in a log book. The clerk at the counter directed them to an office down the hall.

This room had a large table and chairs and not much else, except the gold scale sitting on the table in front of the person who they assumed was the assayer. Over in one corner at a small desk sat another armed guard. In another corner was a tall closed supply cabinet.

The four were directed to sit down at the table and show their I.D's again. The assayer asked if they had one joint gold quantity or individual quantities.

"We've got separate quantities," Bob responded.

The assayer then gave them each a form to fill out, stating where they acquired their gold. They all filled out and signed their forms. Bob then placed their lockbox on the table and opened it again. He handed each of the pouches out to the four of them. The pouches had their names on them. The assayer dumped the gold from Bob's pouch onto the scale's tray and weighed it. His gold weighed in at nearly forty ounces. The assayer wrote the weight in a ledger and on the form filled out earlier by Bob. He took the gold and placed it in a metal container which would be put into a safe in the assayer's basement until it could be securely transported to a gold dealer somewhere in the lower forty eight. He then told Bob to take the form across the hall where a clerk wrote Bob's name in a ledger along with the date and weight of the gold and the amount paid out. He then wrote a check out to Bob in the amount of six thousand dollars.

Meanwhile, Frank had his pouch of gold weighed and processed. He had thirty six ounces of the gold and was given a check for five thousand, four hundred dollars.

Roger was next at thirty four ounces and got a check for five thousand, one hundred dollars.

Richard was next at thirty three and one half ounces and a check for five thousand and twenty five dollars. The four prospectors headed back to Fort Greely under threatening skies. It looked like it could rain at any time. In early September, it could also turn over to snow.

"Hopefully, that will hold off until we got back to Greely. We've had enough of snow already, and winter has just begun." Bob was thinking as he herded the three quarter ton military truck back down the highway, "We've already experienced our first blast of winter, thank you, but, it's late afternoon and we've got to get this boat and other gear turned back in to the Rec. center, and the truck into the Motor Pool."

"You just breezed by the Road House," Frank said, "We're starved. Why didn't you stop?"

"Why pay Alaska prices, when we can get back to our Mess Hall and eat for free."

"We're rich now. Remember!"

"Well, we're not rich quite yet, Frank. We've got to get our checks into the bank, which we can't do today, remember, it's a holiday."

"Oh, yeah, I forgot about that. But when we do, I think we'll each have almost ten grand in the bank from our gold prospecting. Quite a haul, huh? Which will be nothing compared to what we'll be making when the testing season starts again."

"What do you mean, we? You mean, I'll be making that money."

"Well, er - - ah, I'll be getting a commission percent of your take for setting it all up." Frank lied, and Bob thought his friend was indeed lying to him, and it started Bob wondering if, Frank wasn't actually his handler.

The rain held off until they got back to Greely and turned in the boat, motor and all the other gear and the gold panning gear. Bob then turned in the truck at the Motor Pool.

After supper, they all met again at the EM club to celebrate over several beers.

"It's a shame to think that our gold panning season is over. I was just getting to really enjoy it," Roger said, "It's been a lot of fun, in spite of the confrontation with those dangerous criminals. I can't wait until next spring when we can do some more prospecting."

"And, our prospecting has been very profitable," Richard added. "Tomorrow, I'll drive us all in to our bank in Delta Junction to deposit our checks."

"We can only hope that the Sheriff is able to round up the rest of that gang by next spring," Bob said, "So the Army can remove the "Off Limits" flag on Shaw Creek."

"Well, I'm sorry to say, I won't be joining you guys next spring," Frank said, "My Alaska tour of duty here on the "Last Frontier" is over in November, as well as my enlistment. I'll be returning to the good old lower forty eight."

"Well, Frank, let's toast to that," Roger said as they all raised and clinked their beers. "Here's to whatever lies ahead for all of us."

"For all of us, indeed," Bob thought, "I don't even want to think of what will happen when Frank leaves in November. There's too many questions to yet be answered. Will Frank be arrested before he ships back to the lower forty eight in November? Will all of our contact men at the test sites be arrested as well? Will the I.G. have enough evidence by November? Or, will I have to continue to do the pickups and mailings of the duplicate test results after November until they have enough evidence. Will Frank and all my friends ever find out that I'm a double agent for the I.G.?"

CHAPTER 15

Mid October and the temperature was plummeting like an airplane in a nose dive, as 'Old Sol' retreated back south across the equator. It was well below zero at night, and only in the teens above zero during the day. There had been several snowfalls already, leaving a foot of snow on the ground. Daylight hours were rapidly slipping away as well. The sun came up at eight in the morning now, and set at four in the afternoon. The winter testing season was just getting started, but, Bob was already busy picking up the packets of classified test results and signing them over to the ATB headquarters, and mailing the 'other' copies of the test results to Lt. George at Fort Wainwright.

The soldier's winter uniforms were required to be worn by everyone, which consisted of the heavy wool shirts in army olive green color and thermal insulated pants also in the olive green color, of course, and long johns were authorized if you worked outside. The outdoor wear consisted of the arctic, thermal insulated cap with flip down ear flaps that tied under the chin or tied up on top of the cap. The standard cold weather, water repellent field jacket with a wool liner and wool lined hood was now authorized. For the hands there were black leather gloves with wool liner inserts, or, if you worked outside, the 'chopper' mitten with a wool liner and a thermal lined gauntlet. The standard color was olive green, unless you were in a combat unit, then, white was the color. The standard authorized, required boots were the black rubber boots with a built-in felt liner, commonly called the 'Korean war' boot.

However, starting the First of November, all military personnel in the Alaska command were required to begin testing the new extreme cold weather parka. The color was white if you were in a combat unit, for everyone else, olive drab color of course, with a quilted thermal lining and a quilted lined 'snorkel' hood with wolf fur trim around the snorkel hood opening. Also tested were the new military winter boot made of white rubber with a thermal, inflated air chamber. This new boot was quickly nicknamed the "bunny boot", because of the bulbous shape caused by the inflatable air chamber, and, of course, the white color. This new outer wear was required to be worn and tested for the entire winter in temperatures down to minus seventy below zero.

As ever shortening daylight hours slid away along with the remaining days of October, the new winter testing season routines were established. For Bob, the volume of mail increased as the testing units rosters were brought up to strength. There was an increase of mail from the civilian manufacturing companies to the various test sites, and, of course, an increased number of the classified test report packets, to be couriered back to the USAATB headquarters, as well as the 'unclassified' packets to be mailed out to Fort Wainwright. This meant an increased number of trips out to the remote testing sites, as well.

This was shaping up to be a very busy testing season. Thousands of pieces of new military hardware needed to be tested for Arctic worthiness. There were no more off duty recreational trips out into the wilderness on weekends as the testing now went on 'twenty four-seven'. The old army adage certainly applied, which stated that, "a busy soldier is a happy soldier". Any and all recreational activities were set up around busy work schedules. Bowling teams were formed and played one night a week. Basketball competition was under way with competing teams from each army division, such as Infantry, Armor, Artillery, Supply, Transportation and Bob's team, Administration. Games were played two nights a week. The college extension classes provided by The University of Alaska that Bob signed up for; Freshman English and Business Management, were held two nights a week in the ATB Headquarters Building Training Center.

For those who preferred the more unstructured off-duty recreational activities, there was the base theater where the new movie reels were brought in every Friday from Fort Wainwright. There was also pool to be played in the basement Rec. Room or TV in the TV Lounge. The EM club and NCO club were open every evening, although our gang of four sometimes preferred to venture off-base to the infamous Malamute Saloon and Motel on Saturday night for a little change-of-pace R & R to relieve the stress of life on the Last Frontier in this remote, dark, frozen and isolated part of the world.

What transpires at places like the Malamute, is so very typical of off-base 'entertainment' establishments outside of every military base of every army, navy and air force of every country around the world. This is the scenario that has played out for thousands of years, as the young warriors have marched across the planet, pillaging, plundering and raping the women of the conquered country. The resultant 'churning up' of the DNA of the human race has resulted in a world where the human species is more blended today than ever before. You take the isolated locations of most military installations, combined with the very virile age of the young military men with their raging testosterone, screaming for a release and bring them together with the young female of the species, with raging hormones of their own. Now add in an enterprising minded businessman who sees a definite need to be fulfilled for profit. - - - -

* * * * * *

They first took seats at the bar and ordered drinks. They were just in time for the first 'show', as it was called, which amounted to the girls doing their 'pole dances', three girls on three poles on a raised stage above the bar, while the four piece band played the typical stripping music. When their number was finished, the band played regular dance music during the intermission and some couples would dance on the small dance floor in the corner, while the girls would 'mingle'. Roger, Frank and Richard then moved to one of the more 'private' booths along the back wall. Bob followed along. He wasn't yet familiar with how the game was played, being the 'newbie' of the group.

The girls soon joined them. They weren't wearing their scanty stage costumes, but costumes that were tantalizing none the less. They didn't require any extra chairs to be pulled up to the table. They immediately made themselves comfortable on the laps of the three guys. Bob just observed how the game was played. Rounds of drinks were ordered as the girls made small talk. After a couple of drinks, as the band blasted out the sounds of the late fifties and early sixties, the girls began to move and gyrate in the guy's laps bringing certain girl body parts into contact with the guy parts. Soon hands became also involved. Richard and Sylvia immediately went to work getting warmed up good and hot. In a few minutes they got up and left for an upstairs room. Frank and Roger continued getting warmed up and soon the rigidity of the guys became obvious as they got up and proceeded upstairs as well.

Bob sat there for a while, just nursing his drink. After a while a girl came up to him at the table that he recognized from the ATB headquarters office where he turned in the classified packets. They introduced themselves and made small talk for a few minutes while they finished their drinks. Her name was Joanie. Bob asked her for a dance. They danced for a few numbers and she returned to the group that she came with; some of the other civilian employees that worked on the base. Bob returned to his table and ordered another beer and waited. After about twenty minutes, Frank and Roger and their two girls returned from upstairs. The girls moved on to another table of guys as Frank and Roger returned to Bob's table and ordered another drink as they all waited for Richard and Sylvia to finish up and return.

They waited for the rest of the 'intermission' as the girls all returned from upstairs to the stage and were joined by three more girls for their second set. Richard and Sylvia didn't return for quite a while.

"Man, oh man," Roger finally said, "That Richard is either a real stud, or he's paying for a second round of sex with Sylvia, but just talking."

"Yeah," Frank joked, "He's probably trying to talk her into marrying him."

At that point of the evening, the front door of the Malamute opened and three MPs from Fort Greely entered.

"Relax everybody," one of them said, "We're just making our required rounds. Everything okay tonight, Fritz?" He asked the owner of the Malamute.

"Oh yeah, guys. Everyone's behaving and having a good time. Hey, why don't you boys come back after your shift and enjoy some of our fine and beautiful ladies. These fine young girls are of Scandinavian descent and are freshly imported from Minneapolis, Minnesota and Seattle, Washington."

The MPs stayed for a few minutes, talking to some of their friends from the base, then left.

Richard and Sylvia returned from upstairs after a while and Sylvia got changed and returned to the stage where the girls gyrated to the music and lost more and more articles of clothing in the process. The guys consumed a couple more rounds of drinks and soon the girls were all naked and the stage was strewn with the various articles of their costumes as their number came to an end and the girls all went backstage and got changed into their 'working girl' clothes.

"You guys ready for more," Sylvia said to Bob's group, "How about you, Bob, are you ready to try it yet? Don't be shy. I won't bite, now, I promise," As she attempted to crawl into his lap for a lap dance.

"No, no," Bob lied, as he stood up "I'm a married man and we were just leaving,"

"They all are," Sylvia responded, "But, this is Alaska, and it gets sooo cold and lonely up here. Think about it, sweetie, when you're back on base lying in your lonely bunk with your hard cock in your hand. I'll be here waiting just for you."

Richard had his coat on and was waiting by the door and didn't see his 'girl' come on to Bob.

The other three all got their coats and joined him. Outside the temperature was already about twenty five below zero. They rode back to the base in silence, each with their own thoughts about their evening at the Malamute.

ROBB FELDER

CHAPTER 16

Sun Dogs stood guard on either side of the sun in mid November, as the temperature slid even farther below zero at night, and didn't even make it above zero during the extremely short day. The thermometer would not rise above zero until March. Daylight hours now numbered about four hours. The sun came up, just barely above the Delta River Valley at ten in the morning and set at two in the afternoon. In another month there would be no sunlight at all at Fort Greely, only a couple of hours of twilight. In the far north at Prudhoe Bay the sun had already disappeared completely and would not be seen again until next March; four months of almost total darkness. There was about one hour of twilight at twelve noon. Five hundred miles north of there, at the North Pole, there was twenty four hours of total darkness for almost six months.

On his mail runs to Prudhoe Bay and Fort Yukon, Bob's plane had to rely on radar guidance systems to guide it into the Prudhoe Bay and Fort Yukon landing strips. They were already in total darkness. All across the far north, the bush pilots could no longer land at those remote villages that did not have a generator to provide runway lights and run their radios. Those villages now had to rely on dog sled transportation for any emergency supplies or medical emergencies. These bush pilots were basically out of work until spring. Many of them would spend the winter in the lower forty eight states. These "snowbirds" would go as far south as Arizona and Southern California for the winter.

Frank was a very charismatic person who knew a lot of people as he made his supply runs up to Fairbanks every week, so when a going-away party was thrown for him at the EM club, about fifty people showed up to send him off, back to the lower forty eight and civilian life.

After the party, after everyone had left; Frank caught Bob's attention and they found a secluded table in the back corner of the club.

"I know we've talked before about how this operation works and who the players are. Well, I've got some news to share with you before I go. I've decided to take the position of being your handler and head of the entire operation. I'll be setting up an office in Fairbanks to coordinate the operation from there. I'll be making a lot of trips to the lower forty eight to set up the new equipment manufacturing companies on the plan."

"Well, Frank, I'll feel better knowing that you're my handler. I have to admit, I've often thought that you were already my handler. You are the one who set up the whole operation and got me oriented into it. Nobody knows more about it than you."

"I'll call you and give you my phone number when I get set up in Fairbanks. I hope that you are happy with the money you're making so far. I know that I am."

"Yeah, my last bank statement shows that I already have over ten thousand dollars deposited into it."

"Oh, there'll be lots more yet to come."

Bob wondered how much longer the I.G. Dept. was going to allow Frank to continue his operation. Why haven't they made arrests and shut down Frank's industrial spying operation? Maybe they were waiting until Frank got set up with his office in Fairbanks. Maybe they needed more proof. He had no choice now, but to continue doing what he was doing, until he heard from Lieutenant George.

Bob continued his busy schedule of mail and courier runs to the remote test sites. Just after

Thanksgiving on his run to Prudhoe Bay, MSG. McCaffery invited him to participate in a test run of the new snow machines. There were about seven machines to be tested. MSG. McCaffery gave Bob a pair of goggles and explained that they were necessary to prevent his eye balls from freezing in the forty below zero temperature. A face mask was also worn for frost bite protection. A squad of men from Fort Wainwright was assigned to assist in the testing.

"I notice," Bob said, "you've gotten in some new and different types of these power sleds. The ones from the Bombardier Company have a rear mounted engine, where these new ones have a front mounted engine."

"Yes, these new ones came from a company down in Minnesota. I believe the company is called The Arctic Cat Company. You'll be getting separate test results on each of these to send to the opposing companies."

They made several loops around Prudhoe Bay to get everyone acclimated to driving the power sleds. After the warm-up session, they proceeded out onto the Arctic Ocean ice. Because the ocean ice is constantly shifting and moving, huge blocks of the ice are forced up and over other ice creating large shards of the ice protruding up into the air, some as much as ten or twenty feet tall.

It was a treacherous trip, maneuvering through the rugged icy obstacle strewn terrain. While the terrain was difficult enough itself, it was compounded by the total blackness of the arctic night. After a couple of hours, the squad was pretty exhausted from maneuvering the twisting, winding trail and they were somewhat glad to get back off the ice.

"Now, that was fun," Bob exclaimed to MSG. McCaffery when they got back, "albeit a little exhausting. I can still envision a whole new form of winter recreation utilizing these machines."

"Well, right now, these are war machines, and we are testing them as such. We are preparing these and our other larger transport vehicles for the war games that will be held sometime after the holidays; out on the Arctic Ocean ice. We have ordered up several hundred more of these Arctic vehicles of all sorts. There will be about a thousand men participating in the war maneuvers. These arctic war games will be carried out on both the arctic tundra and out on the Arctic Ocean ice, from the Yukon River to the North Pole. This will include units of men from all branches of the Army, from Fort Wainwright and from the lower forty eight states."

The next morning, Bob signed out the classified test documents pouch and took the other pouch of the unclassified copy and returned to Fort Greely. He again delivered the classified packet to the ATB headquarters and mailed the other packet to Lt. George at Fort Wainwright.

While weekends would not be the same without Frank, the other three were anxious to move on and find a replacement for him in their foursome. They all knew that it would be the same for all of them as they each completed their tour of service in Alaska, and would be returning home to the lower forty eight, to their families and loved ones. The Army's standard tour of duty for Alaska was eighteen months, because even though it was now a U.S. state, it was still what the military considered a "hardship" duty station because of the remoteness and isolation of the bases there.

As the December days slipped away, so did the sun. By the twenty first of December; the winter solstice, all that remained of daylight were a few hours of twilight. Without the sun to warm the air, the temperature had plunged to minus fifty below zero. The one plus caveat was that, at those extreme temperatures, it didn't snow anymore. They had already received about two feet of snow for the winter so far.

Down on the Delta River flats at the Missile Range, the testing crews and the factory reps.

scrambled to find a type of rocket fuel that would ignite at those temperatures. Likewise the testing of the Army's new M1 Abrams tank revealed that the tank's turbine engine would not perform at those temperatures. The reps. from Chrysler also scrambled to find a fuel that would fire at minus fifty to seventy below zero.

Meanwhile the chemical warfare crews at the Gerstle River test site worked to find chemical combinations that would carry their deadly toxins through the air at those extreme temperatures and still be effective.

At the Fort Yukon site, testing was all but shut down for their season. With the Yukon River and the muskeg swamps of the tundra frozen over, there was very limited testing to be done across the frozen terrain.

In the far north, at Prudhoe Bay, testing was ramping up and plans were being formulated for one of the largest war games ever held in the arctic tundra and out on the Arctic Ocean ice pack.

Bob was working frantically, ten hours a day to keep up with the increased mail going out to all the test sites with the increased number of the civilian technicians getting mail from their company headquarters as well as regular letters from home, and with the river of paperwork in the form of secret test documents being couriered back and forth between the test sites and the ATB headquarters. He barely had time for his extension college classes provided by the University of Alaska on Monday and Thursday nights. He already had to miss a couple of bowling nights and basketball games. But then, so did a lot of the other guys.

He was getting more and more excited as the Christmas holidays grew near. He had made arrangements for his girlfriend Susan and his daughter Megan to visit him for Christmas through the New Years holidays. However, as he checked with the only motel in Delta Junction, the Midnight Sun Motel, he found that they were already all booked for the holidays; apparently quite a few of the married guys from Fort Greely had the same plans as he did. His only other option was The Malamute Saloon and Motel. He really didn't want his girlfriend, and daughter staying at a brothel for the holidays, but lucky for him, Fritz had one of his small trailer homes available that was vacant. In addition to the Saloon and motel, Fritz had a small mobile home park located adjacent to the bar. There were about ten or fifteen small mobile homes that he rented out to the soldiers from Fort Greely who for whatever reason didn't qualify for base housing, yet wanted to have their wife's, or, girlfriends and family living with them in Alaska, fairly close to Fort Greely. So Bob rented one of the mobile home units for his girlfriend and baby girl Megan for the holidays. Two days before Christmas, he met them at the airport in Fairbanks. Frank Krisinzkey's replacement, Aaron Singleton drove Bob up to Fairbanks and back to pick up his girlfriend and baby girl and dropped them off at the Malamute mobile home park. Aaron also lived at the park with his family of four.

Bob and Susan shopped the next day at the base PX for Christmas decorations along with gifts for each other and baby Megan. The temperature mellowed to a rather balmy minus ten below zero, which of course, allowed it to snow. Not a lot, but enough to make commuting back and forth to base a bit tricky. Bob found the ideal Christmas tree in the woods behind the mobile home park. They decorated the tree and wrapped the gifts and placed them under the tree. Bob was allowed to sign out his mail truck off base during the holidays. He drove his family to the Fort Greely base church for a Christmas Eve service. On Christmas Day the ATB opened the mess hall for all the soldiers and families and put out a fabulous feast for everyone.

The idyllic days between the holidays were busy as Bob and Susan spent time getting to know their neighbors. They had parties for the kids and shared meals at each other's trailers as the temperature slipped back down into the minus forty below zero range. They all planned a big party for New Years Eve. Sergeant Trent and his wife Sherlie agreed to host the party. They had the biggest 'wanigan'(an additional room build onto the side of a mobile home).

New Years Eve and the Malamute Saloon was rocking and packed with soldiers. So was the Sergeant Trent's party. It started out with a meal of barbequed caribou and moose steaks from the moose which Aaron Singleton shot and butchered right behind the mobile home park. After the dinner, desserts were shared. Everyone brought something to share. Then the drinks were shared by everyone until midnight when everyone toasted the new year, nineteen sixty two, then left to put the children to bed.

At about two in the morning, Bob and Susan were awakened by a pounding on their trailer door.

"Now, who in the hell do you suppose that could be?" Susan asked, rhetorically.

"I don't know, Honey, I heard a lot of noise from next door earlier. That party at the Malamute was still jumping."

Bob got up and threw on a robe to answer their door. It was Roger, Richard and Sylvia.

Richard was frantic. "You've got to let us in, Bob, quickly. They're after us."

"Wait, what, who. Who?" Bob asked as he opened the door to let them in.

"The MP's, Bob, The God damn MP's. They raided the place. They, - - they, threatened to arrest my Sylvia."

"Wait, why would they do that?"

"The three of us were just sitting there at our table, enjoying our drinks right after. - - you know. All of a sudden this big ugly dude from the Motor Pool comes up and starts swearing and yelling at me and Sylvia. He say's," "God dammit, you can't have her all night long. You don't own her, ya know. You've got ta share her. I got good money too." "Then he just grabs her by the arm and starts dragging her away. So I jumped up and punched him out. Then, all hell broke loose. A big fight broke out. Apparently he had a lot of his friends there with him that wanted a piece of Sylvia too."

Susan got up to see what all the excitement was about. "You guys, please keep it down, you don't want to wake up little Megan. Miss, are you all right?" she said to Sylvia.

"Oh, I'm fine," she replied, "I just crawled under a table to get out of the way."

"That's when I jumped up and got involved in the foray." Roger continued, "About thirty drunken soldiers proceeded to wreck the place. The MP's who were already there, probably in anticipation of the inevitable fight when soldiers are drunk and celebrating. The MP's hauled away the five or six instigators. That's when we three made a run for it, out the back door. The MP"s then cleared the place out and shut it down."

"Well, let's all get some sleep," Susan said, "Miss, you can take the extra bed in Megan's room, but be quiet please, she's teething and will be a hand full if she wakes up. Richard and Roger you'll have to share the pull out couch."

The next day, New Years Day, the base Commander ordered the Malamute Saloon "Off limits" to all military personnel until further notice. This infuriated Fritz who relied on the Malamute Saloon for most of his income. He, in retaliation, shut down the power generator which supplied electricity to the mobile home park. Not only were the residents left with no lights, their furnaces also would not operate. Emergency shelter was provided at Fort Greely for the mobile home park residents. The Fort Greely commander acted quickly to avoid catastrophic water damage to the soldiers mobile homes when the water pipes would have froze and burst. The base immediately brought out one of their mobile generators and hooked it up to the mobile home park.

Then the stand-off began. Fritz wanted compensatory settlement for the damages done by the base's drunken soldiers before he would turn his generator back on. The commander said he stayed open beyond the allowed hours of the curfew of his soldiers. Fritz claimed there were no regulated hours that he could stay open, and so, on and on, the argument went.

Meanwhile, the day after New Years Day, Aaron drove Bob, Susan and Megan back to Fairbanks, to catch their flight back to Minnesota.

While they were sitting in the waiting area, waiting for Susan's flight back to the lower forty eight, she said, "You know, Bob, up until that bad incident at the Malamute Saloon, I had been thinking of just staying here in Alaska with you for the rest of your tour. I had made some real good friends with some of the wives at the mobile home park. But now, with the problems with the electricity at the park, I just don't want to put our little Megan in danger of freezing to death because of some battle Fritz is having with the Army. I had thought the Army was better at resolving these kinds of issues."

Soon after her comments, Susan and Megan's plane pulled up to the gate. Sad goodbye's and hugs and kisses were shared by Bob and his new little family. On the way back to Fort Greely, Bob began thinking; his family would not have been able to survive with Alaska's prices and his meager PFC's salary. He was only getting one hundred and ten dollars a month. Bob was now eligible for a promotion to the next rank of Specialist Fourth Class. He had fulfilled the 'time-in-grade' requirement already, three months ago. That would have boosted his pay to one hundred and sixty five dollars a month. But, he probably wouldn't be getting the promotion, any time soon. He became very upset thinking about how he was being screwed over by the set-up that the Army had with the relationship between the Army's Arctic Test Center and it's being under the command of Fort Belvoir, Virginia. Promotions were issued by the available openings in each Army command area. Any openings available in the Alaska Command could not be allocated to the Army Arctic Test Center. And any openings available in Fort Belvoir's First Army area were allocated to soldiers on the east coast.

When he got back from Fairbanks, he went back to the Malamute Mobile Home Park to pick up the rest of their things, mostly Christmas decorations and a few groceries and kitchen items, which he gave to Sgt. and Mrs. Trent. Sergeant Trent told Bob that this incident with the electric power goes on about twice a year, whenever there's a big party at the Malamute. It was several weeks later that Bob noticed a letter that came in to his mail room addressed to Richard. He just happened to glance at the return address. He was a bit puzzled, because it appeared to be from Sylvia, Richard's girl from the Malamute. However, the return address was from somewhere in Seattle,

Washington. When Bob handed out the mail to Richard, he just said, "Tonight, the EM Club, let's talk."

The two of them got together later that evening at the club and ordered beers.

"So, Richard, do you want to talk about Sylvia and the letter. I'm sorry, I couldn't help noticing her return address. Com'on, buddy, talk to me. What's going on?"

"Well," he began, "It seems that Sylvia got fired from the Malamute after that fracas on New Year's Eve. Fritz blamed her for being the cause of it all. Right now, I'm feeling incredibly guilty about it all. I'm really the one who started it. Bob, I think I'm developing some real feelings for Sylvia. I might be falling in love with her."

"Well," Richard said, "the question now is what do I do about it? I mean, she's even gotten a job as a waitress at a restaurant in Seattle, instead of a strip bar. I think she really wants to better herself. "

"I think that you really need to get down to Seattle and sort this all out and see if she feels the same way. Hell, Richard, you've got plenty of leave-time accumulated and God knows enough money from our gold prospecting last summer."

Richard went in the next day to talk to the Company Commander and got approved for some leave-time to Seattle. Two weeks later, on a

Friday night, they all got together after work, at the EM club, for beers, to welcome him back and welcome a new member to the group. A new soldier named Henry Murdock.

"So, Richard, how did it go in Seattle?" Bob asked after they all toasted Henry into their foursome, and Richard back from Seattle.

"Well, the one main thing that happened in Seattle, was that Sylvia and I are now married," Richard exclaimed excitedly, holding up his left hand to show off his new wedding band, "We were married on Fisherman's Warf just four days ago. We got a new apartment in the Uptown area, not far from The Seaside Restaurant where she works. And, we took a quick honeymoon trip up the coast for a couple days. Hey, did you know that Seattle is getting ready to host the World's Fair in a couple of years. We noticed, as we drove north, they're starting to build something called a monorail. And the fair will have this really tall structure called The Space Needle. I can't wait to get back there. I've only got four months left on my enlistment, then, I'll get to be with my Sylvia."

CHAPTER 17

In the distance he can faintly hear the sound of the Red Winged Blackbirds calling, - - - - calling out to each other, - - - no? Who are they calling out to? - - - Are they calling to him? - - - And, why are there birds in this frozen place. His ancient, cloudy cerebral matter struggles to process, struggles to separate the real world from his dream world. Slowly, ever so slowly the cerebrum tugs at his dream, pulling it away, pulling him away from Alaska, clouding over his dream and replacing it with, - - - - the calling of the black birds? Reality? But wait, why are the birds shouting words at him? Slowly, slowly, it seems like minutes or hours pass before the reality comes into focus, pulling him away from the icy cold of the Alaska winter. His first realization is that he is freezing. His body shivers, even in the hot July sun of reality. He slowly tries to pull his stiff, cold, sore body up. Still, somewhere in the back of his mind, he is wondering why the birds are yelling to him. As he reaches the sitting up position and opens his eyes, squinting in the bright sun, the real world comes back into focus and he realizes that it isn't birds calling his name, but his grandchildren and great grandchildren.

"Come on Papa, wake up," both Kira and McKenna, his two great granddaughters are shouting and running towards him, "It's time to eat."

"Let's eat, Grandpa," says Zachery, Bob's grandson.

"Yeah, after we eat, Grandma said we can go fishing," Colby stated.

"Come on," says Barb, his wife, as she helps Bob to his feet, "You must have dozed off while you were waiting for the kids and I to explore your family's old farm here on the river. Even though, there isn't much left, just some old crumbling buildings. The kids are loving it though. Brenda and I've told them this place is haunted by the ghosts of your family who used to live here."

"Ryan has added to the ghostly scenario by playing the part of the voices of the family ghosts," Brenda said, "that live here in the ancient ruins."

"Now, let's get something to eat, Grandpa, remember, we packed a nice picnic lunch to eat here on the river bank. The kids and I have it all set up and ready over here under the trees, on the big blanket we brought."

Granddaughter Jenna began dishing up plates for Kira and McKenna. Travis has just finished up cooking the hot dogs on the portable grill they brought. The kids all dished up heaps of Grandma's delicious potato salad. Ice cold sodas and chips were added. Except Grandpa Bob, who couldn't eat the chips because they bothered his false teeth. When they all finished, there was Grandma Barb's fabulous rhubarb crisp for dessert. As the adults cleaned up, the kids got ready to go fishing. When everything was packed up, Barb and Bob spread a blanket out in a sunny spot on the river bank and used another to cover with although the midday sun was quite warm.

"Come on everyone," Zachery called out to the rest of the group as they all headed up the trail, "Colby and I will show you the way to the big horse shoe bend where all the fish are. We've been there before. Come on Ryan and Auntie Brenda, you can explore the many 'wash-outs' in the river bank on the way up to the big spring."

As the kids left, up the river trail, Barb and Bob cuddled up for a nice afternoon nap in the warm July sunshine. Barb began drifting back as she began to fall asleep, back to an idyllic time of her youth with her two sisters, growing up in the iron mining town of Hibbing, Minnesota.

Bob also began drifting off again as he heard the roar of a train on the nearby railroad as it crossed the river bridge.

CHAPTER 18

The roar of the twin engine Caribou Army plane kept Bob awake as it took off from Fort Greely, into the Arctic blackness of the February midmorning. At twenty thousand feet, he could just barely see the twilight of sunrise taking place several thousand miles to the south. But, they were heading about a thousand miles to the north where even a twilight was still two months away. Bob was heading north on this trip, to the test site that was normally at Prudhoe Bay, but was now temporarily located several hundred miles out on the frozen ice pack that was the Arctic Ocean. Here there were war games going on. Here, the Army was testing men and machines in an Arctic Battlefield.

The runway, spread out on a smooth stretch of the Arctic Ocean ice, was equipped with runway lights and radar homing devices. The plane descended out of the arctic night sky and pulled up in front of the Arctic Test Center's headquarters tent. A small village of large tents, thermal insulated, and heated by several large kerosene heaters were clustered around the headquarters tent. In the distance, an electric generator could be heard, providing lights and power for the communication equipment for the arctic base camp. Somewhere off in the far distance, similar small clusters of these thermal encampments, were spread out across the Arctic Ocean, all the way to the North Pole. Over a thousand soldiers were waking up in the black arctic morning, dining on a breakfast of 'K' rations, then donning their extreme arctic clothing. They would then pull down their thermal tents and pack them again, onto the sleds, working under the light of the constant Aurora Borealis, which here, near the North Pole were directly overhead. and brighter than anywhere else on the planet, creating a twilight of sorts to work under.

The squads of men would then climb into their arctic designed vehicles for another day of trekking across the vast arctic ice fields, seeing with the large light bars mounted atop each vehicle, and guided by compass and radio commands from the command center. Each squad vehicle had a scout vehicle out front, one of the new snow-scooters, forging the way through the jungle of the huge shards of the arctic ice. The job of the scout vehicle was to guide the larger troop carriers around potholes of open water and large crevasses in the ice crust.

Powerful forces of nature were at work in the minus sixty to seventy below zero temperatures. The expansion of the rapid freezing of any exposed water at those temperatures coupled with the almost constant powerful arctic winds at the North Pole, moved and shifted the enormous sections of ice, the size of small continents colliding into each other and pushing one 'continent' up and over other segments of the five to ten feet thick crust of the arctic ice that had been broken and refrozen again into a mountainous terrain of jagged peaks of the broken ice. Much of this ice cap near the North Pole has not been thawed for thousands, even tens of thousands of years.

Along with the dozen or more of the troop transport arctic tracked vehicles carrying the infantry, there were another dozen vehicles equipped with artillery weapons. Long and short range howitzers were mounted on the tracked vehicles. Another dozen vehicles carried rocket launchers. All of these vehicles were followed by the supply vehicles. About ten or so more vehicles were equipped with fuel supply tanks for both the vehicles and for the kerosene heaters for the arctic tents. Another half dozen carried the food supply for this excursion.

As this arctic armada made its way across the North Pole, it then began the trek south again, on the other side of the North Pole, heading in the direction of the USSR. The mission was to get close, but not too close to the Soviet mainland. So as to not cause a major provocation, they would stay well away from the Russian international waters.

As this test army advanced deep into the arctic, statistics were gathered at the end of each day. The performance of the vehicles was reported on, as well as things like fuel consumption and the wear and tear on the vehicles and their maintenance and repair requirements. Also monitored was the performance of the soldiers. Their morale after being cooped up in the vehicles all day was closely monitored as well as their ability to perform all of the tasks of survival in this extreme, alien and hostile environment.

The extremely dangerous environment did, however, have its toll on the soldiers involved. While executing their way through the very dangerous terrain, one of the troop carrying arctic vehicles got too close to the edge of one of the many icy crevasses. The protrusion of an ice shelf at the edge of the crevasse gave way and began to crumble. The driver lost control of the vehicle and the large arctic tracked vehicle plunged about thirty feet down into the crevasse. One soldier was killed and four of the squad of eight, were injured when the vehicle overturned on its way down into the crevasse and they were thrown out of the vehicle which crushed them when the vehicle hit the bottom of the crevasse.

The injured were immediately transported back to the test site headquarters medical tent by helicopter and emergency first aid was applied by the medical corpsman. The injured were then forwarded by helicopter to the Fort Wainwright Hospital for further treatment. The deceased soldier; Corporal Mike Johnson, was also flown to Fort Wainwright via the Caribou aircraft that Bob used for trips back and forth to Fort Greely. Bob rode with the body of the deceased soldier to Fort Wainwright and then he went on to Fort Greely. The deceased soldier was processed and forwarded to his home town. The Commander of the Arctic Test Center; Colonel Ray Kimball flew with the body as an escort and to console the grieving family and remained with them for the funeral service and burial.

A memorial service was held at Fort Greely, attended by everyone not on critical duty, as well as the uninjured squad members of the fateful accident. The arctic war games continued on as usual. However, a ton of paperwork was generated as a result of the tragic accident.

As the statistics from the arctic war games were compiled along with the regular daily operational statistics, the paperwork was couriered back to the mobile command headquarters. Here they were organized and categorized. The documents classified as 'Top Secret' were signed over to an officer, to be flown back to Fort Greely. The test documents that were stamped 'Secret' were put into a courier pouch. As Bob signed for the courier pouch, he was also, again given the copied set of documents by Master Sergeant. McCaffery.

"The money from this mission will send my children to college," McCaffrey whispered.

"And also mine," Bob replied as he picked up the two packets and left for his daily flight back to Fort Greely. He was making daily flights up into the arctic now as the war games were in progress. The Pentagon wanted the daily reporting so they could closely monitor the maneuvers. He signed over the packet to the ATB headquarters as usual, and mailed the copied set to Lt. George at Fort Wainwright. He no longer needed to keep the name and addresses of the equipment manufacturers hidden away in the toe of his boots. Lt. George, he assumed was doing the distribution to the individual companies after carefully altering the test results. He still worried every day, however, when the whole scheme would come crashing down on Frank and his crew of industrial espionage agents. How much longer would Lt. George of the Army's I.G. office in Fort

Wainwright wait before he had enough proof to 'pull the plug' and bring down the entire spy ring.

Meantime, Bob noticed; as he received his monthly bank statement from Wells Fargo that his balance was growing by leaps and bounds.

ROBB FELDER

CHAPTER 19

On one of his daily trips to the Arctic Ocean test site, Bob was very surprised to find Frank at the test site headquarters.

"What brings you up here?" Bob asked.

"I'm just up here checking on how our operation is going."

"So, how did you get here? Were you able to catch a flight on a military plane?"

"No, Bob, I guess I neglected to tell you that I now have my own plane."

"Oh, really, Frank, I guess I didn't even know you had a pilot's license."

"Oh, yeah, I've been taking flying lessons in Fairbanks for the past year or so. Last month I found a real good deal on a Cessna twin engine plane, down in Anchorage, so I bought it. When these arctic war games were announced, I finagled a military clearance to fly up here to check things out for myself. I've been doing some reporting for the Army's newspaper; The Stars And Stripes."

"I guess, I didn't realize you were doing that, as well as everything else."

"Well, why don't we get together soon, maybe after the war games. I see you're pretty busy right now with couriering the test results back and forth from the Fort Greely headquarters. Give me a call when you're freed up and I will fill you in on a new venture that I'm working on."

"Okay, Frank, I'll see you then. You fly safely, now."

When Bob returned to Fort Greely, he was called in to the Company Commander's office. He saluted, and Captain Ellis returned his salute.

"At ease, Specialist Fellerer," Captain Ellis said, "It is my pleasure to award you with your new rank of Specialist Fourth Class. You've earned it, Specialist Fellerer. You've been given an excellent rating by the U.S. Postal Service on their annual inspection of your mail room. And I've gotten excellent reports back from all of our test sites and from the Arctic Test Headquarters, on your handling of the courier duties, bringing back the test results from all the remote test sites. Congratulations."

Captain Ellis handed him a copy of the official orders promoting him to the new rank of Specialist Fourth Class,(E-4).

"Thank you Sir," Bob said as he saluted and left to get to the base tailor and get his new arm patches sewn onto all of his uniforms.

As February slipped away, the arctic war games drew to a conclusion. The arctic expedition had reached its destination, near the Siberian mainland, to the island of Severnaya Zemlya and then headed back across the North Pole.

After his final trip to the Arctic Ocean test site, Bob requested some time off. He was eligible for some days off after working through the Presidents' Day holiday. He needed a nice long weekend get-away, so he called his friend Frank in Fairbanks. Bob told him about his promotion to SP4. Frank invited him up to Fairbanks for the weekend. He arrived on a Friday evening in the falling snow and the falling temperature, down to well below zero.

"Bob, I'd like you to meet Nicole Kiselyova, she's my new partner," Frank said as they were seated at The Arctic Fox Restaurant in downtown Fairbanks, "Nicole, this is SP4 Bob Fellerer. He's stationed down at Fort Greely. Like I told you, Bob is the Army's courier at the Arctic Test Center. He is the one who does the mailing of the duplicate test packets to all of the competing manufacturers of the equipment that the Army runs tests on down at Greely."

"I'm very pleased to finally meet you Bob. Frank has told me so much about you."

"I'm pleased to meet you too, Nicole. So what will be your duties as Frank's partner?"

Bob immediately noticed that Nicole was a very attractive young girl with short bobbed black hair, large black eyes and beautiful red lips. She wore a bright red turtle neck sweater which accented her generous bust line and slender waist. She had on tight black slacks, and high heeled black patent leather, knee length boots.

"Well, because of my background and education, I'm currently working on a business major at the University of Alaska, I'll be in charge of coordinating business operations," she replied with a very thick Russian accent, "I'll be mostly in charge of scheduling meetings, keeping the books and scheduling flight operations."
The waiter came to the table, and they ordered drinks. Frank and Nicole ordered Vodka gimlets, Bob ordered a gin and tonic. After their drinks arrived and they all ordered dinner, they engaged in small talk until their dinners arrived.

Frank explained how he met Nicole. "We were both taking the same class at the University of Alaska, a Business Finance class."

"Yes," Nicole continued, "We decided to meet at Frank's apartment one night after class to work on our homework assignment. Well, we started working on more than just homework, if you know what I mean."

"So," continued Frank, "shortly after that, I invited Nicole to move in with me. Soon after that, she introduced me to another income producing venture. We'll tell you about it later at our apartment where it's more private."

Their dinners arrived and they all ate and had several more drinks. Frank and Bob reminisced about last summer's gold prospecting adventure. Nicole told a little bit about her family and background, growing up in Sitka, Alaska, where her parents owned a large commercial fishing boat. She told about working summers, on the boat, helping her father, setting out the crab pots and bait bags and pulling in the pots filled with the King Crabs.

"My parents were immigrants from Russia," she continued, "They came to Alaska from the Soviet city of Minsk just after World War 2. I have many relatives there, in Minsk, we write often. In the Sitka area of Alaska's panhandle there are also many Russians. Some can speak only the Russian language, even today, including my parents. I can speak and read and write the Russian language, of course, as well as English."

"Well, with that," Frank said, "Why don't we continue our discussions at our apartment?"

Frank paid the tab and the trio left the restaurant and headed up Aurora Drive. The snow had been falling while they were having dinner, and about six inches had accumulated making the driving difficult. The temperature was about fifty below zero, typical for a mid-February period. Frank and Nicole had a fourth floor apartment overlooking the Tanana River, which lay below them, frozen almost solid in the long, frigid, arctic night.   Their two bedroom apartment was furnished in the late fifties, mid-century modern, of course. After they all had shed their arctic outer ware and boots, Frank mixed more drinks and they settled in for the night to discuss Frank and Nicole's plan.

"Our original plan is going quite well," Frank began, "We're passing the testing results to the competing manufacturers, and they are returning a fair amount of money in return for the risk that we take in passing that information on to them."

"However, Frank and I have been discussing a proposal for a new plan," Nicole said, "I think that this new plan could make a lot more money for us. Let me give you a little rundown on my background in the espionage business. Like I've told you before, at the restaurant, my family came from the Soviet city of Minsk. Now, what my parents have told me is that our family has been engaging in the espionage business for the last fifty years in Minsk, going all the way back to World War One."

They started during that war, doing espionage work. They worked for the Czar, passing information back and forth during the Great Russian Revolution. Some of my relatives were killed when the Czar was defeated and the Communists took over. They continued to work for the underground resistance up until World War Two, when they actually worked for the Stalin regime, passing espionage papers coming out of Germany to the Communists about the movements of the Nazi Germany army."

"Right after World War Two, my uncle, Nicolai Kiselyova, whom I am named after, went to work for Stalin's war ministry and was a double agent, passing military secrets to the West. But, when he was arrested and sent to Siberia, My father, Mikhail, who worked with him, escaped with my mother Ursula and myself on the Trans Siberian Railway to Vladivostak. From there we boarded a ship and came to Sitka. I was only five years old when we escaped. Father had accumulated a rather large sum of money paid to him by the USA's CIA for his spy work, and he bought a fishing boat, a crab trawler. In nineteen fifty three, when Stalin died and Khrushev came to power, he pardoned many of Stalin's old adversaries, including my uncle, Nicolai. Uncle Nicolai went to work, again setting up a network of spies, passing secrets to the west. My father made contact with Uncle Nicolai and they set up a courier pickup service for the secret documents. These documents would be transported on the Trans-Siberian Railroad to Vadivostok where a Russian fishing boat would pick them up and transport them to the Aleutian Island town of Unalaska. My father would pick them up from there on his crab trawler and would bring them back to Sitka and mail them to the CIA headquarters in Langley, Virginia. Uncle Nicolai told my father, that this was a more secure route than going through Europe."

"When I turned fourteen, I would go with my father on these courier runs out to Unalaska, in the Aleutian Islands. He said the money we got from the CIA for handling these spy papers would go towards my college education. When I graduated from high school, I enrolled in the University of Alaska, where I am now in my senior year. I will graduate in the spring with a BA in business management. Now, my father says he wants to retire from both, the crab boat operation and the espionage business. He wants me to take over both operations. However, I told him that I have no desire to become a crab boat operator, but that I would be interested in taking over his espionage operation.”

“But, how would you take over the business?” Bob asked, “Would you two move down to Sitka?”

“No, no,” Frank responded, “Nicole and I have discussed this at some length already. We’ve discovered that there is a flight from Vadivostok to Fairbanks, once a week. We could pick up the papers right here at the Fairbanks airport and mail them to Langley.”

“That’s right, Frank. I have already contacted Uncle Nicolai and had him set up the change of courier connections to get the papers on the Fairbanks flight.”

“Well, I’m glad for you two,” Bob said, “But, how does all this affect me?”

“Here’s the changes we’re going to ask you to initiate, Bob.” Frank said, “We’ll need you to mail those test results from Fort Greely’s arctic test sites to us, here in Fairbanks, instead of directly to those competing equipment manufactures, and we’ll do the forwarding”

Bob was becoming very conflicted by this sudden request. He didn’t quite know how to respond. He couldn’t very well explain to Frank and Nicole how he wasn’t mailing those test results directly to the manufactures. He couldn’t tell them that he was instead mailing the testing results to Lt. George at Fort Wainwright; because Frank was also a part of Lt. George's investigation. What to do? What to do? How was he going to respond to their request?

CHAPTER 20

So, Bob didn't agree to the change of plans. Instead he said, "I, don't know, Frank, I'll have to think about it. Why is it that you want to do the forwarding?"

"Okay, here's the new plan," Nicole explained, "We'll need those test result papers, so that we can make copies and send a doctored up copy back to my uncle Nicolai in Minsk. The Soviet's KGB double agent is demanding something in return for the papers he is providing to the USA."

"Now, wait just a damn minute," Bob responded, "It sounds like I just keep getting in deeper and deeper. This could get me a life sentence in Leavenworth."

"Well, you think about it, Bob, sleep on it." Frank said as they all finished their drinks. "We better all get some sleep, it's getting late and I have to fly down to Sitka tomorrow and meet with

Mikhail, Nicole's father. We have to work out the details of transferring the flow of the espionage papers to now flow through us here at Fairbanks."

"Nicole, are you going along?" Bob asked.

"No, Bob, I have to stay and study for a mid-term test at the university on Monday."

Bob got up and went into their second bedroom and got ready for bed. He had a hard time getting to sleep, however, puzzling over Frank and Nicole's proposal. But, he was quite tired and finally fell asleep. Frank and Nicole got ready for bed in their bedroom. After they were in bed, Frank waited for a while, to make sure Bob was asleep, he then began talking to Nicole in a whispered tone.

"I think Bob is having a hard time deciding to provide the test papers to us to forward to the KGB. While I'm down in Sitka tomorrow meeting with your father, I want you to work on him, to convince him to join our new plan. Use some of your seductive powers to convince him, if you know what I mean, just like you did on me when we first got together."

"Oh, that won't be too hard to do, Frank, I think Bob is kind of cute. You can bet I'll work him over good, if you know what I mean. I'll have him convinced by the time you get back tomorrow night."

Very early the next morning, the snow had let up. Frank slipped out without waking anyone, and left to get aboard his plane to fly down to Sitka. He stopped for a quick breakfast at the airport. About the time he was on his radio, taxiing toward the runway, asking for permission to take off, Bob was suddenly awakened by someone crawling into his bed with him.

"Nicole," He said very sleepily as he opened his eyes, "Has Frank left yet?"

"Oh yes, Bob, he left hours ago, there's just you and me here now. It's mid-morning and I just thought it was time to get you up."

"Oh, my God, Nicole, you don't have any clothes on," he said, as his lower body extremity suddenly came to life."

"I know, Bob, and it's so cold out, I really need you to warm me up,"

With that, she rolled over on top of him and kissed him, long and hard, and his testosterone flooded his thalamus and began to block out any objections he may have had. He was now completely in her control as she sat him up and tore off his shirt and then went to work on his shorts, like a lioness in heat, she ripped them off and went after her prize. After about a minute of that, she danced the dance of one consumed by the fire, as he met her every movement. while he tried desperately to preserve the moment. They soared higher and higher until fire-works ignited from somewhere deep inside, exploded like the fourth of July and the fiery sparks drifted back to earth as she cried out and collapsed on top of him, both of them, completely spent.

She rolled off of him and turned facing away so he could wrap his warm body around her. They both immediately drifted off to sleep in this spoon position, totally exhausted from the furor of their sexual escapade. They slept for about another hour. Bob awoke first, and with the feel of the closeness of their naked bodies, immediately caused an all too familiar sensation. As he began moving his groin area against her warm buttocks Nicole slowly woke and gave a soft purring sound and began moving her buttocks in unison with his movements.

Soon she whispered, "Okay, Bob, go ahead, I'm ready,"

They both began writhing in unison for just a moment, then she rolled over on her back to accept him again, in the missionary position. Soon pressure in his thalamus was screaming for a release. Then as sparks and fireworks, again erupted, they both cried out and exploded into rapture.

As he rolled over, off of Nicole, and they both caught their breath, they didn't feel the need to collapse into sleep.   This time they felt energized.

"Why don't you get in the shower while I start some breakfast," Nicole said, "Even though it's almost noon," as she got out of bed and reached for her bra and panties.

Bob stood in the shower for a long time, trying to come to grips with reality. "What had just happened?" He questioned, "And where was this leading him?" He asked himself, unaware that he was being played, although, he was mulling over his suspicions; about Nicole's intentions last night, about Frank, about everything that was going on in his life right now. He decided, as he stepped out of the shower and began toweling himself off, that he would play along for a while and see what Frank and Nicole were trying to lead him into.

Just as he finished brushing his teeth and was beginning to smell the coffee perking in the kitchen, Nicole came into the bathroom and began to take off her bra and panties. He began to feel a rise of his penis again as he cupped each of her breasts and massaged them with his tongue.

But she grabbed his growing penis and said, "Sorry, Bob, this'll have to wait till later. I just came in to tease you a little and ask you to finish our omelets while I shower. I've got to get busy and study for my mid-term exams on Monday."

Bob went into the bedroom and got dressed, while Nicole got into the shower. In the kitchen, he found that she had already done almost all the prep work for their breakfast. The omelet mixture was ready and had all the veggies chopped and sauteed and the egg mixture ready. She even had the fry pan on the stove and ready. He turned on the burner and poured in half of the egg mixture, meantime, he set the table, poured the orange juice and coffee, and put two slices of bread into the toaster. As the first omelet was simmering he began thinking about how spoiled he had become.

The army really did spoil it's soldiers when it came to food. They never had to worry about cooking any of their meals, except, of course, when they were in the field and had to heat their K-rations. Luckily, Bob had learned at a very early age how to prepare a breakfast. Growing up on the farm, he had to help his dad fix breakfast before heading out to the barn for the five A.M. milking.

When her omelet was done, he finished up his omelet just as Nicole finished her shower and got dressed.

"Thank you, Bob, for finishing up for me, and thank you, also, for last night. Handy in the kitchen too, I see. My kind of man."

"Yeah, proper upbringing, I guess. Well let's eat, so you can get on with studying for your mid-term."

They both had their orange juice and dug in to their omelets and toast, topping that off with their steaming hot cups of coffee, seemingly too hungry for any small talk after their great workout in the night. Perhaps, each one was processing the events of the previous night, or, too afraid to speak and break the magic of the moment. After they finished, Nicole refilled their coffee cups and broke the silence.

"Well, Specialist Bob, have you thought further about Frank's proposal from yesterday?"

"No, Nicole, I really haven't had much time to think it over yet" he lied.

Because actually he had pretty much thought about their proposal and decided that he did not want to be a part of it and assume the risk of passing military secrets to the Soviets, such a well-known enemy of the USA. The risk was just too great. What would his girlfriend back home think if he got caught? And his daughter, when she grew up and realized her father was a traitor? His family back in Minnesota would probably disown him.

He hesitated, because he didn't quite know how to answer her question, especially after last night. He had to admit, being seduced by her was really having an effect on his decision making process. Even though he pretty much now realized that her seduction was just a ploy to get him to change his mind and join her and Frank in their espionage games. The scary thought was that he felt as though he was actually weakening in his thinking. He began thinking that she was pretty successful as a seductress, and he was starting to like her a lot.

So, he said, "I really need more time to think it over Nicole."

"What do I need to do to convince you, Bob? Would you like to have another romp in the sack? Would that convince you? Because, I'm really starting to like you, Bob, and I could fuck you all day, to convince you. Frank and I really do want you on our team."

"Oh, Nicole, I would like nothing more than to get back in bed with you and spend the day, because, I'm really beginning to like you as well. I think we have a real connection developing here, and I don't mean just sexually. I just think I need more time."

"Well, Bob, our coffee is all gone and it's after noon already. I've really got to get started with studying for my mid-quarters on Monday. You're welcome to stay for the day if you want. Who knows what might develop. Frank won't be back till late tonight." She hoped he would stay for a while. She needed another shot in the sack with him to convince him to join their new plan.

"I'm sorry, Nicole, I would like nothing more than to spend the day with you, but, it's quite a long drive back to Fort Greely, and it's starting to snow again. I really do need to get on the road. I've got to turn my truck back into the Motor Pool at Greely by five P.M. And, I've got to be back to study for my own mid-quarters on Monday, for the courses that I'm taking through the University extension service at Fort Greely and I have to pick up the mail on Monday morning. How about we get back together again next weekend? I would love to have you convince me, if you know what I mean."

He got up and went into the bedroom and grabbed his duffle bag, then came out and put on his parka and boots. She came over to the door and they embraced, and kissed long and hard and her hand found its way down to his crotch where there was already an erection happening.

Bob pulled away and said, "I've really got to go, Nicole. Let's finish this next weekend, okay?"

CHAPTER 21

The trip back to Fort Greely was a very slow trip. The road was snow-packed and very slippery. It was snowing all the way back. The radio weather forecaster said that it would probably snow all night, with over a foot of snow expected. This was pretty typical, the weather man said, for this time of year in central Alaska.

After supper, Bob got together with Roger, Richard and Henry Murdock. They decided to take in a Saturday night movie.

"Don't ya just love those Elvis Presley movies?" Roger commented, afterward, as they stopped at the EM Club for a beer.

"Nah, I'm not too crazy about his movies," Henry said, "They're always so predictable and simplistic. At least he can make good music."

"I love the romance of them," Richard countered, "Boy meets girl, falls in love, almost loses girl, then fights to get her back."

"I think I have to agree with Henry," Bob argued, "Real life isn't that simple, believe me. Love can become really complicated at times."

"Are you talking now, about your own love life Bob?" Roger asked, "Cause you can tell your ol' buddy here all about it. At least you have a love life, and a really terrific girlfriend."

"Yah," Richard said, "All Roger, here has is ol' Betsy Palm and her five daughters."

With that, Roger gave Richard a shove, spilling his beer, "Hey, dude, I used to see you there, upstairs in your bunk in the moonlight, making a tent with your covers. But now that you've got your little 'Hoochie' waiting for you down there in Seattle, you think you're better off than the rest of us poor lonely soldier boys. Sorry about the spill, Richard, I'll buy us all another round."

He called the waiter over and ordered another round for everyone, commenting, "I'm so damn rich, I can't stand not spending all that gold we panned last summer."

"Speaking of spending our gold," Bob said, "I heard that the Malamute Saloon is no longer off limits. Maybe we can get out there one of these weekends."

"Hey," Richard said, "Not to change the subject, away from us all spilling our guts about our sordid love lives. I have to ask Bob, how's our ol' buddy Frank doing? I heard he came back up here to Alaska after his discharge, and you went up to Fairbanks to see him this weekend."

"He's doing just great, guys, he's bought himself an airplane and is opening up a fly-in service," Bob lied.

"That's just great. Good for him," Henry said as their round of beers arrived, "So, it seems, there really is life after Army."

The foursome finished their beers and headed back to their barracks. Bob lay in his bunk for a very long time, however, unable to fall asleep, mulling over the events of last night with Nicole.

"What to do," he pondered, "about Frank and Nicole's plan to get involved in the world of international espionage. That's a whole new level of the game he and Frank were playing up to now. Maybe Nicole was a professional, and knew the ropes, and knew how the game was played, but he, was for sure, just an amateur. At least, up to now he was only involved in a very low-level type of espionage work, but to get involved in the international version of what he was doing was a terrifying thought. And, what about this thing with Lt. George? Why hadn't he heard from him lately? What would happen when he completed his investigation? Would Frank be arrested, and if he was, where would that leave Nicole and himself? There were just so many questions, too many questions."

"Maybe he should just go along with Frank and Nicole, and not worry about Lt George's investigation. He could just make duplicate copies of all the documents and send one to Lt. George, and the other one to Frank. That would just be the easiest solution, problem solved. Let the chips fall where they may. That way, he could continue to see Nicole. Oh damn, there's that feeling again. She really had her claws into him, but good."

It was now after midnight, and with the thought of Nicole, he finally fell asleep. At about two A.M., however, he was awake again. It was the beers. He had to piss. After he returned from the latrine, however, he was right back in his confused state, and couldn't get back to sleep.

There were just too many open issues, too many unanswered questions, and that nagging thought that he might be further betraying his country. He tossed and turned for about another hour and finally fell asleep with the thought that he needed some advice from someone, outside of the problem, someone higher up in the chain of command.

Monday morning, the snow had stopped and most of the roads at Fort Greely had been plowed. Bob had his early breakfast, checked out his mail pickup truck, the usual fifty nine Chevy half ton with the aluminum topper, both painted in the Army's olive green. He made his way, slowly, on the snow-packed roads, out to the main post-office near the air strip. Back in his mail room, he sorted the mail in usual fashion, which left him a few minutes before his delivery down to the Delta River flats, to the artillery and missile test site. He pulled out his wallet and took out a slip of paper with a phone number on it. He picked up his phone and dialed the number. Lt. George answered.

"Lieutenant George, Sir, this is Specialist Fellerer from Fort Greely. I was just wondering, Sir, if you could give me an update on your investigation of Frank Krisinzkey."

"Oh sure, Specialist Fellerer. By the way, congratulations on your promotion. The investigation is moving along quite well. I know, it seems like it's taking a long time, but this a very large scale investigation. I'm still waiting to hear from the I.G. office down in Fort Belvoir. They're sending out investigators to all of the manufacturing companies involved. I hope to have this thing wrapped up by the end of the testing season, in a few months. I know, everyone is becoming anxious for the results, but these things take a lot of time."

"Thank you Sir, I'll try to be patient until then."

He opened the top drawer of his desk and pulled out the phone book with the listings for Fort Belvoir, Virginia, the command center for Fort Greely, he found a number for the Inspector General's office and picked up his phone and dialed it. A Msgt Scott answered the phone.

"Master Sergeant, This is Specialist Fellerer, calling from Fort Greely, Alaska, I would like to speak to someone about a security breach here at Fort Greely."

"That sounds pretty serious, Specialist Fellerer, I'll have our chief investigator, Captain Johnston, call you back. He's currently in a meeting. What time would you be available?"

"I should be back from my courier run by 1000 hours."

"Thank you Specialist, expect to hear from the captain at that time."

Bob completed his mail courier run down to the Delta River Missile Test Site. He returned, once again with a packet of test results stamped 'secret'. and the copied set. He signed the 'secret' packet over to the ATB Headquarters. He brought the copied set back to his mail room. As he was packaging up the packet to send to Lt. George at Fort Wainwright, his phone rang. Captain Johnston introduced himself as the chief investigator of the Inspector General's office of the Third Army Area.

"What can I do for you, Specialist Fellerer?"

"Captain Johnston, Sir, I would like to talk to you about a situation here at Fort Greely. May I ask, Sir, are you familiar with a Lt. George, an investigator out of the IG office in Fort Wainwright, here in Alaska?"

"No, I am not, Specialist Fellerer. I work with that office frequently, but have not heard of him. An investigator, you said?"

"Yes Sir, let me explain."

"When I arrived here, at Fort Greely, last summer, I took over the job of the Arctic Test Board's mail and Courier service. My trainer was a Specialist Frank Krisinskey. As we were going around to the test sites picking up the test results packets to be brought back to the ATB headquarters, Frank would also be given a duplicate packet of the test results. These, he would then mail out to the competing manufacturing companies. For this, he would receive a very substantial payment from these companies."

"Wait, Specialist Fellerer, sorry to interrupt; but it sounds like you are about to discuss something of a security classified nature. That type of matter cannot be discussed over the phone. I'll have to make arrangements for you to come into our office, here in Fort Belvoir, and discuss this further. I'll be getting back to you."

They both hung up, this left Bob wondering, "What am I getting into, now? However, maybe this is progress. Maybe I'll get this issue with Lt. George resolved. I just hope it won't destroy Frank and Nicole in the process. Maybe I won't tell them about Frank's new proposal."

Later in the week, Bob was called into the Company Commander's office.

"I've just received a phone call from Colonel Bingham's IG office down in 3rd Army headquarters," he said, "They want you to report in down there tomorrow. They'll have a flight booked for you up at Wainwright at 0500 hrs. What's going on Specialist Fellerer. Why are you being called down to the IG at Fort Belvoir? Why not their office up at Wainwright? What's going on? Anything I should know about?"

"Well, Sir, I had a question regarding a security issue with the courier deliveries. I actually called IG at Wainwright first, but was told to call Belvoir. They said not to talk to anyone until they resolved the issue." He lied.

"Well, Specialist, let me know if there's anything I can do."

"Yes, Sir, will do Sir."

Bob caught the early shuttle to Eielson Air Force Base at Fairbanks, and got on his flight.

CHAPTER 22

He changed planes at McCord AFB, outside of Seattle, and arrived at Andrews AFB near Washington D.C. late in the day, and was shuttled to nearby Fort Belvoir.   He was assigned temporary quarters for the overnight. Wednesday morning, after an early morning breakfast, a military sedan took him to Fort Belvoir Headquarters for his 0800 meeting at the IG office.

Bob stepped into the conference room, promptly at 0800 and was greeted by a wall of brass. He had expected maybe Colonel Bingham. the IG Commander of the 3rd Army at Fort Belvoir, and Captain Johnston, his chief investigator, whom he had spoken to on the phone, back at Fort Greely, and who had made the flight arrangements to get him here.

He stood at attention in front of Colonel Bingham, saluted, and announced." Specialist 4th Class, Robert Fellerer reporting as requested, Sir."

"Please, be seated, Specialist," Colonel Bingham said.   Bob sat down opposite Colonel

Bingham and he began to introduce Bob to the rest of the participants at the meeting.

"On my right is Colonel Wayne Rogers, IG Commander from Fort Wainwright, Alaska. Next to Colonel Rogers is Colonel Hanson, IG Prosecutor from the Pentagon. On my left, Captain Johnston, whom you've meet when you contacted our office. Then on your right is Major Schwartz, Legal Liaison from the Pentagon. And on your left, we have, Women's Army Corps, Lieutenant Elizabeth Rosen, our stenographer."

"Oh, holy crap," Bob thought, "I've just been invited to a brass party, and I'm the only non-brass person in the room. What the hell am I doing here? These power hungry beasts will feast on me like I was a Thanksgiving bird, and where will I end up after this party is over? Thrown out with the bones I suspect."

"Ok, Specialist Fellerer." Colonel Bingham began, "Here is what we have so far; correct me if I am wrong. According to your conversation with Captain Johnston, you claim to have been training in to a job as the ATB mail and courier person with a Specialist Frank Krisinskey. You told Captain Johnston that in the course of your training; Specialist Krisinskey was accepting duplicate copies of the classified test results from the test sites and mailing them out to the competing manufacturers, and accepting payments from them. Is that correct so far?"

"Yes, Sir, that is correct."

"Okay, then, Specialist Fellerer, why don't you continue on with your explanation of what is transpiring up there at Fort Greely."

"Well, Sir, as Specialist Krisinskey was mailing out these test packets, he explained what he was doing, and how he had set up this network of contacts at the various test sites to supply him with duplicate copies of all the test results. He then stated that he wanted me to continue to mail out the duplicate packets after he had trained me in on the mail and courier job. I told him that I would not continue the mailings. He stated that he could just get someone else to do it for a payment. At that point I decided to contact the IG office at Fort Wainwright and report him for this illegal activity. I called the IG office and spoke to a Lt. George in the Fort Wainwright IG office."

"He set up a meeting at Fort Greely with Colonel Kimball, ATB Commander, himself and me. I reported to them what Specialist Krisinskey was doing and that he wanted me to continue his little espionage operation. Lt George called me several days later and ordered me to comply with Frank's request to continue the mailing of these test packets, only that I was to mail the packets directly to himself at Fort Wainwright, so that he could more closely monitor the situation. He stated that he would gather the information on all the parties involved and then proceed with legal action against them."

"So, why is it that you decided to call our office here in Fort Belvoir?"

"Well, after several months had gone by, and no action was forthcoming that I was aware of, I decided to call Lt. George back and get an update. He informed me that he was waiting for his investigators to complete questioning the companies involved. Somehow I didn't believe him at this point, because so much time had gone by. That's why I called your office, Sir."

"Well, Specialist Fellerer," Colonel Bingham said, "At first I thought we needed to take action against you for your involvement in what looks like a ring of espionage agents at work up there at the ATB. But, it looks like we need to first find out more about this Lt. George at our office in Fort Wainwright."

"Yes, Colonel, I agree," said Colonel Rogers. However, my office has never heard of this Lt George. He is not on our roster of investigators. I don't quite understand how Specialist Fellerer happened to get ahold of him"

"Well," said Major Schwartz, "We can't hold Specialist Fellerer responsible. He was just complying with this Lt. George's orders to forward documents to him. Specialist Fellerer, do you have any documentation from Lt. George stating that you were to be forwarding these testing documents to him directly?"

"Yes, Sir, I do." Bob opened up a folder that he had brought with him and passed around copies of the orders he had received from Lt. George.

"It looks to me, like these are legitimate orders," Major Schwartz stated, "I can certainly see why Specialist Fellerer felt compelled to comply."

"I agree with the Major, here," said Colonel Hanson, Prosecutor from the Pentagon's IG office. I think the person we need to pursue is this Lt. George."

"So, gentlemen, can we safely dismiss Specialist Fellerer, and send him back to his duties at the Arctic Test Board?" Major Schwartz asked.

"In light of this set of orders from Lt. George," Colonel Hanson stated, "Specialist Fellerer you are free to return to your duties at Fort Greely. For now, however, just keep doing what you have been doing; sending these testing dossiers to Lt. George, so as not to tip him off, until we can track him down and see if his investigation is valid, or, build our case against him. One of us will keep you informed."

"Specialist Fellerer, We thank you for coming forward with this information," Colonel Bingham said, "We will be in touch if we need anything further from you."

"Yes Sir, understood Sir," Bob said as he stood and saluted.

"I think," said Colonel Sims, after Bob had left, "That we also need to take a look at this Specialist Krisinskey. It seems to me that he is the one who set this whole espionage ring up. I understand that he has since been discharged from the Army. I'll have to get the FBI involved in tracking him down."

"Okay, gentlemen, we need to put together a plan of action." Colonel Bingham stated, "We can't continue to let these testing dossiers just keep floating around up there in Alaska and wherever they are being sent by this mysterious Lt George. Hell, he could be sending them to the Russians for all we know right now."

CHAPTER 23

Bob returned to Fort Greely, he resumed his mail and courier duties to and from all the test sites, and continued to mail the duplicate copies of the testing documents to Lt. George as directed by Colonel Bingham. On Friday, after his evening mail call, he got a call from Frank.

"We need you to come up here this weekend, Bob. An issue has come up with the changing of the route for the dossiers from Nicolai Kiselyova. We need to discuss an alternative route."

"Well, Frank, I was planning on coming up anyway to discuss that other matter we talked about last weekend."

"Okay, good, and could you get some extra days off, maybe some leave time? We need to take a little trip in my plane."

Bob stopped in the Orderly Room and put in a request for five days of leave time. When First Sergeant Balleu asked why, Bob lied and said he was going down to Seattle to spend a few days with his girlfriend, Susan and daughter Megan. Roger would do Bob's mail and courier service again while he was away, except of course the copied test packets.

Saturday morning, under the eternal black skies of the late Alaska winter, he packed a duffle and caught the early morning shuttle to Fairbanks. It was another cold, dark morning in Alaska. It would be another black day without a sunrise. The temperature though, felt like it had warmed up a bit, to about five below zero. But there was a dampness in the cold, dark air. Bob thought it felt like it could snow again, like maybe there was a storm brewing. Frank and Nicole were already packed when Bob arrived at their apartment. They drove over to the Fairbanks Airport and stopped at the main terminal for breakfast. After they had selected their items from the breakfast buffet and were seated, Frank began to explain his planned plane trip.

"The setup we talked about last weekend with the Russian dossiers coming in from Vladivastok by plane isn't going to work out. The flights are too erratic. They want us to pick them up from a Russian fishing trawler in the town of Kotzebue on the western coast of Alaska, which is Located just north of the Arctic Circle on the Kotzebue Sound, off the Chukchi Sea."

"But, isn't that fishing village and the Kotzebue Sound frozen in all winter?" Bob commented.

"Yes, it is, so what we will have to do is travel by dog sled across the Kotzebue Sound to the Seward Peninsula and out to the fishing village of Shishmaref on the outer banks of the Seward. This village stays open all winter, warmed by the Pacific current coming up the Bering Strait through the Bering Sea."

"That sounds like a lot of extra traveling overland," Nicole said, "That would add many hours to our trip every time we went out to pick up the Russian papers."

"Yeah, why can't we just meet the boat in the town of Nome, they have an airport there," Bob questioned.

"No, they say they can't do that," Frank replied, "They don't have clearance to dock their boat there. They have clearance to dock in Shishmaref, because it's closer to the Russian waters. In the summer we can meet their boat right in Kotzebue where the airport is."

"Well, we better head out," Bob said, "So we can beat that storm coming in."

"Okay," Frank said as they were finishing their breakfast, "But first, I've got to run over to the hanger where I keep my plane and see if my crew has prepped the plane. You guys wait here, I'll be right back."

After he left, Bob turned to face Nicole across the table as he took her hand in his.

"I've missed you so much this past week, Nicole."

"I know, Bob, I've missed you too. I can't wait to get back into bed with you. We'll have to see if we can steal a little time again."

"How are things with you and Frank?"

"Oh, I just don't know, Bob, sometimes I think our relationship is just developing into something plutonic. We've probably only made love once all week. He just gets so absorbed into this whole espionage thing, he hardly has time for me anymore."

Frank returned a few minutes later and asked, "Bob, did you bring those copies of the test results from the Prudhoe Bay war games this winter?"

"Yeah, but I did so reluctantly. I'm just not comfortable with all this exchange of dossiers quite yet."

"Look, I know you are hesitant, but they want those papers as a show of good faith before they start turning over their dossiers to us. You did edit them first, right?"

"Oh, yeah, sure, but that still doesn't make it any easier. I'm just still nervous about all this."

"Well, we better get going, it's a long flight out there and back for one day."

They caught a shuttle over to the private hanger where Frank had his plane prepped and ready.

"Kotzebue is about three hundred and eighty miles, so about a two and a half hour flight," Frank stated after they were airborne, "It should be a fairly smooth ride almost all the way up to the Brooks mountain range, with about a ten mile per hour head wind coming out of the northwest. We'll refuel in Kotzebue for the return trip. They have a large fuel storage facility there, brought in by sea in the summer."

They flew into the inky-black morning. Somewhere a thousand miles south of them, the sun was rising. But, there would be no sunrise here in northern Alaska for almost another two months. To the north, the Aurora Borealis lit up the sky with its ever moving green toned lights. Frank had the 'Omni' signal receiver tuned in to the signal from the town of Tanana, on the Yukon River. Forty five minutes later they flew over the Yukon River town, two thousand feet below them. A few lights were visible in the blackness below, as residents made their way to their daily routines. The next town's Omni signal showed up. The town of Huslia beckoned to them with its signal, about a hundred miles northwest. After that, was the town of Selawik, located on the southeast arm of the Kotzebue Sound, another hour away. Finally, further up the frozen sound, the signal from the airport at Kotzebue pulled them in.

They landed at about 10:00 hrs. and immediately had the plane refueled for the return flight. At the airport they rented a dog sled and hired a guide for the trip out across the frozen sound and across the Seward Peninsula, following the frozen coast line to the coastal fishing village of Shishmaref on the outer banks. They arrived at the village about noon. The only boat at the dock was, of course the Russian trawler, named Aurora. During the long dark days of winter, not too many boats ventured out on the black sea, but the Aurora had Omni signaling equipment and only had to make the relatively short trip across the Bering Strait, past the Diomede Islands.

Captain Vladimir Marenko welcomed the three agents aboard his ship and took them below deck where it was warmer. They showed him their ID's.

"So, I have something for you. You have something for me," he stated in very broken English. "My something comes from your man in Minsk, Nicolai Kiselyova. Your something, I will forward to my Yuri Bezmenov, at KGB headquarters in Moscow."

Captain Marenko produced a sealed packet of Soviet papers, while Bob pulled his packet of the US Army test results out of his backpack. They then exchanged dossiers, while the Captain's first mate got out glasses and poured them each a large glass of Russian Vodka.

"To our countries," He toasted, "Russia and America, the more we are different, the more we are same."

After they all gulped down their vodka, the Captain said, "Till next time then, Madam and Gentlemen. Good Day."

The three couriers left the Aurora with the Russian dossier from Nicolai Kiselyova, to be sent to the CIA. They met up with their guide and had a lunch at a small nearby restaurant where they all had a steaming hot bowl of fish chowder. As they boarded their dog sleds, they noticed that a light snow was falling and the wind was picking up. They mushed their way back across the Seward Peninsula and the Kotzebue Sound to the airfield just outside the town of Kotzebue. By the time they got to Frank's plane, it was snowing quite heavily.

"Are you sure you should take off into this heavy snowfall?" their guide asked.

"Oh, yeah," Frank answered, "It's just starting. I think we can get out ahead of it. Besides, we have the Omni on board to guide us."

They took off at 1500 hours into the inky-black sky, now filled with a driving snow.

"We should have a pretty good tail wind coming out of the northwest," Frank said, "I'll try to climb above the snowfall."

He climbed the plane to two thousand feet, but the snow was still coating the windshield, so he climbed to three thousand feet. That was a little better, but still snowing. He tuned in the Omni transponder and picked up the signal from the town of Selawik at the southern arm of the Kotzebue Sound. After they passed over Selawik, Frank set the Omni to pick up the signal from the next town, Huslia. But what he didn't realize was that the wind had suddenly changed directions and was now coming out of the southwest. This caused the plane to turn about a quarter turn, so that the signal he thought was coming from Huslia, to the south east, was actually coming from the town of Kobuk, due East of them on the Kobuk river. They were now flying east into the Brooks Mountain Range. After about forty five minutes they flew over the town of Kobuk, which Frank thought was the town of Husila. He flew on past Kobuk, but then couldn't pick up another signal. He didn't realize the wind had shifted and turned their plane due east. There would be no more towns emitting signals, they were heading right into the Brooks Mountain Range.

Frank was still disoriented and kept thinking that for some reason, perhaps the snowstorm, that Husila had lost their signal. Still unaware of the wind shift, he was sure that if he just kept the wind at his rear, he would eventually pick up the next signal from the town of Tanana.

To exacerbate the problem, the heavy snow fall, plus the time in the air was causing the wings and props to begin to ice up. The plane slowly began to lose altitude and speed as the engines struggled to try and maintain altitude. Soon, the altimeter was reading twenty five hundred feet, then two thousand feet. Frank began to really panic when the altitude was at fifteen hundred feet. He knew he had to somehow land the plane quickly, before they crashed into a mountain side. He cut the throttle back to prepare to land. Luck was on their side because they were just above a river valley and not in the higher elevations of the mountain peaks. Miraculously, they had barely missed crashing into the eight thousand five hundred foot high mountain peak of Mount Igikpak, the highest peak in the Brooks Range.

Frank could not see what was below them, but cut the throttle again and brought the nose up. The plane bounced off a rocky ridge and plunged about several hundred feet into the river valley. More luck for them, the river valley was at a high enough elevation that the trees were only short scrub trees, so that the plane wasn't totally wiped out. The short trees helped the plane to slow more gradually. After bouncing off another boulder outcropping they came to rest on the side of the mountain, in the deep snow and brush. Unbeknown to them, they were only about a hundred feet above the Alatna River.

Suddenly everything went black inside the plane. There was just utter silence as the engines abruptly stopped. No one spoke for several minutes. They were in shock. Each of them was processing their own situation, coming to terms with what had just happened.

Finally Bob spoke. "Is everyone okay?" he asked, hopefully, from the back of the plane.

"I think I'm okay," Nicole replied from the front passenger seat, "I'm not feeling any pain anywhere, but the plane's pretty badly crumpled up here. Frank, are you okay? Frank? Frank!"

Bob undid his seat belt and scrambled around until he found his backpack and pulled out a flashlight. He shined it up front. Nicole was right, the whole front of the plane was crunched in, right back into Nicole and Frank's laps. The windshield was right in front of their faces. This was one of the problems with twin engine planes. There's no engine in front to absorb the impact in a crash. Bob shined his flashlight at Frank. He looked to be in pretty bad shape. There was blood trickling down from under his helmet. He appeared to be unconscious. Nicole reached over and picked up Franks right hand and felt his wrist for a pulse.

"There's no pulse, Bob," She exclaimed, "I'm afraid he may be dead."

"I think you are probably right Nicole," Bob said, as he shined his flashlight around to the front of Frank, "It appears that the steering wheel hit him in the chest and broke off from its shaft as the front of the plane collapsed. The shaft end looks like it penetrated his chest. At the same time, his head snapped forward and struck the windshield framing. He must have died instantly."

"Oh, Nicole," Bob said, "I'm so sorry. He was your friend and lover."

"I know," Nicole replied, "And he was your best friend."

Nicole tried to undo her seatbelt but the buckle was jammed. Bob pulled out his pocket knife and cut the belts so she could crawl free. She crawled into the back with him and he held her as she began to sob.

"What do we do now?" She sobbed, "Where are we, Frank is gone, now how do we get back? We must be hundreds of miles from anywhere in these mountains. Can we call for help on our radio?"

"No, I'm afraid not, Nicole, the radio was completely crushed when we hit that boulder. We'll have to attempt to hike out of here," Bob tried to console her, "Frank told me he had stashed a lot of survival gear in the back of the plane. When this storm lets up, we'll go for it. "

He continued to hold her, consoling her, both of them still very much in shock. All around them, nothing but total silence, except for the sound of the howling wind and driving snow. It was still fairly warm in the plane which lay buried under a mountain of snow that they had plowed up as they skidded down the mountain side. Soon, they both dozed off from the exhaustion and the trauma of the crash and the warmth they felt in each other's arms. They both slept for four or five hours and then awoke as the plane was cooling down inside. The temperature outside was about fifty below zero at this elevation. The temperature all around Alaska, generally didn't vary much, daytime to nighttime without the sun to warm the air during the daytime hours. The time was about 2300, or 2400 hrs. Not that it mattered, without the sun, the time of day was irrelevant.

CHAPTER 24

Inside the plane, Bob turned on his flashlight and began looking around, for food, first of all. They were both hungry. It had been twelve hours since they had eaten. And they were going to need all the energy they could consume for the long hike ahead of them, down the mountain. He found a backpack full of C rations and other high energy foods, along with canteens of water, also extra mittens, ski masks and mukluks. They both ate and drank all they could. Next, they needed survival gear. They found another backpack filled with a tent and sleeping bags, as well as more flashlights, food and cooking gear. But, most importantly, Bob found a map of western Alaska, all the way from Nome to Fairbanks, and also a compass. He studied the map, but it didn't tell them exactly where they were because they had become so turned around and lost in the blizzard.

"Maybe we'll find some kind of a landmark as we go along," Bob said, "That will tell us where exactly we are."

Way in the very back of the tail section they found two pairs of snow shoes.

They struggled to get out of the plane as they found that it was completely buried in snow from the storm. Bob had to break out a window in the top of the door and use a snowshoe to scoop away the snow so they could open the door. They each put on a pair of the heavy mittens, a ski mask, backpack, and a pair of the snowshoes, after they said their goodbyes to their dear friend Frank.

Bob took out the dossier they had received from Captain Malenkova, aboard his Russian boat, The Aurora. He put it in his backpack along with Franks gun, a 45 caliber military pistol. Outside, they found that the snowstorm had completely abated. The sky was clear and was lit up with billions and billions of stars. Along with the Aurora Borealis, it was as light as a twilight. They found that they could easily see dark objects such as trees against the white snow. Looking down the mountain about a hundred feet below them, they could even see the frozen river, looking like a white ribbon, winding its way between the high mountains.

Their trip down the mountain to the river went quite smoothly. They could practically use their snowshoes as skis, down the steep slope. They just had to avoid the trees, which became larger and larger as they descended. In a few minutes they were down at the river.

"Now, which way do we go?" questioned Nicole, "To the right or to the left?"

Bob got out the map again and studied it, along with the compass.

"This map is still pretty worthless, without some landmark, but, the compass tells me that the river runs pretty much from north to south. Looking at the map, it looks like all the rivers on this side of the Brooks Range flow south toward the Yukon River. I think if we follow this river, we'll end up at the Yukon River, or quite possibly come across some remote village. So, to answer your question, assuming that we had been flying more or less easterly, then, I think we go to the right."

"Okay, Bob, but let's get moving. I'm freezing. I think that as long as we keep moving, we'll keep from freezing to death."

They made their way out onto the middle of the river. Here, they found that the wind blowing up the river valley had swept the ice almost clear of snow. For some stretches of the river, they could take off their snowshoes and just walk on the ice. They made better time without the snowshoes. After hiking for several hours, they stopped for a break. They found that they were getting quite thirsty. In spite of the bitter cold, they were sweating inside their heavy arctic gear from the aggressive hiking down the river. They each had a drink and then replaced their canteens inside their parkas to keep them from freezing. They knew that the food they had in their packs was frozen solid by now. They would have to eat it frozen, or try to thaw it out with the sterno heaters.

Bob and Nicole began hiking again. They knew they must be making pretty good time out on the more or less level ice. But they had no idea how far they had to go to get to any civilization. They hiked for another five or six hours, taking an occasional break, then decided to make camp and get some sleep. It was probably sometime, mid-morning. They had no idea. Without the sun, there was no way to know what time of day it was. The sky looked the same. The light from the stars and the Aurora Borealis was the same. They set up their tent and covered it with a thick layer of snow for insulation. It looked just about like an Eskimo igloo. Inside, they got out some of the c-rations and thawed them with the sterno heater.

"We'll have to eat conservatively," Nicole said, "We don't know how far or how long until we get to another food source."

After they ate a small amount each, they crawled into their sleeping bags, with clothes on.

They needed to conserve every bit of heat they could. They both slept fitfully for several hours, then got up and ate another small amount of the c-rations. They melted some snow on the sterno stove and refilled their canteens.

Performing toilet functions was very tricky at fifty below zero. Any exposed flesh would freeze in about two minutes. Peeing was not so much of a problem for Bob, of course, however, Nicole had to find a fallen tree, scrape off the snow, put her mittens on the frozen trunk and bare her behind to pee. Same procedure was used for both of them for pooping. This had to be completed in about two minutes to avoid frost bite. They would help each other balance on the frozen log. After packing up everything, they set out again, on what seemed like an endless journey through an eternal arctic night.

The river seemed to follow the edge of a large mountain range. At times, sheer cliffs rose up on the west side of the river. This was good, because it shielded them from the bitter northwest winds. It had been a strong southerly wind that had earlier swept the river ice clear of snow.

After about ten more cycles of hiking, eating and sleeping for a few hours, they had no idea what time of 'day', or 'night' it was. Without the sun, there wasn't any measurement of time, it all just ran together. In the eternal arctic night they could only estimate how many hours they spent in each phase of their cycle, hiking, making camp, eating and sleeping. On one of their camping 'nights', they heard the cry of wolves in the distance.

"What will we do if they attack us?" Nicole asked.

"I guess all we can do is see if we can climb up some of these rocky cliffs where they can't climb. From there, maybe I can pick off a few of them with Frank's pistol.

After several more cycles, while they were hiking down the river, they heard a noise in the distance, a thundering noise. As the noise became louder, they saw huge clouds of vapor rising up from the river up ahead. They approached cautiously and soon realized the thundering noise and rising vapor was caused by the river going over a falls.

"We'll have to go around the falls, of course," Bob said, "It looks to be about twenty or thirty feet high."

"We will need to be extremely careful climbing down alongside the falls," Nicole said, "Any slip or fall into the open water could prove to be fatal in this extreme temperature."

From the top of the falls they looked out beyond the falls at a vast valley down below. They wondered if somewhere down below they would find civilization. They both were becoming very worried that their food supply would not hold out until they found civilization and more food.

The two hikers very slowly and cautiously attempted to make their way down the steep rocks alongside of the falls. However, they found that the rocks were coated with ice that had formed from the water vapors given off from the cascading falls and were too slippery to navigate. They had to go along the edge of the cliff and plow their way through the deep drifts for a about a half mile away from the falls. There they found the climbing much easier and safer. Below the falls, the river went cascading over a long section of rapids before leveling out again and freezing over. There, Bob and Nicole could get back out on the ice and continue their hiking journey. But first, they had to plow through more waist-deep snow alongside the cascading river rapids. The rapids went on for about a mile, the river twisting and turning through small canyons, the terrain dropping down as the river churned through a section of numerous boulders and rock formations, sending huge clouds of the frozen water vapor high into the sky.

As they were pushing their way alongside the rapids, they suddenly heard the barking and yipping of what they immediately knew were the wolves they had heard earlier. As the pack of wolves, numbering about eight came closer, they had to take some action. They found their way down to the river and found a place where there were a large number of the boulders fairly close together in the rapids. They climbed out onto a rocky ledge above the chasm, with the rapids about twenty feet down below.

The wolf pack came in for the kill. Bob took out Frank's fourth five and picked off the pack leader. The pack retreated temporarily. They climbed back down and went over to their kill. Bob handed the gun to Nicole to stand guard while he got a hunting knife out of his pack and began to carve up and butcher the wolf. They kept the hind quarters where the most edible meat was. Bob tied it to his backpack and they went back over to the river chasm and climbed down to the rapids. With the wolf pack snarling and yipping at their heels, they climbed out on the large rocks and very carefully made their way from one boulder to another. Miraculously they made it to the other side. The wolf pack did not to attempt to follow. They knew instinctively that the fast moving current and the deadly water temperatures were too dangerous for them to pursue. Bob and Nicole then had to get out away from the river and make their way down the opposite side of the rapids until they lost site of the wolf pack.

Finally, the rapids diminished and the river settled down again and leveled out, and began freezing over again, here they would be able to get back out onto the ice.

Our two survivors were exhausted, however, after navigating, not only the climb down from the falls, but then having to plow through about a mile of snow drifts alongside the rapids, and then climb across the rapids on the rocks. They again made camp on the shore of the river on a high rocky outcropping, in case they had to fend off the wolf pack again. Bob found a deadfall pine tree and broke off a several of the branches. The dried pine needles ignited into a roaring fire. Meanwhile Nicole carved off several pieces of the wolf meat. Bob made a skewer and she cooked the wolf steaks for supper. They were so hungry from the struggle that they ate ferociously.

"I'm, sorry, Nicole, for eating so much," Bob apologized, "I hope that didn't exhaust our food supply. I was just so famished after that struggle, I was beginning to feel faint from lack of energy."

"Yes, Bob, I did the same. I think we were both pretty burnt out and starving. We are getting dangerously low on food. I think we have enough, now with the wolf meat for a few more meals if we cut down to quarter rations, but we have to just keep going to the end. I mean, what choice do we have right now."

With that, they crawled into their sleeping bags again and immediately succumbed into a deep sleep from the exhaustion of the struggle, the battle with the wolf pack and the lack of food.

Many hours later they awoke. They both felt refreshed and energized after their long sleep. After a very light breakfast of quarter rations, they performed their morning routines, dawned their packs and made their way back out onto the river ice. As they looked back up the river, past the rapids, they could see the falls high above them as a strong southerly wind was sweeping away the clouds of the frozen vapor.

"Wow," Nicole exclaimed, "The falls are really high above the rapids. I wonder how far we've descended from the upper river."

"I think perhaps a couple thousand feet, and the temperature seems slightly warmer down here. The good news is that the southerly wind is bringing in warmer temperatures. The bad news, is that the wind is now out of the south. That means that it will bring with it, more snow, of course. Well we better get going. We need to make as many miles as we can before the next snowstorm hits."

The two weary hikers again began their trek down the frozen river that they didn't even know the name of. Occasionally they could hear the wolf pack in the distance, but they were not pursued by them again. After four more cycles of hiking, eating and sleeping, their food supply was almost depleted and so was their energy. On the fourth "morning", as snow was beginning to fall, they ate the last little bit of the food.

"Well," Nicole said, "This is it, this will be our last day. We've got to find civilization and more food or we're done for. They say starvation is not a fun way to die. Maybe we should go back up the river and hunt more of the wolves for our food supply."

"No, Nicole, I think we should just keep going. We're bound to find some civilization soon."

They went back out onto the ice and began hiking again. With the heavy dark snow clouds, they had to navigate in the black dark. No stars were shining through the thick clouds. Nor were the Aurora Borealis showing through. They continued plodding along, their hope and energy waning. The snow was falling at an ever increasing rate. After several hours, they heard the thundering sound of another falls. They approached and found a much smaller falls. This one was only about ten or fifteen feet high, with a similar set of rapids down below. They navigated down the cliff near the falls, and with the last of their energy, plowed through the waist deep snow drifts along the section of rapids. Below the rapids, they again got back out on the ice, but they were so weak from pushing through the snowdrifts that they knew they couldn't go on. Nicole collapsed onto the ice and began sobbing.

"I just can't go on," she sobbed, "I have no more strength. I think we're done for."

Bob began looking to the shore, through the falling snow for a place to set up camp.

"Come on, Nicole, maybe with a little rest," He tried to encourage her, "We can regain enough energy to push on down the river, for a ways, even though our food is gone. There's got to be a village on this river, someplace"

He helped her to her feet again. As they neared the river shore line, they could barely make out, through the trees and heavy snow fall, what looked like a man-made structure. It was sitting up off the river on a high bank, half-buried in the snow.

As they waded through the deep snow and approached the structure, Nicole said, "It looks like a cabin of some sort, a tiny little cabin."

"Yeah, Nicole, I think perhaps it's a trapper's cabin of some sort."

Bob used his snowshoe to shovel away the snow from in front of the door. The door was locked, but Bob slammed his shoulder into it a few times and broke the lock. He got out his flashlight and shined it around.

"This is just like the old trappers cabin over on Shaw Creek that we used last summer. This one looks like it is still used, but not for a while this winter."

The two weary, desperate travelers went in and Bob found a kerosene lantern and lit it. There were bunks along one wall, a table and chairs in the middle, and a cook stove next to a counter and cupboards. Along the back wall was a huge fireplace, and alongside of it was a huge stack of firewood. But best of all, they found, hanging inside the huge fireplace on hooks were several smoked salmon and Caribou jerky strips.

"Oh, my God," Nicole exclaimed, "I think we're in heaven."

"It looks like whoever uses this cabin, is a hunter and a fisherman. I don't quite understand why he would leave all this behind. I'm sure he will be back for it sometime."

They carefully took all the meat and fish down from the fireplace where it had been smoked and placed it on the counter. Bob loaded some of the firewood, along with some kindling, into the fireplace and started a fire. Nicole, meantime found some plates and set them out on the table and served up pieces of the salmon and caribou. They ate the delicious smoked meal until they were full, grateful that they had survived. After they finished their meal, Bob stoked up the fireplace again, while Nicole washed up the dishes. There was a hand pump in the cabin which did not freeze because the pump cylinder was about ten or twelve feet below the cabin. They crawled into one of the bunks and quickly fell asleep in the warmth of their cozy little find of a cabin, as outside, the wind had picked up and a blizzard was raging.

CHAPTER 25

Five thousand miles southeast of the cabin, in our nation's capital, there was not a blizzard happening. It was a bright warm sunny day in early April. The cherry blossoms were budding out. Colonel Bingham gave the command.

Five hundred miles to the southeast of the cabin, there was not yet a blizzard happening, but it was a cold dark morning. At 0800 hours, a squad of MP's pulled up in front of the USAATB test site headquarters at the Delta River Tank and Missile Test Site. They entered the headquarters building and Master Sergeant Ron Davis met them at the front desk. They read him his rights and took him away in handcuffs.

Three hundred, fifty miles north of the Delta River test site, at the Prudhoe Bay Test Site, the same squad of MP's, later arrived by plane and arrested Master Sergeant Gene McCafrey.

Thirty miles east of Fort Greely, another squad of MP's entered the Gerstle River Test Headquarters and took Sergeant Wilson away in handcuffs.

Two hundred miles to the north, that squad of MP's arrived by plane at Fort Yukon and arrested Sergeant Bill Williams.

The four suspects were locked in cells at the Fort Greely MP Station. They would be held for several days while the blizzard closed in on Fort Greely and forced the closure of the highway to Fort Wainwright. The sting operation had, so far, been classified as a secret operation, known only to the Military Police involved in the arrests. No one at Fort Greely knew about the arrests yet.

Back in the Washington DC area, at the CIA headquarters at Langley, an arrest warrant was issued for Frank Krisinzkey, the alleged mastermind of the Fort Greely espionage operation.

At Fort Wainwright, meanwhile, Colonel Rogers, the IG Commander for the Alaska command initiated a search operation for Lieutenant Ray George. He seemed to have disappeared, however. There was no sign of him having ever been on Fort Wainwright. The search team searched the apartment in Fairbanks at the address that Bob had given the Brass at that meeting down in Fort Belvoir. There seemed to be no clue that such a person ever existed.

At Fort Greely, Captain John Ellis, the Company Commander of the Arctic Test Board, sat at his desk and pondered what to do about

Specialist Fellerer, who had been AWOL(Absent Without Leave) for almost a month. After thirty days of AWOL, he would have to classify him as a deserter.

"Why had he gone AWOL?" Captain Ellis wondered, "After his one week leave time? Had he intentionally gone AWOL, or had he gone missing due to some tragedy or accident? Specialist Fellerer, he thought, had been an exemplary soldier. He had an impeccable record of the inspections of his mail room by the U.S. Post Office. He was respected and liked by his peers. What had gone wrong?"

He decided to see if he could get more information on his disappearance. He called in his First Sergeant, MSgt Balleu to see if he could trace Specialist Fellerer's travels on his leave. MSgt. Balleu said that Bob had said something about flying down to Seattle to see his girlfriend and little daughter.

MSgt. Balleu called the Fairbanks airport to see if they had a record of a Specialist Fellerer leaving on a flight near the time that Bob had signed out on his leave. They said that he was listed as a passenger on a private flight piloted by a Frank Krisinzkey who had filed a flight plan to the Alaskan coastal town of Kotzebue and returning the same day. The FAA reported that the flight had left Kotzebue at 1500 hours on the return flight back to Fairbanks. The omni signal stations at the towns of Selawik and Kobuk had picked up their signal as the plane had flown over those towns, but nothing after that. The flight never returned to Fairbanks.

The FAA reported that based on the change in direction of the flight path, the plane had probably been blown off course by the high winds of the blizzard that occurred on that date. The plane, it was assumed, had flown into the Brooks Mountain Range and crashed somewhere in the snowstorm. It was impossible to tell where because they had lost the signal after the last signal transmission from the town of Kobuk. They said that a search plane had gone out several times between the blizzards, but, had found nothing so far.

First Sergeant Balleu wrote up a report stating what the FAA had told him, and gave it to Captain Ellis, who wrote up a MIA(missing In Action) report to be sent up the chain of command. That would have started the whole process of notifying Specialist Fellerer's next-of-kin. He hesitated to submit the report, however. It was late Friday afternoon and he decided to wait through the weekend. He needed time to think about it. Something was bothering him about the whole thing.

"What was Specialist Fellerer doing on a flight way out to the coastal village of Kotzbue on the western coast of Alaska with Frank Krisinzkey? Did they know somebody out there? What was Frank involved in? And why did Specialist Fellerer go with him? And why did he lie to First Sergeant Balleu about his plans for his leave?"

On Saturday morning, as the blizzard was raging through Fort Greely, Captain Ellis called for a meeting with First Sergeant Balleu, Specialist Roger Hammond and Specialist Richard Davis.

"As you all know," Captain Ellis said, "Specialist Fellerer has been missing for almost a month. First Sergeant Balleu and I have been trying to determine where he may have gone. Have either of you two heard anything about where he was headed for on his leave, and why?"

"When he asked me to take over for him with the mail service," Roger said, "All he told me was that he was going down to Seattle to meet his girlfriend and daughter."

"When he didn't return after his week of leave time," Richard said, "I called his girlfriend down in Minnesota and asked her if she knew where he might be. She said they never met in Seattle. She knew nothing about any such meeting."

"What do either of you two know about his friendship with Frank Krisinskey," First Sergeant Balleu asked.

"They were very close friends," Roger said, "Ever since Frank trained Bob in for the mail courier job, they became very close."

"When Frank was discharged," Richard stated, "Apparently he returned to Alaska, and, according to Bob, Frank bought a plane and opened up a fly-in service operating out of Fairbanks."

"Are you saying," Roger asked, "that Frank may have something to do with Bob's disappearance?"

"We can't say anything yet," Captain Ellis said, "Right now, we are exploring all possibilities. That will be all for now, gentlemen. Consider this meeting classified until we know more. You two are dismissed."

After the two Specialists were dismissed, Captain Ellis said to his First Sergeant, "Those two soldiers weren't able to shed much light on why Specialist Fellerer flew way the hell out to Kotzebue on the west coast with Frank. What the hell were those two up to?"

"Well," Sergeant Balleu replied, "If the FAA doesn't find the plane crash, we will probably never know."

"I agree, Sergeant, without any further information, I guess I'll just have to submit the MIA report on Monday."

ROBB FELDER

CHAPTER 26

Nicole woke up slowly after several hours of sleep, then realizing a certain feeling was stirring in her groin, she snuggled up against Bob. After a few minutes, Bob also slowly awoke as Nicole's hand found its way to that sweet spot she knew between his legs. As both their bodies were awakening to the familiar sensations, they kissed long and hard and soon were scrambling to get their winter clothes off while still under the covers. With that task accomplished, they began working on each-others arousal sensations. Bob began softly nibbling on Nicole's excited nipples, while she softly moaned with the pleasure of the sensation, as she worked on his growing shaft. Bob's hand found its way to that magic spot above heaven's gate as Nicole moaned and whispered, "Now, Bob, please, I want you in me so bad." Bob climbed on top and they both rocketed into outer space and exploded into oblivion. He collapsed alongside of her and they spooned as they both struggled to get their breathing back to normal. Very soon they were both sound asleep again.

Bob woke up with a start. It was freezing cold and black dark in the cabin and he had to pee. He grabbed his clothes, coat and boots, and put them back into place on his body, and grabbed his flashlight, then found his way to the door. He opened it and was greeted by about three feet of snow that had drifted against the door as they had slept. The blizzard was still raging. He was hit in the face by a blast of the still swirling snow as he grabbed one of the snowshoes and shoveled away the snow to get outside. There, he walked for a ways through about two feet of new snow from the blizzard and peed into the snow. As he was feeling the relief, he suddenly thought about Nicole. How would she manage? As he shined his flashlight around, looking for a fallen tree, he spotted what appeared to be an outhouse, toward the back side of the cabin. Oh, great, he thought. Nicole will love that. First class accommodations.

Bob hurriedly got back into the cabin. He found the lamp, filled it with kerosene and lit it again and loaded up the fireplace with logs, then got out of his clothes again and crawled back into bed and spooned up against Nicole. She did not wake up and so he fell asleep again. They both slept for about another six hours. The exhaustion from the hundred mile trek down the river, and then the fervor of their lovemaking had left them both completely spent.

Nicole was first awake this time. "Bob, will you come with me outside. I now have to pee. Would you help me please."

"Sure, baby, I'll come with you. I have a surprise for you outside. They both hurriedly got dressed. Bob grabbed his flashlight again and they went out into the cold, never-ending arctic night. But this time they found that the blizzard had passed and the stars and the Aurora Borealis again created that feeling of twilight. Bob escorted Nicole around to the side of the cabin and showed her what he had found earlier.

"Oh, wow, honey. This is first class." As she went into the outhouse, he guarded the door. When she finished, he took his turn. They quickly got back into the cabin, and the warmth. As they removed their outer ware, Bob asked Nicole if she wanted breakfast.

"No, honey, not breakfast yet, but here's what I really want."

She took his hand and led him over to the bed and began to undress him. He followed suit and did her, and soon they found their bodies entwined in rapture again. This time it was her turn on top as they both rocketed into oblivion. After the fireworks, they both needed another little nap. Nicole was up and dressed first this time. She quietly went over to the cupboard and found a box of the Bisquick flour mix and made up a batch of biscuits and began baking them in the stove's oven. Next she found the coffee and a percolator coffee pot.

Bob was awakened by the smell of coffee and fresh baked biscuits. At first he thought he was still dreaming, but Nicole assured him he was not. He hurriedly got dressed and joined her for a hot breakfast of smoked salmon, caribou jerky and hot biscuits and hot coffee.

"Wow, Baby, this is the first hot meal we've had in, I don't really know how many days. Thank you for getting up first and cooking."

After breakfast, bob did the cleanup, and they sat down with cups of coffee to discuss a strategy for the rest of the trip down the river.

I could make another batch or two of the biscuits to pack with for the trip," Nicole said, "Along with the rest of the salmon and caribou jerky. That should get us far enough down river to find a village, or someone who could help us."

"Yeah, It can't be that much further," Bob said hopefully, "For someone to have built this hunting and fishing cabin.

Bob was becoming apprehensive, thinking about getting back. Although they didn't know exactly how long they had been hiking down the river, Bob knew he had been gone long past his leave time and was probably now considered to be AWOL and quite possibly a deserter. They found a deck of cards in the cupboard and played several games of gin rummy to keep Bob's mind off his dilemma, while Nicole baked up another couple batches of the biscuits to pack with.

He got out his backpack and began to go through it. He pulled out the dossier he had received from the captain of that Russian fishing trawler at the port town of Shishmeref and decided to look through it. But he found that it was all written in the Russian language.

"Nicole, Honey, could you interpret this for me, please. You said you were fluent in Russian"

He handed the dossier to her and she began reading it.

After a few minutes of reading, she said, "Oh, my God, Bob. This is unbelievable. It looks like the Soviets are installing guided missiles at sites in Cuba."

"Holy shit, Nicole, we've got to get this information sent to Langley immediately. Come on let's pack up and get going."

"Ok," Nicole said, But it feels like it's getting late again in our daily cycle.

When they had everything packed up in their backpacks, Bob made another pot of coffee and they decided it must be dinnertime. They ate a few more of the warm biscuits and smoked salmon and the elk jerky. After their dinner they were tired again with their full bellies, and decided they better get some rest before setting out again.

After another couple of hours of their timeless sleep in their timeless world, they were awakened by the sound of barking in the distance. Was that the wolf pack again? Had the wolves followed them down the river? After listening to the barking and yipping for a few minutes, they realized that it wasn't wolves, it was dogs they heard barking. Bob got up and got dressed. He made his way to the door to investigate. Nicole got dressed and followed him. They opened the door as the barking sounded even closer. They went to the edge of the bluff overlooking the river. There, down below on the river, in the twilight, they saw not one, but two teams of dogs pulling two dog sleds.

Bob and Nicole waved and shouted frantically as the dog sleds were passing by down below. The two mushers brought their teams to a stop and looked up the bluff and saw them. They turned their teams around and came over to the bottom of the bluff.

"Who are you?" one of the drivers asked as he climbed up the bluff towards Bob and Nicole.

"We're on our way up the river," the other driver said, "We're out searching for that plane that crashed up at Mount Igikpak about a month ago. Have you heard about it?"

"Come on in and warm up and we'll tell you about it." Bob replied.

The four of them enter the cabin and Nicole makes a pot of coffee as the two dog sled mushers introduce themselves.

"My name is John Michaels," one of the mushers began, "I'm with the FAA Search and Rescue Operation out of Fairbanks."

"Hi, my name is Peter Townsend," the other musher said, "I'm with the FAA Search and Rescue from the town of Allakaket down on the Koyukuk River. We have been assigned the mission to find a downed aircraft."

"We were on our way up the river to the Endicott Mountains in the Brooks Range," John continued, "to began the ground search for that plane that went down a month ago in that big blizzard. Our air searchers have reported seeing a wreckage at the base of Mount Igikpak."

"Well, I am Bob Fellerer, and this is Nicole Kiselyova, and we were the passengers on that downed aircraft that you are searching for. We are the survivors. Our pilot, Frank Krisinskey died in the crash."

"We were uninjured," Nicole added, as she poured them all cups of fresh hot coffee, "We've made our way down the river, thus far. We nearly starved to death on the way. The emergency rations from the plane ran out several 'days' ago.

When we were attacked by wolves, we shot one of them and ate it. We barely made it to this cabin. Luckily, someone had left some smoked salmon and caribou jerky, which we've been eating to regain our strength to continue on down the river."

"We were just about to pack up the rest of the salmon and jerky," Bob said, "and continue down the river. We don't know how far it is to that village; what did you say the name was, Allakaket. Hell, we don't even know the name of this river. I tried to look it up on our map, but we had no idea where our crash site was."

"Well," John said, as they all finished their coffee and washed up their cups and the coffee pot, "We'd better get going. We'll give you a ride down river to Allakaket on the dog sleds. By the way, the name of this river is the Alatna River. It runs into the Koyukuk river in the town of Allakaket. It's about a ten or twelve hour run down to Allakaket. We should be in there by midnight, but we will have to come back up the river, later, and retrieve the body of Frank Krisinkey, your pilot."

Bob and Nicole grabbed their packs and heavy winter clothes. As they all stepped outside, they noticed it was slightly lighter out. On the southern horizon they could see a lighter sliver of brightness.

"It must be 12 o'clock noon," Peter commented, "It's early April and we're starting to see the start of a sunrise."

They all went down onto the river. Bob and Nicole each got onto a sled with the mushers behind them on each sled. That sliver of sunrise was already gone by the time they got going. It would keep growing, of course, every twenty four hours, until June when the opposite effect would be in play.

They stopped for lunch half way down the Alatna River and had the rest of the salmon, biscuits and caribou jerky. They made good time, even with the heavier load, because the trail had already been broken through the deep snow. They arrived in Allakaket just before midnight. Bob and Nicole checked into a hostel for some much needed sleep before venturing out on the next leg of their journey back to civilization. John and Peter, their rescuers also found a hostel for some much needed sleep before trekking back up the river to Mount Igikpak to retrieve Franks body.

After finally sleeping for a full eight hours, Bob and Nicole had breakfast at a restaurant before hiring another pair of dog sleds and mushers to take them to the town of Tanana. That was a two day trip. They all stayed at a log cabin again, at the halfway point. They had dinner there, and another eight hour sleep. After breakfast, they were out on the trail again.

They reached the town of Tanana late the second day. Tanana was a much more civilized and larger town than Allakaket. They had electricity and phone service because of their close proximity to Fairbanks. Most importantly there was an airport in Tanana. Bob immediately called the Fort Greely's ATB company orderly room. He spoke to First Sergeant Balleu. While he explained some of his misadventure, he did not tell him why, exactly he had gone out to the coastal town of Kotzebue. In his defense, he claimed that he would have been back by the end of his leave time, were it not for the plane crash. First Sergeant Balleu believed him based on the report he had received from the FAA submitted by his rescuers.

"I'm still going to have to charge you with being AWOL for the thirty days you ran past the original leave," Sgt. Balleu explained.

Bob thought this was unfair, but the First Sergeant explained that it was standard procedure for these types of situations. Bob felt relieved that some of the problems of his absence had been resolved. At least for now, they weren't going to arrest him. They found a motel and crashed for the night, exhausted again after another long day on the trail.

CHAPTER 27

In the morning, after breakfast, Bob got the Russian dossier out of his backpack and found the local Post Office and mailed the packet to the CIA Headquarters at Langley, Virginia. After finally getting the Russian papers mailed off, he and Nicole made their way out to the airport and caught the next flight to Fairbanks. They took a cab to Frank and Nicole's apartment.

t was Saturday, so Bob didn't have to report back in to Fort Greely until Sunday night. This would hopefully give them time to sort things out. They had a lot of loose ends to tie up regarding Frank's espionage business. Without Frank, there would be no more collection and mailing of the ATB test packets. While some issues would be resolved by Frank's death, other issues remained to be dealt with. What to do about shutting down the collection of test documents from all the test sites.

And, what about Nicole? What would be her role, now that Frank was deceased.

They had no idea yet, about the MP raid on all the test sites and the arrest of all of Bob's contacts at those sites. And what about Lt. George? Where was he, and just who was he?

Bob made a pot of coffee and Nicole scrounged up some lunch. She found some old lunch meat in the fridge; a half roll of salami, and some very stale, month old potato chips in the cupboard. Bob found a half loaf of bread, but it had to be thrown out, it was green with mold after sitting out for over a month. But, eureka, the best find was a six pack of bottles of beer in the fridge. So, they ate what lunch they had found, and topped that off with several of the beers.

"We'll have to get more groceries if you stay here very long," Bob said.

"I think I'll just stay long enough to complete the last semester at the college and take my finals. I'll have a lot of catch-up work to do, but then I can graduate this spring. But, beyond that - -, I just don't know. How long before your enlistment is up, Bob?"

"My enlistment is up in August, Nicole. Do you think maybe you could get a summer job here in Fairbanks until I get out? Then, we could go anywhere together. Except not here in Alaska, I'm sick to death of the eternal blackness of these Alaskan winters. Have you ever been to the lower forty eight states? Maybe we could settle down in

Seattle.   At least we'd know someone there. Richard and Sylvia will be living there by then."

"No, I've never been there, Bob. How about Sitka? I've been thinking about taking over my fathers fishing business, you could run the trawler, and we could both work the espionage operation. I'm sure that after us being absent for the last month, he has re-established the old route for the Soviet papers."

"I could live with that, Nicole. That sounds like a good solid plan."

With that they stood and raised their bottles in a toast. They set their bottles down on the table and came together in the living room and their bodies became entwined as they kissed long and hard. They fell onto the couch and then started to undress each other again. But, they only got as far as their underwear, when they heard a noise at their door. It sounded as though someone was trying to get in, maybe picking the lock. Bob ran to his backpack and pulled out the forty-five. They both ran to the door and stood on either side. Nicole stood behind the door. Bob stood back and to the side of the door against the wall. In a few minutes the intruder had the lock picked and began to enter. As he stepped into the apartment, Bob stepped out away from the wall and confronted him with Frank's forty five.

"Lieutenant George, what the hell are you doing here?"

"I'm going to ask you the same question," Lt. George said. He was also holding a gun, a Bulgarian Makarov, 9mm automatic, "What are you two doing in Franks apartment?"

"Frank is dead, killed in a plane crash, his plane. We survived the crash and came back here to clean out his apartment. Now, back to my question, what are you doing here? How did you know Frank?"

"Well, Frank and I have worked together for several years. You see, I am Frank's boss, or was, Franks boss in our operation. I am Frank's handler. I'm the one who sent him on that little run out to Kotzebue for that exchange. I didn't know he was going to involve you two in my plan. When Frank was the ATB mail courier, he would make copies of the test results and send one copy to the manufactures and one to me and I would send it on to the KGB in Moscow. When you expressed reluctance at doing the job, and called me, that's when I had you send me the test documents and I handled the duplication process."

"So, I'll bet you are not who you said you are, are you? I've always suspected that Russian accent that you have. You're not Lt. George. Who are you?"

"No, I am not, that I will say, but that is all will say. And now, Specialist Fellerer, I must be about my assignment of cleaning up Franks little mess."

Bob noticed just the faintest muscle tensing in 'Lt. George's' lower arm just as he was about to shoot him. But, Bob fired just a split second sooner. Bob wanted Lt. George alive and so he aimed low, hitting him in the lower left abdomen. Meanwhile, Lt. George's shot went wide. He had been aiming for Bob's heart, but at the last split second Nicole sprang from behind the door and plowed into Lt. George's back, causing him to jerk slightly right as Bob's round hit him. The result was that Lt. George was struck in his lower left abdomen, but more into the hip area, luckily the shot missed his femoral artery. Bob was hit in his upper left arm near his shoulder, shattering his humerus. Both men went down yelling in pain from the shots and dropping their weapons.

Nicole immediately grabbed Lt. George's gun and quickly went over to Bob.

"Are you alright, Honey?"

"Yeah, I'm in pain, Sweetheart, but I'll live," Bob said as he struggled to sit up, holding his left crippled arm. "See if Lt. George is okay, we need him alive."

Nicole went over to him, still lying on the floor writhing around and moaning in pain. She saw that he wasn't bleeding too bad. She ran into the bathroom and brought back two towels. One she used to put Bob's arm into a sling. The other one she used to make a pressure bandage for Lt. George's hip. Just as she was to about go to the phone and call for an ambulance, they heard the sirens screaming outside. Someone in the building had heard the gunshots and called the police and ambulance. Nicole went back into the bathroom and found some large bandages and applied them to her two wounded patients.

They told the police that the shooting was a matter of self-defense. Nicole told the ambulance driver to take them to Fort Wainwright Hospital because they were both military. She rode along in the ambulance.

Bob and Lt. George were both sent to surgery immediately. Bob's shoulder was repaired quickly. There was no damage to the shoulder joint. But the bullet went through and just grazed the humerus bone just below his shoulder enough to shatter the bone. Not so lucky for Lt. George. The bullet from Bob's forty-five shattered his hip bone. A lot of pins and plates were installed. He would be in a lot of pain and would take a long time to heal. When the two of them came too from their anesthesia, they were put in a room together. Nicole met them there and said she would try to keep them from killing each other.

Dinner was brought in and they all ate, but, Bob and Lt. George were not talking to each other. Understandable for two people who had just shot each other. They all watched TV for the evening. The two wounded argued continually however over which program to watch. Later, Nicole was assigned a guest room and they all finally crashed after a pretty rough day.

Sunday Morning, 0500 hours, our two shooters were awakened and a doctor came in to check their wounds and a nurse changed their bandages. Breakfast came at 0600 hrs. Nicole came in and Bob gave her some money for her breakfast in the cafeteria.

At 0630 hrs., Colonel Rogers from the Fort Wainwright IG office came in followed by two MPs, and a gentleman he introduced as Special Agent, Jim Fowler of the CIA. Nicole returned from her breakfast a short time later and took a seat in the corner next to Bob's bed..

To Bob he asked, as he pointed to 'Lt. George'. "Is this the notorious Lt. George?"

"Well," Bob replied, "That's who he says he is Sir."

Turning to 'Lt. George', Colonel Rogers said, "Before this day is out, we'll know who you really are."

Jim Fowler went over to 'Lt. Georges' bed and asked him, "What is your real name?" He grabbed his wounded leg and began twisting and torqueing it. 'Lt. George' screamed in pain, but would not answer.

A nurse came running in and asked, "What is the problem? What's going on in here?"

Jim Fowler replied, "Your patient seems to be suffering some pain. I think he needs some more morphine."

The nurse went running out and came back with a syringe of morphine. Colonel Rogers stopped her and grabbed the syringe and said, "I'll just administer this as the patient needs it."

The nurse started to object, but, when she saw his rank, she just turned around and left.

Jim Fowler again began to torque on 'Lt. George's' leg again. He again screamed and moaned.

"Oh, please stop, stop. Can I have the morphine please, please?"

Jim Fowler again applied torque to his leg. 'Lt. George' just moaned and passed out. Colonel Rogers gave him the injection of morphine, then took out a small case from his inside jacket pocket and removed a small syringe and gave him an injection of the substance.

To the other people in the room, he simply said, "Sodium pentathol."

Jim Fowler then took a tape recorder and placed it on 'Lt. George's bed.. A few minutes later the 'Lt George' came too. Jim switched on the tape recorder.

Jim Fowler asked him, "What is your real name, Sir?"

"Why, I do believe my real name is Dimitri Sokolovskaya," he replied in a slurred voice.

"Is it correct that you posed as someone else, and what was that name?"

"I used the name, Lieutenant Ray George of the US Army."

"And, who do you work for, Dimitri?" Jim asked.

"Well, Sir, I work for Colonel Ray Kimball, the commander of the ATB in Fort Greely. He's in charge of our whole operation."

"And what did you do with the ATB test documents that Specialist Fellerer was mailing to you?"

"Well, Sir, I forwarded a copy of them to the KGB in Moscow."

"And are you a citizen of the United States of America?"

"No, Sir, I am not. I am a citizen of the USSR."

Jim Fowler said, "Thank you, Dimitri. That will be all the questions for now. You get some rest, now, you'll need it."

Jim took out a pair of handcuffs and handcuffed Dimitri to the bed rail. "You are under arrest, Dimitri Sokolovskaya," Jim said, "for crimes against the United States of America. You will be tried in a military court of law for these crimes. A military court appointed attorney will be assigned to defend you at your trial."

Jim Fowler then switched off the tape recorder. Colonel Rogers called in the nurse and asked if the patient, Dimitri, could be moved to a more secure room. She disconnected everything from Dimitri's bed and began pushing him down the hall. The Colonel and Agent Fowler followed, as Dimitri fell fast asleep. The two MP's stayed behind, awaiting further orders. Nicole and Bob just sat there silently, sort of in shock at what they had just witnessed.

The colonel and Jim Fowler returned some time later. The Colonel posted one MP guard outside Dimitri's new room and the other MP at Bob's room.

"Dimitri Sokolovskaya," the Colonel stated, "when he recovers, will be incarcerated in the Stockade here at Wainwright until his trial. He will then be transferred to Fort Belvior, Virginia for his trial."

"What will become of the ATB Commander, Colonel Kimball?" Bob asked.

"Well, Specialist Fellerer, I have just dispatched a squad of MPs from here at Fort Wainwright to go down to Greely and arrest him immediately and transport him back here to Wainwright, where he will remain in custody until his trial.”

"What about all of the contacts at all of the ATB test sites that have provided the duplicate copies of the test papers?”

"We already have them all in custody and they are being held here, in the Fort Wainwright Stockade awaiting their trials. As for you, Specialist Fellerer, you will be awarded a commendation ribbon for your part in all of this. And now, I think Special Agent Fowler has a few words to say to you. I will be leaving now. I have a mountain of paper to generate on this operation. I will keep you posted on the disposition of our incarcerated traitors.”

After Colonel Rogers left, Agent Jim Fowler stepped over to Bob's bed.

"Specialist Fellerer, on behalf of the CIA, I would like to say, Thank You, to both you and your friend, Nicole, for your exemplary work in bringing this ring of spies to justice. It appears to me that you seem to have a talent for this kind of work. And you, Miss Nicole Kiselyova, The CIA has long been aware of you and your fathers work. I think there could be a position for both of you with The Bureau. I will be recommending you both when I write up my report on this situation.

Expect to hear from either me, or the Bureau in the near future. Good luck to both of you."

After he left, Bob and Nicole just sat there and looked at each other, stunned by what he had said.

"Did you hear what Agent Fowler just said, Bob, I think he just offered us both jobs, with the CIA."

"But, how will I accept the position with my shattered arm?" he wondered.

CHAPTER 28

It was late April. Bob sat alone in the rear seat of the US Army sedan, a 1956 Chevrolet, olive green, standard non-combat type vehicle used primarily to transport officers and dignitaries around military installations.

Although it was nearly the month of May, the temperature was still at about minus 30 below zero. The sun was now just still a thin sliver of orange light on the horizon, struggling to break into the black arctic sky above the Delta River Valley and reclaim it in the blue that it had given up back in September when 'old sol' had retreated into the southern hemisphere. In the next couple of months the sun would make the rapid transition from a very minimal showing, to several months of continual 24 hours of sunlight. That was Alaska, land of ever changing extremes.

As the Army's olive green sedan glided closer to Delta Junction, where the ALCAN highway met up with the Richardson highway,

Bob's thoughts were wandering. Mostly he was having thoughts about Nicole. "What would happen to their relationship, now with Frank out of the picture and the espionage operation shut down? Quite frankly, he felt that it would make life a lot easier for him. But what about Nicole? True, she would be pretty tied up with finishing her last quarter at University of Alaska. But, what about after that? Would she stay in Fairbanks and wait until his enlistment was up in September? Or would she decide to return to Sitka and take over her father's crabbing operation and work for the CIA, passing papers back and forth to Russia? At least, he thought, he could still see her on weekends until she finished her degree program at the university."

As Bob was signing in at the ATB, he was met by First Sergeant Balleu.

"Welcome back Specialist Fellerer. We all heard about your shoot-out up in Fairbanks. We're glad to see you survived. We've been reading about it in the Stars And Stripes paper and The Fairbanks Midnight Sun. You're quite the hero, for capturing that spy, Dimitri Sokolovskaya. That's quite a shoulder injury you received. How are you feeling?"

"Oh, I'm feeling pretty good after a week in the hospital. I'd like to get back to work, but I've got to have this cast on for another couple weeks."

"Well, I think you can ease back into it. One thing that happened while you were gone, I had to get a replacement for your backup person. I need Roger back here in the Orderly Room, so I brought in a new person for you to train in as your backup."

"Okay, that sounds great, Sarge, maybe I can have him do the heavy lifting while I'm training him in."

"Sounds like a good plan, Specialist. Here are the keys, again, to your mail room. Let me know if you need anything. Your new guy is over at Supply, getting all his arctic gear. I'll bring him down to your mail room when he gets back."

Bob hurried upstairs to his bunking cubical and unpacked and changed into his Army arctic clothes again. Next, he unlocked his mailroom and checked to see if there was any mail to be returned to the Post Office for forwarding.

"It looks like Roger has done a decent job of the mail duties while I was gone," he thought.

He went over to the Motor Pool to sign out his mail truck, the 1956 Chevrolet pickup. He had a bit of trepidation at first about being able to drive it with one arm, because it was a stick shift. He managed just fine, however, and drove out to the airfield to pick up the ATB mail. He arrived back at the company and was met by his new trainee, a PFC Willian Johnson.

He introduced himself, and Johnson said, "Hi, I'm PFC Johnson, but please, just call me Bill."

"Okay, Bill, we'll start by having you unload the mail sacks and get them into the mail room. As you can see, I'm kind'a handicapped right now."

As Bob sorted the mail as he had been doing for about a year. His new trainee was seated at the desk and given the mail handler's manual to study.

"This is just like it was a year ago," Bob thought as a wave of nostalgia came over him, "I guess I've come full circle. Only, then, it was me, as the trainee, and Frank, my mentor. I sure do miss my ol' buddy."

He took Bill with him, around to all the test sites and introduced him to all the new contacts. Then, he showed him the procedure for handling all the classified test documents, signing for them and returning them to the ATB headquarters. He remembered what a tangled web he had gotten himself into and was so glad that it was over. He had learned so much about the spy game, in the last year. Now he felt free from all that. He just wanted to finish out his enlistment and get on with his life.

His first week back went by very rapidly. On Friday night, after dinner, he got together with his friends again at the Malamute Saloon and brought along Bill, to introduce him to the group, and to the Malamute. None of them had been there since that New Year's Eve brawl. They had to get a large corner booth, their group was growing.

"Wow," commented Roger, "I like what they've done to the place. Look, they put in a new bar, after we busted up the old one."

"Looks like these tables and chairs are new too," Henry Murdock said.

"The stage above the bar has been replaced," Bob said.

"And refreshed with some new talent," Richard added, "These are all new girls. Don't ya miss the old ones? I sure miss my Sylvia."

"Who's Sylvia?" Henry asked.

"Oh, just one of the old troop of dancers," Richard replied.

"Don't worry Richard," Bob said, "Your little secret is safe with us.

"What little secret?" Bill asked.

"Oh, look," Roger said, trying to change the subject to protect Richard's 'little secret', "The show is starting."

When the show was over, the girls joined the spectators to 'socialize'. Two of the girls came over to their booth and crawled into Henry and Bill's laps. After several minutes of grinding to the music, the four of them left for the upstairs rooms.

"Well, dang," Roger said, "It looks like the 'newbies' get all the action, while us old timers get to just sit around and reminisce about the old days. Richard, you got to get some relief down in Seattle, and you, Bob, had a nice little visit from Mrs. Santa during the holidays. But I gotta tell ya, guys, I am definitely starting to feel the need."

"By the way, Bob," Richard said, "I heard from my sources that you may have a little something going on up in Fairbanks. Maybe taking over where Frank left off. What's that all about? Want to tell us about that?"

"Yeah," Roger said, "First Sergeant said you were planning on going up to Fairbanks again this weekend."

"I've just got to go up to the U of Alaska to take the finals that I missed when I was gone, after Frank's plane crash."

They all had to stay for another round of the dance routine to get over before Roger had his chance.

"And, so, it seemed, things were getting back to normal," Bob thought.

Saturday, early morning, Bob got on the shuttle to Fairbanks. First, he did actually go to the University and complete the finals for the two courses that he had been taking down at Fort

Greely, through the extension program. Under the ever expanding sunrise, he made his way over to Nicole's apartment afterwards. She was waiting for him in her pajamas.

"Shall we continue what we started a month ago?" she asked, as she took his hand and led him into her bedroom, "Before we were so rudely interrupted by that awful Dimitri guy."

They kissed passionately and soon were, both frantically ripping off their clothes. They collapsed onto her bed as his tongue again found all the right places. Bob was already amped up from watching the dancers at the Malamute, the night before.

"Oh, Bob, I've missed you so much. I love you," she whispered.

"I love you too, Nicole, I want to be together with you forever."

Soon fireworks erupted and thunder rolled from somewhere deep inside. After that, Bob rolled over and they both regained their breathing. They spooned again, but only for a few minutes before Nicole broke away.

"We've got so much to talk about, Bob, We better just get to it."

They got dressed and went into the kitchen. Nicole made lunch, ham sandwiches, potato chips and pickles.

As Bob made a pot of coffee, he said, "First of all, let me congratulate you on graduating from the university. I'm so proud of you. I'll bet your parents are very proud of you too"

"Thank you, Bob. I assume you completed your finals at the university today. I hope you can go on and finish your degree program, some day."

"Yes Nicole, me too. You know, if it weren't for this Army enlistment, I could have been graduating next year as well. Most people, including my family, don't even realize just how much a person gives up to serve his country. They think 'well, just go on to college when your enlistment is over'. It is nearly impossible to go to college after you have been virtually a prisoner of the U.S. Army for three years. First of all, everyone else is three years ahead of you. That's three years that you can never get back. Everyone else has moved on. Hell, the world has moved on. And you never quite catch up. Most guys at age twenty two are married and have started a family. That makes it nearly impossible to get into college and finish a degree."

"I'm sorry, Bob. I can't change that. I can only hope that you can finish your degree when your enlistment is over."

The coffee was finished perking and Nicole had the sandwiches finished. They both sat down to lunch.

"I'm sorry, Nicole for going off like that about my issues. What is it that you wanted to talk to me about?"

"Well, Bob, I have some troubling news to share with you. When I called Mom yesterday, she said that Dad has become quite ill, and will be forced to give up his crabbing operation. He's almost eighty years old now. He wants me to come down to Sitka and take over the boat and everything."

"I guess, you should go then, Nicole. You talked about doing that after you graduated anyway. We'll just have to work it out, somehow. I mean, the you and I thing. I've only got three months left on my enlistment. Maybe I can fly down to see you most weekends. I've got a ton of money, you know."

"That sounds like that would work. Thanks for being so understanding, Bob. I do love you so much, and I want to have a life with you in it."

"I feel the same way about you, Nicole. Maybe I could help you pack up here this weekend."

"So, Bob, how did it go with your absence from Fort Greely? Are you still AWOL, or whatever?"

"Oh, it's just crazy, Nicole, it looks like I'm somewhere between being a deserter and being given an award for valor. It'll be like, here's your medal for valor, now take it and off you go to Leavenworth. Right now, I haven't heard anything yet, which way it'll go."

"Well, you're my hero, Bob, after our struggle for survival after Frank's plane crash. I certainly couldn't have survived without you."

"Well, thanks to Frank's survival kit, we made it. I sure do miss him though. Did they ever recover his body?"

"Yes, they did. His family had it shipped back to Pittsburg for burial."

"Well, thanks for the lunch, Nicole. I guess we should go out and get some boxes and get started packing you up."

They spent the rest of the day, Saturday and most of the day Sunday packing up Nicole's things for her move back to Sitka. Sunday afternoon, before Bob left, they made love again, hot and furious. They said their goodbyes and Bob caught the shuttle back to Greely. All the way back, he sat there feeling the pain of their departure and wondering what was in store for him,-- for her,-- for them.

The next work week, and the week after, went by painfully slow. Bob talked to Nicole on the phone to see how she was doing with her move back home and taking over her father's crab boat and espionage operation. Friday, she called and said not to come down. She would be out on the boat all weekend.

Bob met up with the gang Friday night, but not at the Malamute. They wanted to talk about their plans for the summer, namely trips up Shaw Creek again, to their gold camp. They didn't want the distraction of the strippers at the Malamute. They met instead, at the EM club. They talked about the fact that their group was shrinking. Richard was leaving for Seattle next week, his enlistment was up. Roger would be leaving the end of June, his enlistment would be up. That would leave Bob and the two newbies until he left the end of September.

This was all too typical of military life; always in a state of flux. People were coming and going in and out of your life, constantly. With all the turmoil, they decided to have another planning session next week. They had several more beers, shot a couple games of pool and then called it a night.

Saturday, there was a big party at the EM club for Richard. Everyone had plenty to drink. Richard got drunk on his ass and passed out. Bob drank way too much. He was 'stress drinking'. They all were, their world of comradeship was coming apart, and there wasn't a damn thing they could do about it. In the military, you didn't get to decide about where you lived or who your comrades were. You had to take what the Army Brass assigned to you.

(Little did Bob know at this time, he was celebrating his own departure). Bob got puking drunk and had to be led back to the barracks by also drunk Roger. Sunday was a day of recovery for everyone.

On a Monday, late in May, Bob was summoned to the ATB headquarters. He was escorted to a conference room. Bob got an ominous feeling when he saw two MPs standing outside the door. Inside, he was again met with a wall of brass. He noted that Colonel Kimball, former commander of the ATB was replaced by a Colonel Bill Williams. On his right was the Fort Greely base commander; Colonel John Martin and Bob's company commander, Captain John Ellis. Next to him was MSG. Robert Balleu. On Colonel Williams left was CIA Special Agent, Jim Fowler. Bob had a bad feeling about seeing him here.

Bob stood at attention and saluted the table of brass. "Specialist Fourth Class Fellerer, reporting as ordered," he said.

"Remain at attention, Specialist Fellerer," Colonel Williams said as he came around the table and gave Bob the command, 'right face'. Bob turned to his right facing Colonel Williams.

The Colonel began reading from a sheet of paper. "Specialist Fourth Class Robert Fellerer, for exhibiting valor and extreme bravery in a hostile situation, confronted by an enemy of the United States, you are hereby awarded this Bronze Star. Signed; Robert McNamara, Secretary of the Department of Defense of the United States of America. Colonel Williams stepped forward and pinned the ribbon on Bob's shirt just above his left pocket. The Colonel stepped back and picked up another sheet of paper and read from it. "For injuries sustained in a hostile confrontation with an enemy, you are hereby awarded the Purple Heart Medal." Colonel Williams again stepped forward and pinned the ribbon above Bob's left pocket. Colonel Williams stepped back and saluted Bob and Bob saluted back. The Colonel then said 'at ease'. He then shook Bob's hand and said, "Congratulations, Specialist Fellerer.

Colonel Williams then returned to his seat and Bob turned to face him again.

"Have a seat Specialist Fellerer, for the next phase of the program."

Bob already knew what was coming, and he shuddered at the thought.

"It has come to the attention of this panel that you have an outstanding violation of the UCMJ(United Code of Military Justice). You have been absent one day past the maximum thirty day AWOL period and could be prosecuted for desertion from duty, a criminal offence. However, we on this panel, have discussed your situation at great length and have arrived at a solution. Agent Jim Fowler, would you like to explain to Specialist Fellerer, his options."

"First of all, let me congratulate you on earning the medals just awarded to you by Colonel Williams. As the Colonel said, we have three options available to you."

"The first option, is for you to be stripped of your rank and all medals and immediately dishonorably discharged."

"The second option, is for you to be reduced in rank by one grade, serve ninety days in the stockade at Fort Wainwright, and still achieve an honorable discharge. Assuming you have no other violations between now and your discharge date."

"The third option, and we all highly recommend this option: would be for you to accept an honorable discharge right now. Your medals awarded you, would remain in your service record jacket. You would then sign an agreement to immediately enlist yourself in the Agent Training Program at Langley, Virginia. I have highly promoted this option to the panel, Bob, because I really believe you have great potential as an agent. Think about it, you have actually been working at this role ever since you arrived at Fort Greely. Here is a very positive caveat, Bob, when you finish the training and complete three years of service in the Agency, your military record will be scrubbed clean of any violations, you would be credited with your full three years of your Army enlistment, and your three years of military time would be added to your time in the agency toward your retirement. Take a minute to think it over while the rest of us take a coffee break."

Bob sat there in shock and puzzlement. What they were offering him was almost exactly what he thought they would, only instead of time in Leavenworth, he had been offered time in the CIA. He wondered if the CIA would be like the military, where you have no say where you will work, you are assigned a place to work by the agency, just like the military. The other question was the issue about Nicole. Would he be allowed to continue his relationship with her? Could he be assigned a location where he could at least see her, maybe work with her if she too decided to join the CIA?

In the end, he decided he would accept their offer. He thought it was his best option.

With his mind made up, he got up and went over to the table in the corner and poured himself a cup of coffee and returned to the conference table. In a few minutes the brass all returned and Bob gave them his answer.

"You've made the right choice, Specialist Fellerer," Colonel Williams said, "You won't regret it. You'll proudly serve your country as an agent of the CIA."

With that, Colonel Williams opened a folder and slid the first of several slips of paper across the table for Bob to sign. The first was a document, spelling out the terms of Bob's agreement to accept the terms of their offer. Bob read it and signed it and passed it back. The next form was a legal document releasing the US Army of any liability resulting from their agreement. Bob also read and signed that form and passed it back.

Agent Fowler then opened a folder and slid a slip of paper to Bob. It was a CIA form, an application for employment with the CIA. Bob also signed that. Next, came an agreement to accept all the terms of his employment with the CIA. After that was signed, it was back to Colonel Williams. He took the last slip of paper out of his folder and slid it across to Bob. It was a form DD-214, the military form stating that he was now officially and immediately, honorably discharged from the US Army. He did not receive a copy of any of the forms he had just signed. Colonel Williams informed him that all of the forms he had just signed, along with all of his military records would be forwarded to the Army's Record Center in Kansas City, and would be classified as 'secret'.

With that, everyone stood and the brass all congratulated and shook hands with Bob. and then the brass all filed out of the room.

Agent Fowler shook Bob's hand and said, "Congratulations, Bob, and welcome to the CIA. Well, let's get you out of here and on your way to Langley."

Agent Fowler drove Bob over to the ATB barracks and accompanied him up to his third floor cubicle. Bob changed out of his Army uniform and into his civilian clothes. As he packed a duffle bag with the rest of his civilian clothes and personal items, Agent Fowler said, "Just leave all your Army uniforms. Someone from Quartermaster will pick them up and process them, probably strip off all your ID tags and other insignia and probably send your army uniform to the Salvation Army."

They discreetly left the barracks and got into Agent Fowler's car. It was 1400 hours and the sun was setting the southern sky on fire. Bob asked if he could at least say goodbye to his friends.

Agent Fowler replied, "No, that's not a good idea. It only gets everyone's emotions all stirred up. Better if you just leave quietly."

But, Bob was devastated by Agent Fowler's refusal, and as they pulled out through the main gate of Fort Greely, he sank into a very sullen and depressed mood. Dammit, he thought, those were his best friends for the last year and Fort Greely had been his home.

Little did he know, he would not return here for over fifty years.

He remained in his funk and depression all the way to Fairbanks, as the brief daylight hours were melting away, and so was life as he knew it, especially as they boarded the plane for the first leg of his journey to a new life. Agent Fowler tried to cheer him up, but it only got worse as they flew over Mount McKinley and Bob realized he was leaving this strikingly beautiful Alaska behind for good.

As they flew down the panhandle of Alaska, Bob began to wonder what Nicole was doing, down below them. Probably out on her crab fishing trawler. What would she think when she found out what had happened to him? Moreover, would he ever see her again? He thought of his friends he had to leave behind. Richard was probably already in Seattle and with Sylvia, beginning a new life. Roger would be leaving the ATB in a month for his new life as a civilian. Would he ever see them again? Would they ever realize what happened to him? As the plane descended into the flight path for Seatac airport in Seattle, Agent Fowler pulled out a pair of handcuffs and handcuffed Bob to himself.

"Just a precaution Bob, you just seem to be a bit unstable right now and I don't want to lose you in the crowd. I'll just see you to your plane to Washington, D.C. Then, I'll catch a flight up to Sitka and have a talk with Nicole."

ROBB FELDER

CHAPTER 30

George Washington Memorial Parkway runs mostly north to south along the Potomac River on the Virginia side. The Washington National Airport is located on the south end of the parkway on the River. Langley, Virginia is on the north end of the parkway, about a forty five minute drive from the airport. The drive offers a spectacular view of most of the famous monuments across the river to the east, in Washington, D.C.

In the very early morning hours of an early June day; June 7th 1962 to be precise, as the overnight fog was being melted away by a very hazy morning sunrise, the sedan, a very ordinary navy blue, nineteen sixty, Chevrolet model, slowly slipped out of the Washington National Airport and got on the north bound lane of the George Washington Memorial Parkway. In the rear seat there were two very groggy, bleary-eyed young men, who had never met before and had not yet been introduced. Nor, had they had any breakfast yet. The sedan rapidly picked up speed on the parkway, as if to urgently get these two young recruits to some breakfast. As they sped northward, on the left, a ways away from the parkway was the Pentagon, with it's labyrinth of halls and offices, not yet visible through the fog. Fifteen minutes further up on the right, The Jefferson Memorial, only its' dome visible out of the fog. Next, the back side of the Lincoln Memorial, Abraham facing into the hazy morning sunrise and the towering Washington Monument, rocketing up through the fog. The White House, on the north side of the mall, was totally buried in the fog, as usual, I suppose. At the far end of the mall, or, at the beginning, depending on your perspective, our nation's capital dome visibly floating above the fog, reflecting the golden glow of the hazy sunrise. Past Arlington National Cemetery on the left they flew. Somewhere nearby, the bronze-cast Marines were still raising the flag to greet a new day on Mount Suribachi, IwoJima.

Our nations capital, so much history, and so, so many monuments, saluting so, so many great leaders. And yet, so many monuments to the great failings of those leaders, the war memorials stand as a testimonial to their failed diplomacies. Bob wondered, as they sped along through the early morning fog, if there would ever be a monument erected to his war, The Cold, Cold War.

Thirty minutes later they pulled into the parking lot of the CIA complex, the central command post of that war, and up to the front entrance.

Bob and his recruit buddy, of whom, he had not yet been introduced, entered the front door, a door that would lead them into oblivion. To their families and their friends and anyone else that had known them, they had now mysteriously disappeared. They would be disappearing into a mysterious world, where their past identities would be purged from the real world and they would become, - - - somebody else.

As they entered the world of false, they would be assigned false names, false ID's, false families, false jobs, false backgrounds, false educations, false connections to false handlers, passing sometimes, false information to and from other false entities. And all of this information, both true and false would be funneled back here, to this building to be sorted out, deciphered, decoded, reevaluated and reformatted into reports passed to the heads of our own government for evaluation, and utilized in their decision-making process.

The two strangers went up to the front desk, walking past the famous emblem imbedded into the floor in center of the lobby with its eagle head above a shield with the sixteen point compass star, surrounded by a sixteen foot round circle. On a nearby wall, engraved into the granite; a Bible quote, John 8:32, And Ye Shall Know the Truth and the Truth Shall Make You Free.

They showed their IDs. The guard had them sign into a visitors log book and another guard escorted them into an elevator. They went down, three floors below the building. Here they approached another desk and again showed their IDs. This guard kept their IDs and gave them temporary IDs containing what was to be their new names, and said they were to wear them at all times while in training. Bob's new 'CIA name' was: Ronald Lobruck. The other man that came in with him, became: Todd Anderson. Another guard took their bags and informed them that they would not be returned. Your civilian clothes and personal items, along with the clothes you're wearing today, he said, "Will be donated to the Salvation Army." He gave them each a navy blue jump suit and another travel bag with several changes of the jumpsuits along with several sets of underwear, socks and black polished shoes. He directed them to changing rooms down the hall. When they emerged dressed in the navy blue jumpsuits, they were led further down the hall to a small conference room. Seated at the head of the table was the Director of the CIA, John A. McCone, and two other people, on either side of him. Behind them were The American Flag and The CIA Flag.

The two new recruits took their seats. The Director introduced himself and said, "On my right, is our Superintendent of Training: Army Colonel James Sutten. And on my left is your Training Chief: Marine Sergeant William Johnson. Gentlemen, on the table in front of you are several papers that you will be signing today. Take a few seconds to read them over and then sign them."

Their new names were already typed onto the forms. One was an agreement to abide by all the rules of the CIA Agent Training Course. And to hold all training material and all material taught during the training as 'Top Secret'. If they completed the course, or flunked out, the training material they would study was to be considered 'Top Secret'.

Another of the forms declared that they would never divulge to anyone, at any time, their former names, nor any of the names of any and all family members or their locations.

Lastly, they agreed that any and all information gathered was to be considered property of the CIA and the United States of America.

"Gentlemen," the Director said, "Also on the table in front of you are copies of the CIA's oath. Keep in mind, this is a legally binding oath and agreement of loyalty. Please stand and raise your right hand and read the oath."

Bob and the other recruit stood and raised their right hand and said the CIA Oath.

"I due solemnly swear to uphold and defend the Constitution of the United States of America and abide by the laws and regulations of the CIA and those appointed over me. So, help me, God."

Next, they read the Pledge of Allegiance. The Director, the Superintendent of Training and their Training Chief got up and came around the table and shook their hands and said, "Welcome to the CIA, gentlemen, you are now Agents-In-Training.

"Follow me, now," their Training Chief said. "Let's get some breakfast."

They followed him to the elevator and up two floors to the CIA's cafeteria. Their training Chief gave them their meal tickets and they had a very hearty breakfast. They noticed others in the cafeteria in the blue jump suits. After breakfast, they all went back down to Level 3-B. The two newbies followed the rest of the 'blue suits' down the long hall to their squad room and sleeping quarters where they were assigned bunks and lockers The others, they found out had come in just a day or two ahead of Bob and his mystery friend. After they had stowed all their new clothes, they followed their Chief down the hall to the main training class room. There were 30 recruits in the class.

"As most of you know, my name is Sergeant Bill Johnson. I am your training chief. You will have new trainers for each phase of your training. Now let's get to know each other. Let's go around the room and each state your name. Remember, Newbie's, your new name, only. Right now all you have is a new name, nothing more. As your training progresses, you will learn new facts and information about your new life. All the facts about your old life have disappeared. You have been re-born with a new identity and a new prior life."

As they went around the room, Bob gave his new name; Ronald Lobruck.

"Now let's go over your training schedule for the next six months, a printed copy is in front of you. I have to warn you, it is a very rigorous schedule. You will be tested at each phase of the training. If you cannot keep up, or cannot grasp the training material, you will be washed out of the program and returned to civilian life. Only about one third of you will graduate. The first three months will be spent here, in house, at Langley. You will be learning the four major languages;

Spanish, German, Russian, and Mandarin Chinese. These classes will be intermixed with the other classes. You will spend a great deal of time upstairs, observing how your information is processed. Other overlapping classes will be weapons training and Judo, karate, boxing, and other self-defense methods. Since electronics is such a big part of surveillance, you will be trained in all the latest electronic equipment, as well as the equipment of our enemies and allies."

"At the end of the in-house training, if you are still with us, we will begin the external phase of your training. You will first spend time in our mock-up city, right here on the Langley grounds. You will learn how to live in a hostile environment and how to move about undetected. In the next phase, you will progress out into the countryside in groups of three. One of the three will be your handler. Your threesome will find lodging in a smaller town and gain the trust of the local citizens. You will find employment and began reporting, back to your handler, the specific information about that company and the products they manufacture or sell. You will attempt to acquire details and specifications about those items. You will be graded on how well you do on acquiring those technical details and reporting this information back to your handler. Some of you will acquire jobs in the local government and report on the workings of those government bodies."

"In the next and final phase, again, provided you are still with us; you will be assigned to acquire a position with a major defense manufacturer, probably in a larger city, such as, Lockheed/Martin in St. Louis, or General Dynamics Corporation in Norfolk, or General Motors Weapons Division in Michigan, or the Rockwell Corporation's Rocket Division in Huntsville, Alabama. Some of you will be placed in the Pentagon, itself and will be assigned to acquire specific information needed by Congressional Defense Oversight Committees. Some of these positions may last up to a year, some may become for you a career position. However, after one year, you will be considered a graduate of the CIA Training Program. So, as you can see, you won't all finish your training at the same time. Keep in mind that the CIA has as many agents deployed right here in the US as it does in foreign countries."

"Some of you that exhibit talent for the foreign-service will spend your final year in training assigned to a foreign country handler. This could be in any country in the world, friend or enemy. It will be any country that your government wants or needs to keep its eyes on.

You will be the eyes and ears of your government and of your country."

CHAPTER 31

The Brandenburg Gate; erected by Prussian King Frederick William II, in 1788, as a gate to the city of Berlin, to replace the original gate built during the middle ages when cities needed gates, and fortified walls surrounding them. Today it stands as an iconic landmark of the city of Berlin, Germany.

In the winter of 1963 the Brandenburg Gate stood as an ugly reminder, along with the Berlin Wall, of the division of Berlin and all of Germany, and the failings of the world leaders to come to terms with the peace they had just won and the threat of the all-consuming cancer upon humanity; communism.

In this divided city, at this point in history, it is estimated that fully one third of its citizens were involved in the espionage trade, in one form or another, passing information from both East to West and West to East. You could say that Berlin, both East and West was a 'City of Spies'.

On a crisp January day, temperature about 10 degrees above zero, Fahrenheit, Ron Lobruck's plane landed at Ramstein Air Force Base located in Rhineland-Palatinate, near the towns of Kaiserslautern and Ramstein-Miesenbach. He was directed to immediately board a bus for Berlin. Several hours later the bus exited the Autobahn and drove up the Kaiser Strasse and around the Victory Column which commemorated the Prussian victory over Austria and France in the Franco-Prussian War of the 1870's. Ron's bus continued up the Strasse des Juni to the Brandenburg Gate. There he got off and because it was a bright sunny day, he decided to walk over to Checkpoint Charlie, just a 20 minute walk from the Gate, along the Berlin Wall, where he presented his ID and met his handler; Eric Zommerfeld. Eric introduced the person who would be Ron's mentor in East Berlin, Joseph Brenner.

They had dinner at a cafe on Friedrich Strasse, in the Western Sector, just outside of the checkpoint. At dinner Eric discussed with Ron, his assignment as an agent in East Berlin.

"Ron, you will be staying at the Brandenburg Hotel tonight," Eric told him, "In the morning, Joseph will take you across the border into East Germany at Checkpoint Charlie. You two will board a northbound bus there that will take you up Friedrich Strasse to Ziegal Strasse. At that corner is a very large apartment complex. Joseph will help you get signed into your apartment, and help you shop for food, utensils, clothes and furnishings. You will also need to sign up for phone service. I will remain here in West Berlin and set up meetings for you to pass off the microfiche that you will receive from your contact in East Berlin. I assume the CIA has provided you with adequate Deutsche Marks to get started."

"Oh, yah," Ron replied, "I'm all set, I can't wait to get started."

"Well, don't get too excited," Joseph said, "Appearing too anxious in East Berlin could get you in trouble. We'll take it slow and easy, so as not to attract too much attention. One other thing, Ron, when in East Berlin, you must always speak only in the German language."

"What about employment for me? How soon should I look for work?"

"Well, not to worry too much about that, I already have something lined up for you."

In the morning, Ron and Joseph signed out of West Berlin and into East Berlin. They boarded the bus which took them north to the apartment complex at Ziegal Strasse. Ron rented an apartment on the third floor directly above Joseph's apartment. But, he didn't use his CIA name. He rented the apartment under the name of

Mike Grundhoffer, using another set of ID's. It was a name that he didn't tell his mentor, Joseph Brenner about. His apartment overlooked the Spree River.

"Although frozen over in January, it will offer a great view for the rest of the year," he thought.

Ron unpacked his small duffle bag that contained only one change of clothes and of course his picture of Nicole which he carried with him everywhere he went. He placed her picture on his bedside table. God, how he missed her. It had been almost a year since he had abruptly left Alaska. He hadn't even been able to say goodbye to her. He had made several attempts to call her, but each time, she had been out on her lobster trawler. He couldn't even leave her a phone number for her to call him back. He had been moved around so much during his training, spending only a day or two in any one place.

After they went shopping and stocked his apartment with food, Ron bought some more clothes to better blend in with the East Berlin attire. He found a used clothing store and purchased a medium length black leather coat with a heavy lining for the cold days of January, along with matching black leather, fur lined gloves and a black, wool knit watch cap. He also purchased a medium blue, wool turtle neck sweater, a pair of twill, military green trousers, and finally a pair of slip-on rubber, over shoes for the slushy and snowy days. He and Joseph had lunch at a small cafe on the corner and talked.

"We'll spend the next several days for you to get to know your way around East Berlin. Then I'll show you where to apply for your job. But, most importantly, I'll show you where you will meet your contact person, who will be handing off the microfiche which you will then transport back over to West Berlin through Checkpoint Charlie, and turn over to Eric, our handler. One other thing you must do, you must sew a special secret pocket into the lining of your coat in which to carry the microfiche, in case you are stopped by the East Berlin Police and searched. It's almost inevitable that you will be stopped from time to time. Good job, by the way on purchasing the used clothes. You should blend in quite well."

Ron spent the next two days wandering around East Berlin on his own in the subzero temperatures. Then, the weather warmed up somewhat, to above zero, so Joseph took him over to the Monbijou Park, just two blocks from their apartments, where Ron would be meeting his contact person for the hand-off of the microfiche. There was a skating rink in the park with a warming house where the transfer would take place, once a week at precisely 7:P.M. on alternating days. Ron was to rent a pair of skates and leave his street shoes under the bench, at the end, in the corner, then skate several times around the rink.

His contact person was to skate up to him and ask, "You skate quite well, do you play hockey?"

To which Ron was to reply, "Yes, I do, but only on weekends. I just practice during the week."

When Ron went into the warming house to change into his street shoes again, he would find a small envelope with the microfiche, in the toe of his shoe. He was to leave immediately for Checkpoint Charlie and hand off the envelope to his handler, Eric Sommerfeld.

The next Monday, Ron applied for a job at the Waldorff Paper Company. He would work as a forklift driver, moving large pallets of paper products into waiting trucks, and unloading huge rolls of raw paper, imported from Finland. Starting on Wednesday evening, he began picking up the microfiche and transferring it to Eric in West Berlin.

And, so went his days, as the days melted into weeks, the weeks into months, and the winter snows melted into springtime. Now when he looked out his apartment window he could see boats and barges traveling up and down the Spree

River.   He and his contact at the skating rink changed their meeting place to a spot outside in the Monbijou Park, near the playground. Ron would wait for his contact at a bench under a large Linden tree as he read his newspaper.

The key phrase that his contact used was, "Lovely weather we're having. Do you think it will rain?"

To which Ron replied, "No, the sun will keep shinning."

They would both sit there silently for a few minutes while the contact read his newspaper. The contact would then leave his newspaper on the bench. Ron would quickly grab the paper and walk away, leaving his paper on the bench, as he quickly transferred the microfiche envelope from the contact's paper to the secret pouch in his now lighter summer jacket. Several times already he had been stopped by the East Berlin Police, on the east side of Checkpoint Charlie as he was passing through to the West. They would search him and ask where he was heading. To which he replied that he was a furniture manufacturer's sales rep. from the Munstadt Furniture Company on his way to meet a client furniture store rep. from the Schoenberger Furniture Store in West Berlin to sell furniture. He carried with him, a briefcase with pictures and order forms of the furniture he was selling.   The police never did find the microfiche envelopes hidden in his secret jacket pocket.

On one such trip over to the West, Ron asked his handler, Eric, where the microfiche that he was passing to him was coming from. Eric told him that they were coming from a Soviet tank manufacturing plant located in eastern Poland and the Malyshev tank factory in Ukraine. The microfiche contained Soviet tank blueprints, specifications and material lists for the Soviet tanks, the T-64, T-72 and the newest heavy tank, the T-80.

Ron arrived back at his apartment rather late that night. As he got off of the bus and began walking towards his apartment building, he noticed a couple of the East Berlin police cars parked outside. They were talking to his partner and mentor, Joseph Brenner. Ron immediately tensed. This was a red-flag situation that his training had taught him to be aware of. He immediately entered his building by the back door and raced upstairs to his third floor apartment. His Langley training had also taught him to keep a go-bag always packed and ready for just such an occasion. He grabbed his tooth brush and his picture of Nicole and threw it in his bag. He grabbed his bag and quickly ran down the back stairs and out into the night through the back door, just as the police and Joseph were entering the front. He ran for several blocks north and came out back on Friedrich Strasse. There he boarded another bus which took him north all the way to the northern checkpoint in the wall. He checked out of East Berlin and got a cab back to the Strasse des Juni and checked into the Brandenburg Hotel. He called his handler, Eric and explained his situation.

"Good work, Ron," he said, "There are some things developing over there. I don't think you can go back. We'll talk more in the morning."

Eric came over to his hotel the next morning and they met in the hotel restaurant for breakfast.

"Here's what I've learned last night and this morning," he said, "It looks like your mentor Joseph Brenner is a double agent, I've learned from my sources in East Berlin that he was setting you up to be arrested last night. He worked with the East Berlin police to set a trap for you. Lucky for you that you came home and spotted him talking to the police. They raided your apartment, but found nothing, and of you of course, got out just in time."

"You know, I've been wary of him for quite some time. He seemed just a bit too preoccupied. Some of his friends it seemed were too connected to a lot of others in East Berlin, like they had lived there for a long time, like they were citizens of East Berlin. One time I saw him following my contact after he had handed off the microfiche to me. I can only assume that my contact lost him, because the next week my contact showed up again at our meeting place."

"Well, Ron, here's what has transpired; My superiors have decided to collapse the operation. mostly because Langley feels they have enough information on that new Soviet T-80 tank. They'll be issuing you a new assignment shortly. Meantime, they want to place you in a safe house for a week or so, sort of a 'cooling off', while they develop a new operation for you. Right now you and your contact are considered to be too "hot" to be working in Berlin any longer after what has just happened. I have filed a very favorable report to Langley on your work. You should be getting a new very 'choice' assignment shortly. You will take a bus to the airport today and catch a Lufthansa flight to Amsterdam. Your safe house is somewhere in that area. Someone will meet you at the Amsterdam airport. Someone will again, come get you from the safe house for your next assignment when it is set up."

With that, Eric stood up followed by Ron. Eric shook Ron's hand and said;

"Ron, it's been a pleasure working with you. You have done a great job here in Berlin. You are going to be an excellent agent, and quite possibly a handler someday soon. Good luck to you, Ron."

"And good luck to you too, Eric. I hope everything goes well for you here in Berlin."

With that, Ron went to his room and grabbed his 'go-bag' and checked out of the Brandenburg Hotel. He caught a bus to the airport for his flight to Amsterdam.

ROBB FELDER

CHAPTER 32

The powerful R-7 rocket engine thundered to life at the Baikonur Cosmodrome in the Soviet state of Kazakhstan in the spring of 1963. It lifted the Vostok-6 spacecraft containing three cosmonauts into orbit. One of which was the first woman to enter outer space, Valentina Tereshkova.

At the same time, a Lufthansa flight was taking off from Amsterdam bound for the Soviet Union city of Kyiv, in the Soviet state of Ukraine. On board this flight was Special Agent Ron Lobruck on his way to a new assignment under his new name; Yuri Malenkova, beginning in Kyiv. There, he would put together a team of three agents and travel southeast by train, to the Soviet, Russian city of Volgograd.

Volgograd is located on the western side of the Volga River about a thousand miles south of Moscow. Two hundred miles to the east across the Volga, lied the Soviet state of Kazakhstan. From Volgograd, he would dispatch his new team across the border into Kazakhstan, a thousand miles east to the city of Leninsk, adjacent to Baikanur, the home of the Soviet Cosmodrome, and home to the Soviet's space program. Yuri would be their handler. At the Kyiv airport he was met by a Soviet citizen working for the CIA, Nicolai Kiselyova. Yuri, of course knew Nicolai through his niece, Nicole.

"Nicolai would be a very valuable asset," Yuri thought, "because he was, of course a Soviet citizen and could speak the language fluently. He, himself could only just stumble through the Russian."

"So pleased to meet you, Yuri," Nicolai said, "my niece has told me so much about you. It will be an honor to work with you. My new name, by the way is no longer Nicolai. My new name for this mission is; Dimitri Sokalovskaya."

Dimitri then introduced Yuri to another Russian citizen. "Yuri, this is Walter Ulbricht. He is an Astro Physicist who is a graduate of the Academy of Science in Moscow. I met Walter through some connections I had in Moscow when I worked there and he was still a student."

"Pleased to meet you, Yuri, I look forward to working with you. I have been accepted for employment with the Soviet Space Program at the Baikanur Cosmodrome and I'm anxious to get to work."

The three agents boarded a train and after a three hour trip, arrived in Volgograd. They were met by the fourth agent, Boris Chelomi, an electrical engineer. After all the proper introductions, Yuri's newly assembled team of agents all proceeded to the Hotel Stalingard, where Yuri had made reservations for all four of them. After they all had an early morning breakfast in the hotel restaurant, they all met in Yuri's room for a strategy meeting.

"Here are your assignments," Yuri began, "Dimitri, you will be the courier. Your job will be to set up a meeting place in Leninsk for Walter and Boris to hand off the microfiche files that they acquire at Baikanur. You will then transport those microfiche back here to Volgograd and hand them off to me on a weekly basis. When you arrive back here in Volgograd, you will call me with a secret code and I will set up a meeting place for the handoff. We will have a secret phrase for each other when we meet. After we transact the handoff, I will give you a new code for the next weekly meeting."

"Walter Ulbricht,you are already employed at the Cosmodrome as a jet propulsion engineer, working under Sergei Korolev, who is developing the new powerful N-1 rocket engine. This new booster rocket will propel the new Soyuz spaceships on future missions. You will be meeting with Dimitri somewhere in Leninsk on a weekly basis. The two of you will set up your meeting protocol based on the same format as with Dimitri and myself and pass on your files of microfiche."

"Boris Chelomi, You have stated that you have been accepted for employment at the Baikanur Cosmodrome, presumably, you will be working on the manned flights of the new Soyuz spacecraft project. When you get settled into your new job, you will contact Dimitri and set up weekly meetings also based on the same protocol as Boris and Dimitri."

"When our meeting is over today, you will be leaving here, one by one. One of you will leave each day on the train to Leninsk, to your assignments. If any problems should arise, you will discuss them with Dimitri at your weekly meetings. Okay, gentlemen, are there any questions?"

"What about a "Fail-Safe" procedure for us, if we were to be discovered?" Walter Ulbricht asked.

"You will use the code named "Red Dragon". Under this code, you will attempt to get out of Baikanur, and out of Kazakhstan by any means possible and as quickly as possible. If you can possibly reach Dimitri, give him the code 'Red Dragon' to let him know you are in trouble. He may or may not be able to help you escape. Don't wait for him to respond, get out immediately. You are on your own to find a way out of Baikanur; plane, train, auto, or on foot. Once you have gotten out of Kazakhstan, try to make your way back to Kyiv. Call me then, on the number that Dimitri will give you shortly. After you have all left this hotel for your assignments, I will check out and get an apartment to live in here in Volgograd. I will have an additional phone line installed at my apartment that will only be used for any 'Red Dragon' calls. If you are in trouble and have to call, use the code, 'Red Dragon' and I will answer with the code 'White Cloud'. You will reply, 'Blue Sky'. State only your first name and the name of the hotel you are staying at. Dimitri, or myself will meet you there and wait for further instructions from my superiors."

"What about if we are arrested, or captured by the KGB?" Boris asked.

"Dimitri and I will do everything we can to help you escape. But once you have been convicted, it will take higher powers to negotiate your release. We will work with the CIA and the USA political powers to get you freed."

"If there are no further questions; good luck gentlemen. Remember, you are doing a great service to all mankind by attempting to equalize the scientific knowledge between the super powers and thereby preventing future wars caused by the dominance of one country over the other."

Two days later, after the two agents left for Kazakhstan, Yuri and Dimitri got together in the hotel bar for drinks. Yuri wanted to know if Dimitri had heard anything from Nicole. He had tried repeatedly to get hold of her while he was at the safe house outside of Amsterdam.

"No, not recently," Dimitri said, "The last I heard from her was when my brother Mikhail, her father had passed away. When I received a letter from her, she mentioned that she was planning to come to Minsk for a visit. She said that she was doing quite well running the lobster boat."

"Well, I haven't heard from Nicole for over a year, I miss her terribly. It's good to hear that she's doing well on her father's boat. When I can get a break on this mission I intend to travel to Sitka and see her again."

"Meantime, I guess, all you can do for now, at least, is write to her. If I get another letter from her, I'll let you know."

Dimitri left two days later for Leninsk, Kazakhstan and the Baikanur Cosmodrome to make connections with the two new agents. Meantime, Yuri found an apartment in Volograd at the intersection of Ulitsa Khirosimy and Ulitsa Marshala. He acquired phone service and had an additional phone installed for the 'Red Dragon' phone. He kept his hotel room, however, until Dimitri returned to report that all the connections were set up and ready to begin operations. They rented apartments across town from each other. The two agents then gave their phone numbers to each other, but not their addresses. This was for security reasons, in case either one was captured, they had no knowledge of the others location. Yuri also gave Dimitri the Red Dragon number to be passed on to the two agents in Baikanur.

Both Yuri and Dimitri acquired employment in Volgograd. Yuri went to work for the Rokossovich Fertilizer Company which imported potash from mines in Kazakhstan and processed and packaged it and shipped it west into Ukraine. Yuri's job was driver of a semi truck, hauling the loads of fertilizer from the plant in Volgograd to a warehouse in Kyiv. This job would work out perfectly for him. He would make connections at the warehouse with his CIA courier and pass off the microfiche files to be flown all the way back to Langley. Soon the files from Baikanur were flowing like a river through Volgograd and on to Kyiv and then on to Langley.

And so the spring of 1964 turned into summer. It was a very busy time for the fertilizer business and for the espionage business. NASA, through the efforts of Yuri's team, was able to monitor the progress of the Soviet space program as the space race heated up, and the race to the moon heated up. NASA was developing the Saturn-5 Rocket and space ship for the Apollo moon program and the Soviets were developing the N-1 super heavy booster rocket for their Soyuz moon program.

By the end of summer and early fall, as the agricultural season drew to a close, the shipments of fertilizer dried up and Yuri was laid off of his truck driving job. He found another job with the Volga Manufacturing Company, a manufacturer of plumbing and electrical supplies. However, now he had to make the trips to Kyiv by train to deliver the micro fiche files to his contact agent. He also had to come up with the necessary papers to enter Ukraine. He made up papers and an ID posing as a sales representative for his plumbing company based in Volgograd and selling bathroom fixtures in Kyiv.

Early in the new year, NASA and the CIA upped the ante on his espionage game. They decided that they would be passing microfiche back into Baikanur that had doctored up copies of the files that Yuri's team passed to NASA. These copies of design plans of the Soviet Soyuz-1 contained flaws that would cause some of the systems on the Soyuz-1 to fail. By mid-1964, several N-1 test rockets blew up on the launch pad. The design team leader Vasily Mishkin, under pressure to keep pace with the USA's Apollo program. pushed forward with the testing program of Soyuz-1 in spite of the risk. Walter Ulbricht continued to work for the N-1 Rocket team. The design team that Boris Chelomi worked for was developing the space capsule and the lunar lander that would carry the Soviet Cosmonauts to the moon.

* * * * *

"So, Yuri, would you like to see Nicole again?" Dimitri asked at one of their weekly meetings at an all-night diner to hand off microfiche, "I just received word that she will be coming to Minsk next month to visit the family."

"Oh, yes, yes! Of course I would. I haven't seen her in over two years."

"Okay, good, I will let you know when she arrives in Minsk."

"Thanks, Dimitri, I can't thank you enough for helping me reestablish my relationship with your niece."

"I know Yuri, in this business, it seems almost impossible to have a personal life. Believe me, I know what you are going through. I feel that I must warn you. When we leave to serve our countries, for the loved ones that we leave behind, time does not stand still. Time moves on, sometimes changing people. It seems like the work that we do can change governments and perhaps alter the course of history, but we have to give up our personal lives and sometimes relationships to achieve those goals and destinies."

For Yuri, the months of January, February and March crept by at a snail's pace. After hearing Dimitri's spiel he kept wondering, would things ever be the same between Nicole and him again? Would she have waited for him, or would she have moved on? He couldn't wait to see her again, yet he was now terrified of seeing her again. He kept thinking of all that they had been through. How in love they were before the Army and the CIA tore them apart.

Finally, late in the month of April of 1965, Dimitri told him that Nicole and her mother had arrived in Minsk. He gave Yuri the address of the family home in Minsk.

"You go now, Yuri. Don't worry about the microfiche packets from Baikanur. I will just make the trip up to Kiev with the packets for the handoff while you are gone. Just give me the passwords for the meetings. I have already told Nicole that you are coming. I have also gotten papers for you to get into Belarus."

Yuri trusted Dimitri, so he gave him the passwords and packed a duffle bag for the trip to Minsk in the Soviet state of Belarus. He had to change trains in Kiev, and after a twelve hour ride, he arrived in Minsk on April 22nd. At the station, he was given the shock of his life. Meeting him was, of course, Nicole. She looked so different now, somehow. They immediately embraced and kissed long and hard. Tears of joy were shed.

"Oh, Bob, I am so happy to see you again. It has been so long. I have missed you so much."

"Nicole, Nicole," He said, struggling with being called 'Bob' again. "I have missed you too. I have dreamed about you every night for the last two years."

He was so excited to see Nicole again that he didn't at first see the small carriage that she had pushed along the train platform to meet him. Nicole went over to the carriage and picked up the baby and handed him to Bob.

"Bob, I would like you to meet our son, Mikhail Robert Kiselyova."

"Oh, my God, Nicole. When was he born?"

"Mikhail was born on March 7th, 1963, exactly nine months after we were in Fairbanks together. I named him Mikhail after my father who passed away just before he was born. And, of course, he has your name as his middle name."

"So, our son is two years old already. Oh God, Nicole, I've missed the first two years of our son's life. I'm so sorry."

"Don't feel sorry, or guilty, Bob, you had no control over your destiny. Those choices were made for you by the US Army and the CIA. Now, you can only make the best of it."

The happily reunited family got a cab and proceeded to the Kiselyova house at 471 on the Tomskaya Vulitsa, a street in the south east quadrant of the city. The house was a large three story Craftsman Style house, build in the 1920's.

"This is the house that I was borne in," Nicole stated, as they unloaded young Mikhail Robert, along with his stroller. They entered and Bob was introduced to the Kiselyova family,

"Until we had to flee to America," She continued, "after the war and Stalin's purges.

Dimitri's wife Valentina appeared to be in charge of the large family home in the absence of Nicolai. Living in the house were five of Nicole's cousins and their spouses, along with eight or nine of their children. Bob couldn't even count them all.

"Come along, Bob, I'll show you to your room. "My room?" he said, "You mean, we won't be sleeping together?"

"No, I'm afraid not. We Kiselyova family are a very strict Russian Orthodox Catholic family, and they would not condone us sleeping together while we're not married."

They began climbing the stairs. Bob carried up his newly discovered son, Mikhail. Nicole brought up baby Mikhail's stroller. On the second floor was Nicole and Mikhail's room. As they entered, Bob could understand why he couldn't be sleeping there with Nicole, for more than just religious reasons. The bedroom was about eight by eight feet square. Nicole's single bed in one corner and baby Mikhail's crib in another corner. He began to lay his son down in his crib.

"Ah,ah," Nicole said, "He will need a changing first."

Bob then laid baby Mikhail down on Nicole's bed, while she went to a dresser and pulled out one of the cloth diapers.

"Do you know how to do this?" she questioned.

"Of course I do, sweetheart. Don't forget, I grew up with a lot of younger, baby siblings."

She handed him the diaper and he began to fold it into the famous triangle. As he removed baby Mikhail's diaper, she watched him for a reaction. There was none, and she looked surprised, because it was a stinky one.

"Don't forget, my dear," Bob said, reading her reaction to his non-reaction, "I also grew up on a farm, handling tons of smelly cow and hog poop. We are all just animals in that regard, after all."

Bob removed the stinky one, and cleaned Mikhail's bottom. He handed it to Nicole to go down the hall to the bathroom and rinse, flush and wring out the stinky one. Bob, meantime, applied powder to Mikhail's bottom, pinned up the new diaper and put a set of pajamas on his son for the night. Nicole came in with a bottle of milk and Bob began feeding him. After his son finished, he kissed him goodnight and laid him into his crib. Young Mikhail Robert was asleep in minutes. Nicole and Bob tip-toed out into the hall and quietly closed the door.

They climbed the stairs to the third floor and Nicole showed Bob his bedroom under the slanted ceiling. It was nothing more than a large closet, about six by seven feet square, with a single bed, tiny dresser, and a small octagon window.

"I, apologize, Bob, this bedroom has always reminded me of a prison cell."

"Well, it'll do just fine for now. Anywhere is fine when I'm with you, darling."

With that, they kissed, long and hard and passionately. They were just about to take it to the next level, when there was a knock at the door and a young voice said, "Come on down to dinner, Auntie Nicole and Uncle Bob."

They descended the two flights of stairs and walked into a room of total mayhem. At the rear of the huge house was an equally huge dining room, with a dining table set for twenty two people. They were directed to two chairs next to the head of the table. Nicole's aunt, Valentina sat at the head, while at the other end was an empty chair.

"That chair is not ever sat in, "Nicole whispered to Bob, "It's reserved for Uncle Nicolai, whenever he returns."

Aunt Valentina rang a dinner bell several times and the room became silent. "Our guests, Nicole and Bob will lead us in saying our dinner grace."

Everyone folded their hands and they began, "Bless us O' Lord and these thy gifts, which we have received from thy bounty, Amen."

After which, the room once again erupted into a roar of chaos, with everybody passing everything to everybody. There was a large beef pot roast, mashed potatoes, gravy, two kinds of vegetables, beets, and corn. and lots of bread, two or three kinds of bread. There was milk for the children, while all the adults had water.

"How do you manage such a wonderful meal?" Bob asked Valentina, "I thought things were very austere under communism."

"Well, we don't eat this lavishly every day, believe you, me. This is a special meal to welcome Nicole and you and baby Mikhail. But we have learned to survive under the punishing communist 'Five-Year' system. That's why we live like this, all of us crammed into this house. There is not enough housing available, so adult children have to live with their parents until the next 'Five-Year' program builds new housing. We normally have to eat whatever the system puts out, without much choice. Many times, grocery stores run out of certain foods. In late summer into fall, we drive about forty or fifty miles out into the country and buy fresh food directly from the collective farms. We then can all the fresh vegetables and fruits for the winter months. In the basement, we have several hundred jars of canned goods. We also buy flour in large quantities and bake our own bread. Meats are sometimes very scarce. There are some meals where all we have is bread and vegetables. We used to have wine at our meals, but alcoholic beverages are almost impossible to buy. You have to get it on the 'black market', same with coffee and cigerettes."

After dinner, Bob and Nicole helped with the cleanup. Everyone settled into their evening routines. Some of the kids went to the basement to play until bedtime. Most of the adults and older children gathered in the living room for TV. Some sat at the table for card games, or board games.

Nicole suggested to Bob that they should go for a walk, to have some privacy so they could talk, even though the temperature was barely above freezing.

They first went upstairs and checked on baby Mikhail. He was still sleeping soundly. After putting on their heavy winter coats, hats, mittens and rubber boots, they ventured out into the falling snow.

As they began their walk, Nicole said, "I'm going to perfectly honest with you, Bob, I don't know how much longer I can keep living like this."

"You mean living in that crowded household?"

"No, no. Bob, not that. I've always lived in a crowed household growing up. I mean trying to live, not knowing where you are, or what you are doing, or if you are safe or not. I know that what you are doing is a very dangerous job. I have talked to Aunt Valentina and she tells me about how Uncle Nicolai is almost always on the run from the KGB and the Russian police. She says she doesn't know how she has put up with it all these years, never knowing if he will be arrested or killed for what he does. She said she keeps begging him to retire, but, she says that he is like an adrenaline addict and just keeps going on these dangerous assignments. Bob, I don't want to live like that anymore. I don't want that for our son, growing up not knowing his father, or, if he even has a father, and I sure as hell don't want that for you and I. It's one thing if you want to risk your life for your country, but it's not just about you anymore, Bob. Now it's about us. Three of us. I am not going to live with that empty chair at our dining room table."

Bob thought long and hard about what Nicole had just said. As they walked along in the falling snow, he didn't say anything for a long few minutes.

"Nicole, I love you, you know that, and I want more than anything for us to have a normal life together. Truthfully, I didn't want this life for me in the first place, and certainly not for my family. I was coerced into this whole damn CIA thing after that incident in Alaska, with Frank and that plane crash. They told me I had a choice, prison or joining the CIA. I chose the CIA because they told me that I would be free after three years of service. So now, I've done my three years of service with the CIA, and I do believe that I should be able to quit at this point. I will put in for an immediate discharge as soon as I can get hold of my handler."

They continued on around the block in the falling snow. When they arrived back at the Kiselyova house, they stomped the snow off their boots and took them off and took off their winter clothes and hung them in the hall closet. The house was growing quiet and all of the children were already in bed. Nicole and Bob tiptoed up the stairs to her bedroom. Bob went over to his son's crib. He bent over and gently kissed little sleeping Mikhail on his forehead and whispered, "Good night my son. I'll see you in the morning."

Nicole kissed Bob and whispered, "You go on ahead up to your bedroom and I'll join you after everyone is asleep."

At 2: A.M. the house had been silent for a while. Bob heard his door open. He had been up reading to stay awake. Nicole tiptoed in and quietly closed the door and crawled into bed with Bob.

* * * * *

On this snowy spring night, the two love birds, Nicole and Bob made passionate albeit, quiet love in Bob's bedroom, on the third floor of the Kiselyova house at 471 on the Tomskaya Vulitsa, in Minsk, Belarus, in the Soviet Union.

At 2:35 a.m., about two thousand miles away, to the southeast, a manned test fight of the Soyuz-1 spacecraft, powered by the N-1 rocket, lifted off from the launch pad at the Baikanur Cosmodrome, on board was the cosmonaut, Vladimir Komarov.

At about 5:A.M., after Nicole was again back in her own bedroom, and everyone in the

Kiselyova house was again asleep, the phone in the third floor bedroom awakened Bob from a sound sleep. It was Dimitri(Nicolai) Kiselyova.

"You must return to Volgograd at once. There will be a cab waiting for you in the street out front. The driver will have your train ticket for your return. Leave immediately, do not say goodbye, just leave, now."

Yuri(Bob) immediately shook the sleep from his head and got dressed and repacked his duffle bag and tiptoed down the stairs. He stopped for just a second on the second floor debating with himself about stopping and waking his new little family to say goodbye, but ruled himself against that decision realizing it would incite too much emotion from the parties involved, and himself included. So, instead, he got out a slip of paper and scribbled a note to Nicole.

"I have been called back into duty for an emergency. I will explain later when I have secured my release from the CIA. I love you, my darling Nicole. Please hug our precious little Mikhail from me."

He slid the note under the door of Nicole's bedroom and quietly left the house.

CHAPTER 33

Soyuz-1 thundered off the launch pad at the Baikanur Cosmodrome in Kazakhstan and into outer space at 3:35 a.m., Moscow time on April 23rd, 1965 and successfully achieved a satisfactory orbit.

The Soyuz at the time of its maiden flight was still afflicted by hundreds of design problems. Many of them brought about by the sabotaged plans provided by the US CIA. Unfortunately, there was little time to solve them; the impending 50th anniversary of the Bolshevik Revolution in May, 1965 increased pressure on the Soyuz program to conduct a flight. The Politburo wanted a successful flight at any cost. In order to make headline news around the world, Russia had adopted a bold mission plan. In addition to the Soyuz-1, a second Soyuz would be launched into orbit the next day, carrying three cosmonauts; Alexei Yeliseyev, Yevgeni Khrunov and Valeri Bykovsky. The two spacecraft would then perform the first ever docking in orbit. Two of the cosmonauts, Alexei and Yevgeni would space walk from Soyuz-2 to Soyuz-1 and return to earth with Komarov. Later, Valeri Bykovsky would return alone inside Soyuz-2.

Four hours later, the Soviet news media; Tass, reported the successful launch and that the flight was proceeding normally. A second update at 10:00 a.m. brought similar good news and everyone awaited news of the launch of the Soyuz-2 which was scheduled to dock with the Soyuz-1 spacecraft.

The USSR was on the verge of upstaging the Americans as it launched its new Soyuz spacecraft, designed to eventually ferry cosmonauts to the moon. The US space program had just suffered its most serious setback brought about by the Apollo-1 fire and the Russians now seemed to be well ahead in the race to the moon with this launch.

Meanwhile, on board the Soyuz-1, things were less than normal. Cosmonaut Komarov reported that one of the ships solar arrays failed to open properly, depriving Komarov of more than half of his power supply. A backup telemetry antenna also failed, leading to sporadic radio reception, and glitches with solar and other sensors meant that the cosmonaut could not even maintain effective control over his orientation. (Later it would be discovered, that the faulty sensor had been improperly installed by the designed team.)

The antenna failure was a minor irritation, but the orientation sensor issues were much more seriously problematic. This would make it virtually impossible to dock with the Soyuz-2. Komarov tried to visually orient his craft, using the Earth's horizon, but with no success. With only one solar array wing deployed, the Soyuz-1 spacecraft had assumed an asymmetrical orbit shape making orientation even harder. Komarov, at one point, knocked his boot against the side of the spacecraft in a futile effort to free the stubborn deployment mechanism for the stuck solar array, but with no results.

Unfortunately for Yuri Komarov, the assembly and installation of many of the components of the spacecraft were installed utilizing the altered design plans returned by the US CIA. This meant that not only did Soyuz-1 have corrupted systems, but also Soyuz-2 which had mirrored systems and would have also been destined for failure.

By now, cosmonauts Yeliseyev and Khrunov's launch of the Soyuz-2 scheduled for April 24th had to be cancelled and planning was begun to bring Komarov and the Soyuz-1 safely back to Earth.

Attempts to perform a de-orbit retrofire were made on Soyuz-1's 16th, 17th and 18th circuits of the planet, but were frustrated by an inability to control the ship's orientation. At this point, Komarov began swearing at his "devil ship", and complained that "nothing I lay my hands on works properly." Unlike his earlier 'Vostok' trips, the Soyuz-1 decent module was not spherical, but had a distinctly flattened base and an offset center of gravity to provide greater aerodynamic "lift" during reentry. Unfortunately, it also required more precision as it began to encounter the upper atmosphere, and with an ineffective attitude-control system, this was virtually impossible to achieve. The first retrofire attempt began at 2:56 a.m. on the 24th, but the orientation problems caused Soyuz-1's automatic control system to halt it. A decision was made to cancel the attempt on the 17th orbit and use that pass instead for the ground controllers to plan for another try on the 18th orbit.

At this point, both the controllers and Komarov himself had a feeling that his survival was unlikely. The cosmonaut even spoke to his wife, Valentina, and to Soviet Premier Alexei Kosygin. In the exchange, Komarov told his wife how to handle his affairs and what to do with their children. He was becoming more aware that the problems he faced were probably insurmountable.

He knew that his re-entry orientation was far from perfect, because of the asymmetrical shape of Soyuz-1 and its inability to exercise effective attitude control.

In order to land, a spacecraft has to reenter the atmosphere with the correct orientation. A very low reentry angle would cause it to skim off the top of the atmosphere, whereas a too steep angle would cause it to burn up from too much friction caused by the terrific high speed of the capsule. Therefore, it needs to have the correct attitude or orientation before the retrofire engines are used.

The Soyuz had three orientation systems; the astro-inertial system, rendered useless by the un-deployed solar panel blocking it, the unreliable 'ion' system that Kaomarov had unsuccessfully tried to use for correction, and a manual system. The third option could be used only on the daytime side of the orbit while 17th orbit reentry would be from the night side of the planet. If orientation using the ion system failed, a manual orientation attempt would be made during the 19th orbit, which would fall on the dayside of planet earth. By then, the Soyuz would be drawing power from the backup battery, so it was imperative to get it right on the 17th orbit.

Unfortunately, things continued to go wrong for Komarov. During the reentry burn, the faulty ion attitude control system allowed the vehicle to deviate too far from its designated path, causing the automatic system to halt retrofire. The pilot performed the manual initiation and fired the retrofire engines. But the unusual asymmetric shape of the vehicle caused it to drift during the reentry burn. The automatic system detected this variation from the desired flight path and shutdown the engines before completion of the burn.

Still, the retrofire that had begun at 5:59 a.m. Moscow time had run for long enough to ensure entrance into the upper atmosphere. Thirteen minutes later, the Yevpatoriya control station in the Crimea picked up voice communications from the spacecraft, in which Komarov apparently advised them of the results of the retrofire and his loss of attitude control. Communications then fell silent as Soyuz-1 became sheathed in the super-heated plasma, and entered a period of radio blackout.

During the reentry, the descent module carrying Komarov would have separated from the remainder of the Soyuz orbital module and the instrument module, about a dozen minutes after retrofire. This would have been followed, 14 minutes later, by the deployment of sets of parachutes and touchdown in the Soviet Union about 25 minutes later. Sometime between 6:18

and 6:20 a.m., Komarov's voice seemed calm and unhurried in spite of the 8G gravity load imposed by the steep ballistic reentry.

Having overcome all of the earlier problems, Soyuz-1 might still have made a safe and successful landing, - - -,

Then its parachutes failed.

* * * * * *

As the vehicle tumbled through the atmosphere, its brake and drag chutes began to deploy. However, the drag chute failed to pull out the main parachute from its container because of a sizing problem the sabotaged chute door was jammed. The reserve chute, which was deployed as a backup, got entangled with the drag chute, effectively turning the space capsule into an unstoppable projectile. Instead of floating under a parachute, the capsule hit the ground at the speed of freefall. The impact flattened the two-meter tall decent module to an astonishing 40 inches, causing the solid fuel rockets at the base of the Soyuz to explode. The resultant ball of fire destroyed anything that may have survived the impact, leaving only a pile of molten wreckage.

Gruesome eyewitness accounts narrated that Komarov had been reduced to a lump. A heel bone was the only recognizable body part retrieved from the crash site. Post-crash investigators conducted an autopsy of sorts and revealed the cause of death to be severe injuries to the skull, spinal cord and bones.

* * * * * *

This bold but dangerous mission could quite possibly have given the Soviets an unassailable lead in the race to the moon. Sadly though, largely as a result of the CIA's effort to sabotage the Soyuz spacecraft, the mission intended to push the Russian space program to a whole new level, ahead of the Americans, instead, pulled it down into defeat.

The creation of the Soyuz spacecraft mission, like everything else during the space race, boiled down to political pressures and ambitions. The Soyuz, the Russian equivalent of the US Apollo, had been in development for a long time. It was a very complex piece of equipment with capabilities such as long duration flights, rendezvous, and docking, and like the Apollo, had suffered numerous problems and delays.

CHAPTER 34

On another cold March night, about two days later, at his apartment, in Volgograd, at 2:A.M. Yuri was again awakened by the ringing of a phone, this time, the 'Red Dragon' phone. He picked up the phone and heard the code word 'Red Dragon'. He responded with 'White Cloud'.

"Blue Sky," came the reply, "This is Boris."

"What can I do for you, Boris?"

"The Soyuz-1 space capsule has crashed after re-entry and has killed cosmonaut Vladimir Komarov. The operation has collapsed," came the reply. "Vasily Mishin, my boss, has fired most of the Soyuz-1 development team. They suspect sabotage. Other members of the team are pointing a finger at me."

"Were you able to get out?"

"Yes, for now. I am in the city of Oral, in northern Kazakhstan. I'm at the train station."

"Can you get to Kyiv?"

"Yes, I think so. I checked. It's about a two day trip."

"Very good, Boris, get on the train to Kyiv, Dimitri will meet you at the train station."

"Thank you, goodbye."

Yuri hung up the Red Dragon phone and immediately called Dimitri. When Dimitri answered, Yuri said, "We have a 'Red Dragon' situation."

"Meet me at our usual place in twenty minutes," came the reply.

Meanwhile Yuri called his handler in Kyiv and explained the situation, "Have everyone meet here in Kyiv. Collapse the operation. We'll regroup and wait for word from Langley. I'll call them immediately and let them know what has transpired."

Yuri then called a cab. He got out of the cab five blocks away from the all-night diner where they used to meet for the micro-fiche handoff. He zig-zagged through the streets, to shake off anyone that may have been following him. It was a crisp, cold, dark night and the streets were silent. It usually didn't snow in Volgograd, but the temperature would go down to just about freezing this time of the year. When he got to the diner, Dimitri was already there.

"I just got back from Leninsk," Dimitri stated as Yuri joined him at a table and ordered coffee, "It doesn't look good for us. Our operation is a disaster. I couldn't get ahold of Boris, he had already fled. I did get ahold of Walter, though. I told him to get out also, when he had a chance. He worked on the N-1 rocket and launch systems which wasn't affected by the re-entry failure of the Soyuz space capsule. So at least he's safe for now. I told him to meet us in Kyiv when he gets out."

"Very good, Dimitri. I just talked to our handler in Kyiv. He told me to collapse the operation and meet in Kyiv, and wait for further orders from Langley. Why don't we catch the early morning train to Kyiv and see if Boris makes it. There's one leaving at six. You go ahead, I'm going back to my place and pack. I'll meet you at the train station."

* * * * *

Boris Chelomi hung up the pay phone at the Oral train station after talking to Yuri. He went over to the ticket window and purchased a ticket to Kyiv. At 5: A.M. he got on the train. In an hour the train crossed the Kazakhstan border into Russia. Six hours later the train made its first stop at the town of Saratov. He had lunch and an hour later he changed trains heading for the Russian city of Voranezh. At midnight, the train pulled into the station at Voranezh. Boris was asleep and didn't see the exchange of passengers, some got off, new ones got on. He didn't see that among the passengers getting on, were about half dozen KGB agents. As the train pulled out, they went to work, walking up and down the aisles checking all the passengers. They each had a picture of Boris, from his file at the Baikanur Cosmodrome. In a short while they spotted him, asleep in his seat. They woke him and told him that he was under arrest. They put him in handcuffs. One of the KGB agents took the seat next to Boris and handcuffed himself to Boris. The other five KGB agents took up seats all around Boris. They all reclined their seats and as the train speed on into the night, they all fell asleep.

At about 6:A.M. the train pulled into the town of Kursk. The five KGB agents and Boris got off the train and had breakfast. For bathroom breaks, the agent handcuffed to Boris would accompany him into the bathroom and another agent would stand guard outside. They then all got on the northbound train heading for Moscow.

* * * * *

Yuri caught a cab outside the diner where he had met Dimitri, and headed back over to his apartment. He unlocked the door and went in and began to hurriedly pack. He paused momentarily, as he thought that some of his things were out of place and thought that maybe the landlord was snooping around. He tossed aside that thought, however, because there wasn't anything missing, and he would soon be leaving and wouldn't be worrying about snooping landlords.

He looked at the clock and decided that it was too early to leave for the train station, the train wouldn't be leaving until 6:A.M. so he laid down for a short nap. He was awakened, however, about 4:30 A.M. by someone banging on his door. He got up to answer it still fully dressed, thinking that it might be Dimitri coming to pick him up and give him a ride to the train station. Dimitri had his own car in Volgograd. He opened the door and five armed KGB agents pushed their way in. They pushed him down onto his couch.

"We are here to question you about your activities connecting you to Baikanur in Kazakhstan," The agent in charge stated, "Have you been to Baikanur recently, Mr. Malendova?"

"No sir, I have never been to Baikanur."

"Well, we think you are lying, Mr. Malendova," another agent shouted. getting very close to Yuri's face, "You see, Mr. Malendova, we have tapped your telephone here and have heard your conversation with someone named Boris Chelomi, an employee at the Baikanur facility."

Yet another agent went over to Yuri's 'Red Dragon' phone and turned it over and showed everyone the 'bug' attached to the bottom of the phone.

"Oh, shit," Yuri thought, "I could be in big trouble here. It sounded like they found out about his connection to Boris. He must have been arrested already, also, and perhaps he talked."

"And, why do you have two phones here, in your apartment, Mr. Malendova?"

"That phone is my business phone, the other one is my personal phone. I have it set up that way so I can track business expenses. I am an independent sales rep. for the Volga Manufacturing Company. I sell their plumbing and electrical products all over the area, including at the Baikanur facility. Boris Chelomi is a buyer for the facility, that is, until he was fired recently. I don't really know why."

"Well, Mr. Malendova," The head agent said, "I think your behavior is very strange, and your connection to Boris Chelomi is extremely suspicious. We're going to have to take you in to our head office in Moscow and try to get this sorted out. You are under arrest for suspicion of sabotage."

Two of the KGB agents grabbed Yuri under each arm and stood him up. The agent number two handcuffed him and they led him out of his apartment and down to the street. There, in the early morning hours, as the sun was just coming up on a crisp, cold Russian morning they loaded him into a big black sedan and took him over to the Volgograd Train Station. The five KGB agents all boarded the train with Yuri handcuffed to the head agent.

"Oh fuck," Yuri thought, "I'm totally screwed now."

He did not see any sign of Dimitri at the station, although, he would be boarding another train at another time. Yuri had learned in his training at Langley, that once they start questioning, or arrest you, you are assumed to be guilty. His only hope was that Dimitri could get away free and would contact Langley to start getting him and Boris some form of defense against whatever charges they were about to issue on them. Hopefully, he thought, Walter was still in the clear because he worked on the N-1 rocket project and not the space capsule.

* * * * * *

Dimitri left the meeting at the all-night diner and got into his car. He did not, however, go back to his apartment. He was an old pro at the espionage game and could sense when the situation was getting too 'hot' and it was time to make a run for it. Not to many espionage agents lived as long as he had without a true sense of the dangers of the job. He filled up his car with petrol at an all-night petrol station and headed west, out of Volgograd. He did not however, head for Kyiv. He could sense that, that city was also going to be to 'hot' after what had happened. So, he headed west into the early morning hours, toward the southern part of Ukraine.

He crossed the border into Ukraine near the town of Luhansk at about 6:20 A.M. He had breakfast and again filled his car with petrol and continued his westward trek across Ukraine. By noon, he was in Donetsk. He had lunch and again filled up with petrol, and headed west again.

Eight hundred miles later, a very weary Dimitri Sakalovakaya pulled into the town of Kirovohrad at midnight, had a bite to eat and got a motel room for the night. At 6:A.M. he ate breakfast, filled up with petrol again and continued on. He had lunch and filled with petrol in

Vinnytsya and continued on toward the town of Lviv. Late evening he had diner and spent the night in Lviv.

On the third day on the road, he arrived at the Polish border crossing at the town of Rzeszow for lunch. He filled up with petrol and lunch and crossed into Poland. By mid-afternoon, he pulled into the city of Krakow. He called his CIA contact in Poland and explained his situation and checked into a CIA safe-house.

ROBB FELDER

CHAPTER 35

Boris Chelomi was led out of the train station in Moscow in handcuffs, after a 2 day train ride. He was put into another large black sedan and taken to the KGB headquarters in the Kremlin and put into a cell in the basement. A few hours later he was taken to a second floor interrogation room. Here a panel of three interrogators began questioning him about everything from where he was born and went to school to how he got the job working on the Soyuz-1 space capsule program at Baikenur.

"Where were you born?" Asked the first interrogator.

"I was born in St. Petersburg, in 1935. I left in 1953 to attend the Academy of Science in Moscow."

They used the 'soft' approach at first, with the more mundane questions, then intensified the approach when they began the questions about his job at Baikenur. Boris continued to proclaim his ignorance of any wrongdoing. He kept insisting that he was just basically an electrician, working on the electrical systems of the space capsule of the Soyuz-1's lunar landing craft..

"I have a major in electrical engineering, but all I worked on was the wiring." he stated, over and over again.

"What was your connection to a person named Yuri Malenkova? When did you have contact with this man?"

"I only met Yuri once, when I was in Volgograd to purchase electrical supplies from the Volga Manufacturing Company. He was their sales rep."

"Have you ever met with anyone else from Volgograd?"

"No, I have not."

"You are lying, Mr. Chelomi, all lies!" the second interrogator shouted and slammed his hand down on the table. "You see, we a have a recording of a phone conversation you had with someone called 'Red Dragon'."

"Yes, that was my friend from college. He invited me to work for his company at their Kyiv office after I was fired at Baikenur."

"Lies, Mr. Chelomi, nothing but lies." the interrogator shouted and again slammed his hand down on the table again. "We will get the truth out of you, Mr. Chelomi, one way or another."

The interrogators continued the questioning for the rest of the day and into the night. They sent in a backup team to work him over during the night. They sent in a heavy thug who used Boris as his punching bag. Even after that, Boris was able to stand up to his story. They continued their questioning for another day. He wasn't allowed to sleep, and they gave him nothing to eat, only an occasional glass of water. However, late the third day, they gave him an injection of sodium pentothal. He appeared to be resistant to the first injection, but after another injection, he crumbled.

* * * * * *

The train carrying Yuri and the five KGB agents pulled into the Moscow station about 3:A.M. He too, was ushered over to the KGB Headquarters at the Kremlin and put in a cell in the basement. At 6:A.M. his interrogation began. Using the same approach they used with Boris, they began with questions about his background.

"Where were you born?"

"I was born in Manchester, England."

Part of his training at Langley had taught him to choose a place somewhere other than the US as your birth place to direct attention away from the USA's CIA. He had chosen Manchester, and had been memorizing facts about it as he was being transferred from Volgograd to Moscow. He had been repeating those facts and the other facts of his life in Volgograd over and over in his mind so as to burn them into his sub conscious, so that even under sodium pentothal they would be his life facts.

"Where in Manchester did you live?"

"I lived at 492 Bramwell Drive."

"When did you move to Volgograd and why did you move there?"

"My uncle lived and worked in Moscow after the war. He wrote to me after I had graduated with a degree in electrical engineering and told me about an employment opportunity in Volgograd at the Volga Manufacturing Company.. So I came and applied and got the job."

After those basic questions, the interrogation got more intense, just as it had with Boris Chelomi.

"Are you a member of the British MI6?"

"No sir, I am not."

"I think you are lying, Mr. Malenkova. Have you ever had contact with a Boris Chelomi?"

Remembering his interrogation in Volgograd, Yuri didn't fall for the same trap again.

"Yes sir, I have."

"And where did you meet Mr. Chelomi?"

"He came to our office in Volgograd to purchase electrical supplies for the Soyuz-1 project in Baikanur."

"Have you had contact with him since that time?"

"Yes sir, He called me recently after he was let go from his job in Baikanur. I attempted to help him out by suggesting we meet in Kyiv and get him a job at our sales office there."

"Lies, all lies." The interrogator screamed at him as he slammed his hand down on the table. "We have it all on tape, Mr. Malenkova. Isn't it true that you were in fact, helping Mr. Chelomi escape from Baikanur after he sabotaged the Soyuz-1 project?"

"I know nothing about his Soyuz-1 project."

"Lies, lies, all lies," the interrogator screamed again, "Get this liar out of my sight."

After they interrogated Yuri for the rest of the day and on into the night; about midnight, the same team of thugs that had worked Boris over began using Yuri as their punching bag. They left him then, bloody and bruised, handcuffed in the chair where he had passed out from the beating. He remained slumped over in the chair until about 6:A.M. An interrogator came in and woke him up and gave him an injection of sodium pentothal. While they were waiting for the drug to take effect, the KGB office got a call from the office of

Premier Mikhail Gorbachev. He wanted both of the prisoners to appear with him in a television news release that evening.

At 6:P.M. the two prisoners, Boris Chelomi and Yuri Malenkova were transported under heavy guard to the Kremlin's TV studio. At 7:P.M. the Moscow news agency, TASS, interrupted the regular evening broadcasting to broadcast a message from Premier Gorbachev.

The two prisoners, battered and bruised looking, stood next to Gorbachev at the podium while he made the announcement.

"These two spies have attempted to sabotage the Soviet space program. They have sabotaged our Soyuz mission which resulted in the death of our Cosmonaut Vladimir Komarov. These two will stand trial and I will ask for the death penalty."

* * * * * *

Five hundred miles to the southwest of Moscow, at the Kiselyova house at 471 on the Tomskaya Vulitsa, in the city of Minsk, Belarus, the family had just finished dinner and were gathered at the TV to watch their favorite evening show. Suddenly the broadcast was interrupted and Premier Gorbachev appeared, along with the two prisoners.

Nikole gasped as she recognized Bob.

"Wait, isn't that Bob?" said one of Nicole's cousins.

"Oh, no,- -no,- -no, no," Nicole said, "That can't be right. There must be some mistake. That can't be Bob."

"No, no, no, oh God no," she screamed," as tears began streaming down, as she was now certain that it was him,

She scooped up baby Mikhail and his blanket that he was playing on, on the floor and ran to the stairs, now too embarrassed and ashamed to face her family any further. She ran crying and screaming all the way up the stairs.

All she could do was scream, "No, no, no, this isn't happening, oh God, no."

Nicole ran into her bedroom at the top of the stairs and slammed the door. She sat on the edge of her bed holding and rocking baby Mikhail and sobbing violently, tears streaming down her face.

"Oh God, why? After all we've been through together? Why does it have to end this way? Why?"

"Oh, sweet baby Mikhail, what will we do now? You will grow up without a father," She continued sobbing.

She continued to just sit there bawling, in shock and disbelief, and rocking her baby Mikhail. She kept on rocking and bawling until her tears went dry. After about an hour, her mother, Ursula came upstairs to see if Nicole was okay. She found her daughter still sitting on her bed, rocking her baby and sobbing. She sat down on the bed next to her. She put her arm around Nicole and tried to console her.

"Nicole, honey, I'm so sorry. I'm at a loss for words. I don't know what to say. I know how much you loved Bob, and now it's over. They may execute him, or send him to prison for a very long time. There's nothing we can do now, except try to make a good life for ourselves and yours and Bob's son Mikhail."

"But why, Mom, why? Why didn't he get out of the CIA while he still had the chance? I know he wanted to. He told me he was fed up with them and wanted out. He said he had served his time and was going to give his notice. Why didn't he just do it, Mom, why? Why did he go back?"

"I don't know, Honey. We may never know what he was thinking, and why he went back and got caught."

* * * * * *

Five hundred miles to the southwest of Minsk, Belarus in Krakow, Poland at the CIA safe house, Dimitri Sokakovskaya again packed his bags. After watching Premier Gorbachev's speech and showing of the two CIA agents responsible for the Soyuz explosion and death of a cosmonaut, he knew he had to offer them some form of help. He got in his car and drove to Warsaw. There he caught a midnight train bound for Moscow. Two days later, he arrived in Moscow. He got a hotel room and immediately went to work. He called a friend of his who was a Russian lawyer, who went to work getting in touch with other lawyers in the Kremlin and began setting up a defense team.

Dimitri, meantime, got ahold of people in Langley, Virginia, who, in turn got ahold of political people in Washington, D.C. These political people in turn, contacted political people in the Kremlin.

Now, the stage was set for the biggest political showdown since the Francis Gary Powers incident. Three world powers; The USSR, The U.S. and Great Britain were about to do legal battle in one of the biggest battles of the cold war. Great Britain was involved because Yuri had claimed to be from Manchester, England.

A date was set for the trial, by a Russian Tribunal. Rumors floated around the Kremlin that the heads of two of the world's superpowers; President Lyndon Johnson and Premier Mikhail Gorbachev had words on the "Red Phone Hot Line".

Four months after the 'infamous' Soyuz-1 lunar capsule incident at Baikanur, on a relatively warm day in May, in Moscow, the trial began. So much pre-trial haggling and political negotiations had already taken place that the trial results were a forgone conclusion.

Boris Chelomi was brought to trial first. The Prosecution opened with a statement that said that Boris had engaged in sabotaging the Soyuz-1 space craft, where he worked as an electrical technician, resulting in the explosion of the failed Soyuz-1 spacecraft re-entry that killed Valdimir Komarov, the Astronaut.

The defense contended that Boris had nothing to do with the explosion. They contended that based on the history of the Soyuz-1 spacecraft, that it was already flawed and exploded because of internal flaws in the parachute system itself and not the electrical system.

After the opening statements, the courtroom was cleared and the rest of the trial by the tribunal was held in secret because of the sensitive and secret nature of the Soviet space program. The Soviets were not willing to admit openly, that the incident with the Soyuz-1 capsule re-entry malfunction and explosion had quite literally knocked them out of the race to put a man on the moon ahead of the U.S. Several more attempts with the Soyus-1 rocket would be made, but ultimately the Soviets abandoned the N-1 program and the moon landing program. Walter Ulbricht was transferred to the Mir space station project and never again had contact with the USA's CIA.

The trial by the tribunal lasted with only three days of deliberations. The doors of the courtroom were again opened for the reading of the verdict and the sentencing of Boris Chelomi. They sentenced Boris to be put to death by firing squad in three days.

On the 25th day of May, in a courtyard of the Kremlin, Boris Chelomi was blindfolded and stood against a wall. The firing squad of six men lined up about twenty paces from the prisoner. Yuri was required to watch the execution from a second floor window overlooking the courtyard. The command, 'Fire' was given and as many bullets pierced his body, he fell to the ground, immediately dead. What went through Yuri's mind could only be imagined.

Yuri's trial began the next day. Unbeknownst to Yuri, his trial would have a predetermined outcome. This was the result of such a large number of pressures brought to bear on his trial, both internally and externally, as opposed to Boris's. In Boris's case, he was a Russian citizen, so they could treat him as they saw fit. Boris had to be set up as an example, a deterrent, to protect the security of its space program.

Other pressures came into play in Yuri's case. Because he was not a Soviet citizen, he had to be treated differently. The Kremlin always played everything to the Russian self-image with the rest of the world, so his trial had to be played on an international stage. It was determined even before the trial began, that he would not be executed. He was to be used as a pawn in the international game of 'Spy Swapping'.

The trial began the same as Boris's. However, the charges against Yuri were different. Because there was no proof that he had ever been to Baikanur, there was no charge of sabotage, only of espionage. The courtroom was filled with international politicians, and of course, reporters from every major news reporting agency in the world. Among the media crowd was Dimitri, who had papers identifying him as a reporter from the Warsaw paper Dziennik, he was going under his original name of Nicolai Kiselyova.

The wiretap was really the only piece of damning evidence presented that linked him to having contact with Boris Chelomi, but, it was enough for a conviction.

After only one day of deliberations, the Tribunal came back with the expected verdict of guilty of the charge of espionage. Yuri was sentenced to 10 years in prison. He was held in the Kremlin jail for a day, awaiting transport to the Kresty prison in Saint Petersburg. Nicolai visited him and told him to keep his hopes up for an early release.

"We're already working on a possible prisoner swap," Nicolai told him, "I will be visiting you in Saint Petersburg."

ROBB FELDER

CHAPTER 36

"No, no, no, I will not go to Helsinki," Nicole declared, after her uncle Nicolai offered to take her and baby Mikhail with him to Helsinki where he would work with the CIA and the U.S political negotiators on a prisoner swap. From there, it was only a short distance to the Kresty prison in Saint Petersburg where she could visit Yuri from time to time.

"No, no, I don't think I ever want to see Bob again, after what he did. We had agreed that he would quit the CIA for our sake, but he decided to go back anyway. Why, why, why would he do that to us? I can never forgive him for what he did to us. I'm just so sick and tired of this God damn spy games. I don't want any part of it anymore, ever."

With that she began sobbing all over again and ran upstairs and slammed the door to her bedroom. Nicolai just threw up his hands in bewilderment.

"Maybe she will come around in time," he said to Ursula, Nicole's mother, his sister in law.

"I wouldn't count on that happening, Nicolai, she's pretty broken up about what has just happened with Bob, and she's pretty stubborn. She may never get over it."

Nicolai tried again, the next day, to get Nicole to change her mind but she refused to even talk to him, so later in the day he left for Helsinki without her. When he arrived in Helsinki, he went to work immediately, rounding up negotiators. He was able to get hold of one of the negotiators that had brokered the release of Francis Gary Powers. Powers was the pilot of a CIA U-2 spy plane that he was piloting over the Soviet Union when he was shot down by a Soviet Sam missile and captured in 1960. He also, was sentenced to 10 years in prison, but was freed in 1962 in a spy swap for the Soviet spy, Rudolf Abel.

Nicolai worked tirelessly for the next three years to attempt to broker a spy swap deal with the Soviets. Finally, in 1968, as the U.S. was in the final stages of their moon landing program, a swap deal was put together.

Yuri, meantime, was becoming deeply depressed in the Kristy prison. He had written to Nicole many times, but always, the letters were returned to him unopened. With nothing but time on his hands, he was beginning to see what a horrible mistake he had made in going back to Volgograd that fateful January day in 1965, after he had promised Nicole that he would get out of the CIA. Especially when he heard from Nicolai that she had refused to come and visit him in prison.

Finally, the swap deal was finalized. Premier Gorbachev approved the deal.

* * * * * *

Early on a chilly fall morning in 1968, a fishing trawler left the Helsinki Harbor. On board was Nicolai Kiselyova, several CIA agents and a Russian spy. His name was Vladimer Marenko from Vladivostok. He was captured by the CIA accepting espionage papers from the USA in the far western Alaska port city of Kotzebue. He was tried in Fairbanks and had spent the last five years at the U.S. federal prison in Sheridan, Oregon.

At exactly the same time, on that chilly October morning, another fishing trawler left the Saint Petersburg Harbor. On board were several KGB agents and an American spy. His name was Yuri Malenkova. He was captured by the KGB in Volgograd and spent the last three years in the Kristy prison in the Soviet city of Saint Petersburg.

The two trawlers set off across the Gulf of Finland. They met up just off of the island of Kingiseppskiy, halfway between Finland and Russia. There was a light fog surrounding the island and the sun was just starting to burn through the fog on that chilly morning, as the two boats pulled alongside each other. They dropped anchor and tied up together. The two prisoners were brought up on deck by their entourages of heavily armed agents. The head agents of both the CIA and KGB shook hands and first swapped photos of the prisoners to verify that these were indeed the two former agents that they were each exchanging. No words were spoken. The leg shackles of both the prisoners were undone and each stepped over the gunwales of the joined trawlers onto the deck of the opposite boat and were immediately taken below deck. The anchors were raised and the trawlers departed the rendezvous area and headed back to their home ports. When the two boats were out of sight of each other, Nicolai went below deck to be with Yuri.

"Are you okay?" Nicolai asked.

"No, I'll never again be okay for the rest of my life," came the reply.

"We'll get you back home again as soon as we can."

"I don't even know where home is anymore. I don't think I even have a home," He responded in a broken voice, "I don't even know who I am."

With that, Yuri(Bob) slumped down in the seat and began sobbing, long painful convulsing sobs with tears streaming down his cheeks. He was a completely broken person. His pain was palpable. Nicolai came over and put his arm around Bob. He loved Bob like one of his own sons. They both just sat there in silence with Bob sobbing for the forty five minute ride back to Helsinki.

When they pulled up to the dock in Helsinki, Nicolai said, "Come on, Bob, let's get you fixed again. They have a really good rehab program at Langley."

They got a cab and immediately headed to the airport. Nicolai already had tickets for their flight to Langley.

* * * * * *

The plane had no more than reached its flying altitude, when the two now former agents fell asleep. They slept for the whole way back across the Atlantic. These two broken CIA agents fell into a deep exhaustive sleep after what they had been through. The two agents, Bob and

Nicolai, didn't even realize the ramifications of what they had done, what they had accomplished. They didn't yet realize that the mission they had successfully completed had changed the course of history. After the failure of the re-entry of the Soyuz-1 space capsule, which their espionage work, through the work of Boris Chelomi, had caused. The Soviets were knocked out of the race for the moon. At the Baikanur space center, the Soviets had made two more attempts to launch unmanned tests of their moon mission. But both attempts with the N-1 rocket had failed. Finally, the Soviets scrapped the N-1 rocket program and cancelled their mission to land a man on the moon.

After their ten hour flight, the two agents landed in Washington D.C. They caught a shuttle out to Langley, Virginia. The two broken agents checked into the CIA rehab program. They were shuttled out into the countryside of Virginia. There, on a farm, they began their program of deprogramming. They spent half of their days in therapy and the other half of their days doing light farm work, which was also part of the therapy. They plowed fields and planted and harvested crops and cared for the live-stock. The farm work was especially helpful for Bob. It brought him back to his youth, growing up on a farm. This was important therapy his therapist told him. It would help him establish a starting point on which to rebuild his life.

As Bob's mind began to heal, and after six months of therapy, he was finally able to face the question of his relationship with Nicole and his son Mikhail Robert Kiselyova.

On a bright sunny day in April, after he and Nicolai had finished their morning chores on the CIA farm in the rolling hills of Virginia, they sat down on the patio of the farmhouse with a cup of coffee, to talk. Nicolai had finished his de-programming, therapy and rehab program and was about to be released and returned to the Soviet Union. Bob, on the other hand, had several more months to go. The main issue he still had to deal with was his relationship with Nicole. He and Nicolai had worked together doing the farm work for the past six months, but, had never discussed her. Now, he and his therapist had agreed, it was finally time to address this issue.

He finally was able to approach the issue. He said to Nicolai, "I notice that you get letters from your family in Russia from time to time. Do you ever hear anything about Nicole and Mikhail?"

"Well, I'm glad to see you are finally strong enough to start asking questions about her. The answer, sadly, I'm afraid, is that I don't hear about them. It seems that shortly after you were sent to prison in Russia. She took young Mikhail and her mother and just left one night. Nobody knows where she went. She didn't tell anyone where she was going. They just disappeared. Everyone thinks that they might have gone back to Sitka, Alaska. But, nobody has heard from her, since. I'm really sorry, Bob. I wish I had better news. But, you know, shortly after your trial, things got really rough for my family. Friends and neighbors who are loyal Communists started giving them a hard time. They started threatening the family. They painted a red hammer and sickle on our front door. Two of my sons lost their jobs. Finally, just before I had worked out your release in that spy swap, we were forced to sell the house and move. I can't tell you where. The pressure got to be too much for me. That's why I checked myself into the CIA rehab program, here on the farm."

"Gee, I'm so sorry, Nicolai, I had no idea that things got so rough for you and your family."

"Yeah, Bob, I guess that's the price we all had to pay for what we did. We brought down the Soviet space program. But, it seems that we brought our lives down in the process."

The next day, Nicolai was discharged from the CIA and the rehab program. They said their tearful good byes and he returned to the Soviet Union, no one knew where. He was officially retired. But, after he left, Bob started becoming depressed again. It took several more months of therapy to de-program his broken relationship with Nicole before he could be released, from the program and the CIA.

* * * * * *

On a very warm day in July, as the USA's Saturn 5 rocket was lifting off from Cape Kennedy, on its way to mankind's first walk on the moon. Bob was released from the program and from the CIA. He returned to his hometown of Perham, Minnesota to try to pick up the pieces of his broken life.

His father had passed away while he was in the Saint Petersburg prison. The farm that he had left behind had been sold. His mother now lived with his sister.

Susan and Megan were still there, still waiting for him. They had not communicated since Bob got sent to prison in Saint Petersburg, Russia. His daughter Megan was now ten years old and ready to go back to school in the fall, into the third grade. He had missed so much of their lives. It took months, if not years, to repair their relationship. They had three more children together, but, their relationship was a stormy one and ended in divorce twelve years later.

- - - -Then he met Barbara.

ROBB FELDER

CHAPTER 37

On the bank of the Ottertail River, the old man was partially awakened by someone calling to him. Was it those pesky blackbirds calling again? No, - - - -? Then who was interrupting his dream this time? He tried to get back to sleep, but the calling continued, - - - -. "Papa, Grandma," Kira and McKenna were calling out from up the river trail as they approached. "Look, we caught fish."

The old man tried to process it all, tried again to separate reality from his dream world. In his half-awake, half-conscious state, he raised himself on one elbow and turned to still asleep Barbara and whispered in her ear,

- - - - - "Nicole,- - -, Nicole, I love you."

THE END

ROBB FELDER

EPILOGUE

- - - - - - Life – is but a dream, Sweetheart.

The best kinds of stories, I believe, are those with a mix of facts and fiction.

The facts of this story are that 'Bob', the main character of the story did in fact serve in the US Army during the Cold War and was in fact stationed at the US Army Arctic Test Board at Fort Greely, Alaska. Many of the escapades in that part of the story did in fact occur, (With just a tiny bit of embellishment thrown in for spice and excitement).

ROBB FELDER

ACKNOWLEDGEMENTS

Thanks to my beautiful wife Barbara, for the love and support she gives me, in this and all my writing adventures. Barbara is my quintessential chief editor.

Thanks to Daughter Brenda Fellerer, for her work critiquing and editing the story.

Thanks for the inspiration of all the fellow soldiers who served with me in Alaska, in the "Cold Cold War", at the US Army Arctic Test Board at Fort Greely in the 'Land of the Midnight Sun'. Most especially Frank, Richard, Roger, Ralph, Robert, MSGT Jackson, MSGT Steel and SGT Trent and the folks at the Malamute Saloon and Mobile Home Park at Delta Junction, Alaska, as we all struggled through the long winter nights and days without seeing the sun. We all struggled to keep all of our digits in tact while the temperatures plunged to minus 74 below zero. Your memories remain alive today, even after sixty years,

To all of our children, grand and great grandchildren, some of whom appear in the story: namely Brenda, Ryan, Jenna, Travis, Zachery, Colby, Kira and McKenna.

ROBB FELDER

* * * * * * * *

ROBB FELDER is the author of the books in the Otter Falls series:

PIONEERS ON THE OTTERTAIL
MYSTERY ON THE OTTERTAIL
ADVENTURES ON THE OTTERTAIL

These are the new releases by; **ROBB FELDER**

LAST FLIGHT OF THE SNOWBIRDS.

THE COLD COLD WAR,

ROBB FELDER

ROBB FELDER Is a Vietnam Veteran. He attended the University of Alaska and the University of Minnesota. He is the author of THE OTTER FALLS SERIES. a trilogy of historical novels.

Robb has just released two new books; LAST FLIGHT OF THE SNOWBIRDS and THE COLD COLD WAR. Robb is retired from a successful career as a computer applications software designer. He and his wife Barbara live in a suburb of the Twin Cities of Minnesota.

ROBB FELDER